Something Good In The Dust

Something Good In The Dust

A Novel

Michelle J. Mann

This book is a work of fiction. All of the characters, names, organizations, places, and events in this novel are either products of the author's imagination or are used fictitiously.

Book Cover Design by Katriona Jaspersen

ISBN 979-8-9924683-3-5 (EBook)

ISBN: 979-8-9924683-4-2 (paperback)

ISBN 979-8-9924683-5-9 (hardback)

First Edition: 2026

Trigger warning: This book has a chapter that includes a memory of an officer involved shooting which may be triggering for some readers.

This is book two of the Good Ones Series.

These books are interconnected standalones and can be read in any order.

Other book in this series:

Everything Good That Happened

For all the girls looking for men at the hardware store.

Look for the ones that don't just give you a bouquet of flowers, but will plant an entire flowerbed for you. Those are the good ones.

Chapter 1

Lilly

Looking for love in the hardware store...

The forecast predicted blowing dust this week. If I guessed correctly, everyone in town would be out in full force, stocking up on toilet paper and bottled water as if we were going to be shut in for a month, when in reality, it would be over in a matter of hours. Dust storms. It's a phenomenon that people love to hate. But unlike everyone else I know, I love dust storms; from indoors, of course, because I'm not a psychopath. Not the regular, everyday dusty skies; those are just annoying. I'm talking about the big ones, the haboobs. There's nothing like watching the towering wall of dirt from a good West Texas dust storm roll in. It's fascinating and you never know what kinds of surprises might come flying in with the shifting sand.

Instead of pursuing a career in meteorology or storm chasing, I opened a bakery, something I'm incredibly proud of. It's a warm, welcoming place that has grown far beyond what I ever imagined. What began as a humble food truck eventually blossomed into a full brick-and-mortar shop. I make a mean cream cheese Danish, and there is no shame in requiring stretchy pants after becoming dependent on them for breakfast every day, and for a midmorning snack after that. However, the best-selling item that I have in my bakery are my teacakes. I call them Grandma's Teacakes and people go crazy over them. The recipe came straight from my grandmother, and it's written on a yellow paper folded neatly in my recipe box. My bakery allows me to afford my favorite things in life: travel and good food.

Traveling to places I've never been to, seeing things I've never seen, and eating foods I'd never find in my own town. It's freeing, exhilarating, and gives me the opportunity to live in the moment, embracing new experiences.

Not everyone is as on board with exciting new experiences. My best friend Jo, being one of them. I mean, suggesting she eat foods without any idea what they are seemed to be a little much to ask of her. My plan is to randomly order something on a menu that I cannot even read because it is entirely in German. The whole point of traveling is eating, tasting the foods that the locals eat, and adding to my Best Foods Ever Consumed list that I diligently keep up with in the notes app on my phone. And of course, see some breathtaking scenery and explore the historic sites, but still, mainly it's the food.

"What if it's haggis?" Jo asked. Jo and I had been best friends since high school, but she didn't share my adventurous and open-minded palette.

"Haggis isn't even a German dish. I believe it's Scottish, but the plan is to have an adventure, not eat the same boring old foods we could get right here in Willow Creek. It's all part of the culinary experience. Live a little, Jo." I've known people who travel out of the country and eat the same things they could get back at home. My brother, Will, is one of them. He seeks out hamburgers on every menu he picks up, no matter where he is or what type of cuisine the restaurant serves.

"So, you're sure about Germany? We don't even speak German," she added, already sounding skeptical about the plan, but still willing to entertain it on my account. Of the two of us, I was the risk taker, and Jo was the cautious planner. We balanced each other out.

"Joann Kennison, the agreement was we would pick a destination out of a hat and go there, no matter where it is or what language is spoken there. It's Germany, fair and square. It's only July now and we aren't going until

October, so we have plenty of time to learn a few words." I took out my phone and googled the 'word for restroom in German.' "Ok, look. The German word for restroom is 'toilette.' See? We'll be fine; besides, it says online that a lot of people speak English in Germany."

I'd been fortunate to catch her in a moment of weakness when I came up with this plan for the two of us to go on a trip together. We'd been talking about doing something like this for years. We couldn't decide on a location, so we decided to draw from a hat. Well, we used an empty frozen waffle box instead of a hat, but that's beside the point. The winner was Germany; this was perfect because it was on the top of my list of places I wanted to travel to. It didn't seem to be on the top of Jo's list, but I'd do my due diligence to teach her that she does, in fact, desperately want to go to Germany.

I looked at pictures of a city called Weisbaden. It seemed elegant with the beautiful buildings and landscape. My love life was nonexistent, but I could imagine a romantic getaway there; sipping coffee at the quaint little outdoor cafes and later drinking sparkling wine at a hilltop winery.

Jo sighed heavily into the phone, but I knew this sigh. She wasn't backing out; it's more of a giving into the situation kind of sigh. Jo's problem is she was too cautious, and it got in the way of the fun she could be having. My job was to make her realize how fun the proposed activity was and enable her to live her best life in spite of her constant need to explore the what-ifs.

"Oh, stop with the sighing. I'll be sending you some YouTube videos to watch and a list of fun things for us to do. At the end of the week, we can revisit this. If you still aren't sold on Germany, we can draw again. But at least give it some thought. I just know this could be so exciting, Jo!" I hung up the phone and immediately started searching for information online to send to her. This was going to be both of our first real trip overseas.

My motto is if you don't take the time to enjoy life, you might miss it. Living is a lost art, something people have forgotten how to do while they are busy surviving. I want to experience everything, travel to places I've never been, get the spontaneous tattoo, and of course, taste all the food. Sure, I might one day get food poisoning from a questionable street vendor or end up with a hideous tattoo right on top of my hand. It's also possible I could break my clavicle in a freak hang-gliding accident, despite my mother's warnings. Or, most likely, none of that will happen, and I'll have the time of my life.

I've always been relatively spontaneous and carefree and kept my parents in a constant state of panic when I was younger. Now, at 32 years old, I'm not quite as chaotic as I once was, but I still enjoy a good adventure. I've only broken a couple of bones, and I've only needed stitches once. Not too bad in my opinion; especially when you take into consideration the broken bones were from a freak tricycle accident, and the stitches were from simply walking too close to a piece of metal sticking out of a parked, wrecked car.

A year ago, I was diagnosed with Systemic Lupus Erythematosus. Lupus for short. For the most part, I can handle vacationing very well. Usually, it's when I return that it hits me, causing a flare up. I almost never talk about my health issues because it's not a fun topic, and people expect me to be the fun one. Honestly, sometimes I feel like they might think I'm making it up or wanting attention and that is definitely not the case. But I know how it is, when you have an invisible disease, other people don't always take it seriously. Aside from Jo, not many people have acted particularly interested in my health, so I just don't bring it up for fear they will abruptly change the subject or brush it off like it's not a big deal.

Speaking of not having anyone to share certain parts of my life with, I haven't had a date in over a year. It's the longest I've been without a significant other. It was easier to find dates when I was younger; especially in college when there were parties and social events overflowing with eligible bachelors. I'm the only one of my friends and family that is single right now and that can feel lonely.

My last boyfriend, Harrison, was a gambling addict. I didn't know about his gambling addiction until we had already been together for almost a year. I started thinking something was off when he kept asking me to borrow cash. He earned a decent salary, more than I did, but kept asking me for money. He also bailed on our dates frequently, giving excuses like his mother needed something or an emergency came up at work. Later, I learned that in reality, he was spending all his time and money at an illegal game room, the kind that has all the windows blacked out and the police raided all the time. One just surfaced in Willow Creek a few years ago. Every time it gets raided, it just opens up at a new location. Gambling isn't legal in Texas so that was his only option other than scratch-off tickets, which he also spent an absolute fortune on.

I'd like to find that person that I want to grow old with. I don't like the saying "settling down," though. To me, that means sitting in matching electric recliners every night after dinner until you go to bed at exactly 8:30 PM on the dot. That's not what I have in mind. I want somebody that wants to *do* life with me, not just exist with me; somebody who will still want to have fun with me even when we are gumming up our senior citizen discounted meatloaf.

There aren't a lot of places to meet men in Willow Creek unless you want to hang out at the Iron Bar, which I do not. I'm not much of a drinker, except for the occasional glass of wine or margarita, and I don't like the bar scene. My brother, Will, used to DJ and met his wife at the bar, but that was just pure, random, unexplainable luck. His wife, Sydney, wasn't even a bar goer, she was just dragged there by her cousin. It was actually Sydney's first time in a bar, and she ended up meeting Will, and the rest is history. It was one of those love stories that you only see in movies but never happen in real life. The kind of sweet that makes your teeth hurt.

I am on the hunt for a long-term relationship. First and foremost, I want a man who sees me as his equal. This isn't 1950 and I'm not going to wait on him hand and foot or treat him like he's helpless. I'm just not that girl. If he can't take care of himself then he isn't the one for me. I want to be a girlfriend and maybe a wife someday, not their mother. Don't even get me started on that conversation because it *will* spiral into an all-day long rampage.

I want a real man, not a boy, somebody who knows what he wants in life. Somebody who is handy with a drill but also with an air fryer, can hold down a respectable job, isn't swimming in debt, doesn't have a gambling addiction, and who helps his elderly neighbors open their jars of pickles.

Obviously, the only place to meet somebody like that is at the hardware store.

Willow Creek has two hardware stores: Mikey's Lumber and Nails and K&A Hardware. I've scoped both and found that Mikey's customers tend to be in the over 50 crowd, K&A's clientele is more of what I'm after. I make my rounds at K&A's at least twice a week. I've been doing it for over a month now. I never actually need anything there, but sometimes I make a small purchase just so nobody thinks I'm suspicious. I'm accumulating a nice collection of bottles of glue, finishing nails, a few potted plants, and a variety of lightbulbs.

I've also learned that there is a certain way to dress when picking up men at the hardware store. One shouldn't be dressed up. It's essential to be dressed down enough that you look like you are there to gather supplies for a home project but still looking decent enough for men to notice you. There is a certain amount of science to it.

Tonight, I dressed in jeans and a nice T-shirt, neat but not dressy. Then I spent way too long making my makeup look like I didn't have any makeup on and fixing my hair to where it looked cute but messy at the same time. It's a windy day anyway, so a purposely messy style is the way to go. It's fool-proof, they will think I'm just an effortlessly attractive woman at the hardware store to get things for a little DIY home project. I don't even do DIY home projects, but that's beside the point.

I like to start out in the lumber section, but there was nothing to see there so I made my way over to the power tools and stopped dead when I saw what had to be God's gift to women standing with his face turned away from me, admiring the saw selection. Tanned, muscular, dark brown hair, grey sweatpants, black T-shirt, a hat turned backwards, no wedding ring. Oh. My. Gosh. I stood staring that this magnificent being for a few minutes before picking up a drill-looking object and started studying it, in hopes that a conversation could be sparked about it. Maybe I'll ask him if he knows if this is a good brand. Then he'll offer his advice on it, tell me what project he is working on, invite me out to dinner...

"Lilly?" a familiar voice said my name, snapping me out of my daydream.

I looked up and immediately wanted to wash my eyes out with soap. Grey sweatpants man was just Kip, my brother's best friend whom I'd known since I was fourteen years old. I'd been staring at Kip's ass. I'd been trying to pick up Kip, who is practically a brother to me. Has Kip always looked like that? I've completely lost it, not to mention that he is also engaged to my sister-in-law's cousin, Leanne.

"Oh, um. Hi," I said, disappointedly, going back to studying the drill and trying to erase the vision of Kip's sweatpants clad buttocks from my memory.

"Are you lost? You realize you are at the hardware store, right?" he asked, a slight smirk on his face.

"I know where I am, freak. I was just needing to get this drill," I said, confidently showing him the tool. The real reason I was there was none of his business.

"That's a brad nailer," he said, raising his eyebrows.

I smiled nervously, heat rushing to my face. “Well, yes, I meant I need to get this brad nailer.” What the heck is a brad nailer?

“And may I ask what you will be doing with the brad nailer?” He scratched his jaw, clearly not fooled.

“I’ll be nailing some brads for a project I’m working on.”

“Mmhmm. Whatcha building?” He smirked with a bemused smile. He’d known me long enough to know that I had absolutely no patience for home projects.

I had to think fast. “A shelf... for my, um, for my... shoes. Well, I’ll see you later then.” I nervously waved and turned, bumping into the display stand behind me, then hurried off red faced to the checkout to purchase the brad nailer. I had no idea what it was for, but by that point, my pride would not let me put it back on the shelf.

Chapter 2

Lilly

Driving skills, or lack thereof...

There's a yogurt shop down the street from K&A's. I stopped there on my way home for a large cup of birthday cake flavored yogurt with chocolate sauce, strawberries, and granola. The fruit and granola cancel out the sugary yogurt and chocolate, so it's still healthy. At least that's what I tell myself. I took it with me instead of eating it there, but they were out of lids. There isn't anywhere to set it down in my car because the cup is too big for the cup holder; therefore, I had to hold it in my lap.

Halfway home I saw the red and blue lights flashing behind me. I glanced down at the speedometer, relieved to find I wasn't speeding. They probably just needed to go around me to pull somebody else over; except there was nobody else on the street and they were still right behind me. I cursed under my breath and tensed up on the steering wheel. It would appear that I was in fact getting pulled over. It was nothing short of a miracle that I'd lived my entire thirty-two years without getting a ticket and I didn't necessarily want to destroy my perfect record.

As I turned onto the next street to pull over, my yogurt tipped over in my lap, spilling the strawberries and chocolate sauce onto my pants. Distracted by trying to pick up the yogurt cup while pulling over, I accidentally ran over the curb before coming to a stop. This mishap wasn't going to help anything. "Ok, settle down, it's fine. Everything's fine," I muttered to myself through clenched teeth. Then, to make matters worse, and to my complete horror, I realized my car was not stopped but was slowly moving backwards. Panicked, I slammed my foot on the brake just in time, avoiding contact with the front of the police car. I'd been so flustered with the yogurt and curb incident that I'd put the car in reverse instead of park. Looking at the officer's unsmiling face in my rearview mirror, I could tell this was not going to go well for me.

I rolled down the window and smiled, hoping a good personality would win him over.

"Good evening Officer! It's a nice night, isn't it? Did I do something wrong?" I flashed my best, most innocent looking smile.

"Ma'am, my name is Officer Wayland. I originally pulled you over because you have a taillight out..." He paused and looked at the yogurt cup in my hand and chocolate mess spilled out all over my leg. "However... Then you proceeded to run over the curb, you put the car in reverse and almost hit my car. You seriously missed it by like three inches," he said, flatly. Apparently, my cheerful demeaner did absolutely nothing for him.

Flustered, I could feel my face and neck flush. "Sorry, Officer, it was an accident, I was just..."

He interrupted me before I could get the rest of my sentence out. "License and insurance, please." Wow, a real conversationalist, this one. I pulled my license out of my purse and fished around in my glove box for the insurance card, spilling out all kinds of miscellaneous items that I'd managed to cram in there. Once I handed them both to him, he took them back to his patrol car, then returned a few minutes later.

"Here you go." He handed the cards back to me, still with a stern expression. "Ma'am, have you been drinking?"

My eyes widened in disbelief. "What? Drinking? No, I was at the hardware store and then stopped at the yogurt shop. I was just heading home, Officer."

He looked again at the mess in my lap, then back to my face, expressionless.

"I spilled my yogurt. They really need to make places in the console for things like that..."

"Mm hmm. I'm going to need you to get out of the car, ma'am." Was he serious? It isn't like I hit his car. And holding an open container of yogurt in the car isn't illegal, or was it?

I put my yogurt down in the passenger seat and got out of the car, the mess all over my pants looking much worse with the light of the patrol car shining on them. The officer was considerably taller than me and a little intimidating, especially since he wasn't particularly friendly.

He held up his flashlight and shined it on my face, making my eyes burn.

"Why are your eyes red?" What the heck is wrong with this jerk?

"Well, maybe because you are shining your flashlight in them?" I said, irritated and no longer trying to use a charming personality to get out of a ticket.

"I need you to take nine heel to toe steps in a straight line with your arms down to your side. Then pivot on one foot and walk nine steps back to me," he said, ignoring my comment.

"Seriously?" Had he lost his mind? I wasn't drunk! If he acts like this with the sober law breakers, I can't imagine how he treats the ones who had been drinking.

"Seriously." He nodded sarcastically with a hard jaw line.

Reluctantly, I did as I was instructed, completing my first ever field sobriety test, then returned to the officer, crossing my arms across my chest. “See? Clean and sober.”

He stared at me for a moment and finally said, “You can get back in your car, ma’am. Get your taillight fixed. And next time get a lid for your yogurt.”

I started to tell him that I tried to get a lid, but they were out of lids. Except he turned and walked back to his car before I could respond.

Wow. He’s Mr. Personality, and what a winning smile he has... But at least he let me off the hook and hoped I wouldn’t have to deal with him again. I guess I could be grateful for that, anyway. Even though I’d never had a ticket, I’d been pulled over a few times, and the officers were always much more friendly to me than he was.

.....

Back at home, I took off my yogurt covered pants and changed into my comfiest pajama pants, still disturbed by the events of the evening. Eyeballing Kip’s butt and completing an unnecessary field sobriety test were both equally unsettling. I put my shiny new brad nailer on the counter along with my collection of other hardware store finds. Then, I sat down to finish what was left of my yogurt.

I love being in my house. It’s old, built in the 1950’s, but it’s cozy and it has character. I’m not a minimalist by any means; more of a maximalist, and my décor style is eclectic. I want my home to have personality, look lived in. It's a mix between vintage, modern, and everything in between, but I think I've done a good job of styling it tastefully. Hanging from a rack of wooden hooks in the kitchen is my collection of vintage aprons. Over that is a shelf that showcases my vintage teacup collection. For my birthday, my mom gave me the cutest antique canister set with mushrooms painted on them and some antique salt and pepper shakers shaped like roosters. I have modern red kitchen chairs and handmade red tea towels that have my name embroidered on them, given to me by Kip's fiancée, Leanne. On the walls are scenic oil paintings that I've found at thrift stores, vintage mirrors with ornate gold frames, and photos from my vacations. I have a grouping of them over my velvety red and gold striped couch that I found at an estate sale. I love the pops of color and all the little details that my guests can look at. My favorite thing is my recipe box that my mom gave me. It contains all her old, handwritten recipes in it, the ones I grew up with, along with some from my grandmother and my aunt.

My failed attempts at picking up men at the hardware store haven't been a total loss; a few of my store finds have come in handy. After I finished my yogurt, I used my new hammer to hang the decorative world map I'd ordered online. It's the kind that is made of cork for sticking little pins in to mark where you have traveled to. I had it personalized, and it reads 'Lilly's Gallivanting Around the

Globe.' I stood back and admired it where it hung on the wall, right over my kitchen table. I'm a particularly visual person, and watching the map slowly filling up with little red pins will be oddly satisfying to me.

I stand firmly behind my theory that people are happier when they have a trip planned. People need things to look forward to, to be excited about, to get away from the mundane day-to-day tasks. My goal is to vacation in every state in the United States and as many countries overseas as possible. My problem is that I have a hard time finding anyone to go with me. While I do know a lot of people, I don't have many close friends that would be able to go with me because they are all married or have kids, and they save their vacation time to do things with their families. I'm fortunate that Jo will be able to go with me to Germany in October.

Two years ago, I went on a solo trip to New York. I've been on trips alone before, but New York City differs greatly from the small town of Willow Creek, Texas; as if it's an entirely different world. My mother became unhinged when I told her my plans, convinced something horrific was going to happen to me. She practically threatened me with death if I didn't keep my location shared and then she undoubtedly stared at her phone the entire time I was gone, making sure my location dot was moving. Needless to say, she had never been to New York and had an unrealistic mental picture of what I was getting myself into. I survived the big city unscathed and experienced all the classic NYC must do's: rode the subway, ate pizza in Time Square and a bagel in Central Park, saw a Broadway show, and looked down at the city from a skyscraper. Trips taken alone create an exhilarating sense of freedom, but I'd still rather share the experience with somebody.

My parents think they have a good reason to believe I need supervision on vacation, all because I might have fallen off a moving catamaran during a family cruise excursion in Cozumel three years ago. I was simply trying to lean over to get a good video of some dolphins that were jumping out of the water near the boat. Just as my mother was yelling at me to get away from the edge, we hit a bumpy wave, and I toppled overboard. They had to stop the boat and throw the life ring out and rescue me, sternly reminding me of the boat rules. Fortunately for me, my phone was attached to my wrist in a waterproof case, and I had the video I was trying to get, but I remained informally on an enhanced level of supervision by the crew member for the rest of the excursion.

The most recent vacation was Las Vegas, Nevada with a couple of friends who were able to find somebody to watch their kids. Harrison's gambling addiction taught me what not to do and I was able to avoid bankruptcy at the slot machines.

The Vegas trip didn't sit well with my parents either with it being "sin city" and all... Again, they'd never been there and assumed the worst. Honestly, I need to stop telling them what I'm doing.

"Please tell me you aren't planning to get a bunch of tattoos. You don't know if the tattoo artists are any good and you could end up with a tulip that looks like an anus." My mom had said to me when I casually stated that Vegas tattoos are one of the touristy bucket list items.

I didn't get a *bunch* of tattoos when I was in Vegas. I got *one* tattoo. Yes, it was a spontaneous walk in and no, it didn't look like a butthole. It's a cute cupcake to represent my bakery. It's on my left ankle. My right ankle has a tattoo of my dog, Beatrice. My parents are very old-fashioned and do not approve of tattoos. I do not care if you are completely covered in ink as long as you are a nice person.

Niceness. That's really all that matters to me. Good people who do good things for other people. My brothers are like that. Kip is too. They are just good men with good hearts. There aren't many men like them in Willow Creek that aren't married or engaged. Actually, from what I'm seeing at the hardware store, there are no single men at all that that fit my criteria. Knowing my luck, Officer Wayland could possibly be the only single man in Willow Creek. With his personality, I just assumed he would be single. I mean, I love a man in uniform, but they also need to not be assholes.

Chapter 3

Lilly

The haboob...

I'd made two more visits to K&A's since the whole mistaking Kip as a sexy beast in grey sweatpants fiasco. I did get flirted with by the guy that works at the paint counter. That was fun for about five minutes, until I found out he was only 20 years old and lived with his parents. I don't think I'm old enough to be considered a cougar, but my date needs to at least be of legal drinking age.

I decided to give it another month at K&A's and then I may have no other choice but to move on to Mikey's Lumber. It's silly that it's come to scouting out dates at the hardware stores but seems like the only logical place to look other than the bar and I'm not comfortable with online dating sites.

Single or not, I try to stay somewhat active. By that, I mean I take my dog, Beatrice, for a walk around our peaceful little neighborhood every morning. We only walk about a mile which is farther than she can handle, and I have to carry her most of the way. I really need to look into a dog stroller. Beatrice is a Chinese Crested mix; it's a mystery as to what she is mixed with. She's getting old, and her tongue hangs out the side of her mouth due to missing a few teeth. She isn't what anyone else would call beautiful, but we don't take offense. Will entered her in an ugly dog contest and I decided to embrace the whole experience, even getting Beatrice and I matching shirts that read "Vote for Beatrice." My fabulous girl won the contest and proudly possessed the title of "Willow Creek's Ugliest Dog" for a full year. Her trophy and photo are prominently displayed on my fireplace mantel.

My other pet is my beloved tarantula, Penny. She's a Chilean Copper tarantula, hence the name. I used to keep her on the fireplace mantel, but I've moved her into my bedroom. I like to watch her while I fall asleep.

Next to my fireplace is my reading chair, which is huge and fluffy, complete with a cupholder and a place to charge my phone. It was my Christmas present to myself, and I could literally live in it. I usually read for a while after my walk. I tried to get a book club going, but it seems there just aren't a lot of avid readers in Willow Creek. I'm the only member of the Willow Creek Book Club at the moment.

Today, I'd taken off the entire morning to get some things done around the house. I planned to go into the bakery after lunch. My assistant manager, Caitlyn, can handle everything when I'm not there. If the truth were told, she probably handles it better than I do. She also takes care of all of our social media content, advises on shop decor, and keeps up with all the latest bakery trends. She is also my beauty consultant. She doesn't actually *know* she's my beauty consultant. I just use her as my inspiration for my own hair, makeup, and clothes because she is gorgeous and stylish, and I am still on my never-ending quest to find a date.

My phone rang, startling me out of the daydream I'd been having. It was my sister-in-law, Sydney.

"Lilly, now listen to me. I know you love a haboob, but do not, I repeat, do not go out in this one. I think it's going to be a bad one," she warned. Sydney is one of the most cautious people I've ever known. Why is it that all my friends are like that?

"Haboob? When? Today?" How could I have not known about this?

"Lilly..."

"I was not aware of this haboob that you speak of," I said innocently. If I had known, I would have planned accordingly.

"Promise me. Remember what happened last time? You almost got yourself killed," Sydney went on. Oh, good grief, you make one mistake and nobody lets you live it down.

"Oh, settle down. I'm not going to do anything stupid," I responded, although Sydney and I have very different opinions of what 'doing something stupid' is.

It seems that some people just don't appreciate the magical wonders of a haboob. How can they not be excited about a beautiful, massive, dense wall of dust reaching miles into the sky? Sometimes, there is a little purple mixed with the brown, a beautiful contrast against the blue sky. The part I love about it is that sometimes there is a clear line between the dust wall and the sky as if it is a dark storm cloud instead of dust. It's magnificent, like a painting instead of reality. Here, in the flat lands of West Texas, in the absence of tall buildings, haboobs can be seen from far away and you can watch it rolling in. To me, It's the most spectacular meteorological occurrence that we have in Willow Creek. It's an unpopular opinion, but I love haboobs, not the part where the dirt sandblasts your skin and gets in your teeth and eyes. Watching them roll in is the good part, the rest is more annoying than anything.

I may have purposely ventured out onto a dirt road during the last haboob because I wanted to make a video with a completely unobstructed view of the spectacular dirt wall coming, but the visibility was reduced to nothing, and I couldn't see anything in front of my car. It was too dangerous to be on the road. I had to pull off the road into a ditch, which was even difficult to locate. Of all the places I could have been, I was parked next to the one tree in the area. The wind was so strong that it uprooted and landed on my car, trapping me inside and denting the roof several inches deep. After the dust cleared up, Will and Kip had to come with chain saws to rescue me, both unamused and agitated by my carelessness, preaching to me repeatedly about how the tree could have killed me. I wasn't hurt, but my little storm chasing expedition cost me my car, which was a total loss. Lessons were learned from that one. I must admit, the tree falling on my car was rather frightening, and I've made a solemn promise to myself and others to enjoy the haboobs safely and securely from indoors from now on.

My phone dinged. It was Jo. **Stay inside...**

I shook my head. It's like they don't trust me or something.

I needed to get to work, even if a haboob was supposedly coming. The bakery was only a few minutes from my house. It isn't like it was going to be here before I got to the bakery; the sky looked perfectly blue and clear from what I could see. I had plenty of time.

I gathered my things, noticing my phone only had two percent charge left on the battery but that was fine, I wouldn't need it in the five minutes that it takes to get to work. The one charging port in my car doesn't work, and I haven't taken it in to get it fixed.

My bakery is located on Main Street, in the center of town. The street is paved with red bricks and lined with unique and historic buildings, many of which were once houses and have since been turned into businesses. My bakery was a Victorian style home at one time until it was sold and turned into a daycare center. After the daycare moved, I bought it.

Backing out of my driveway, I finally saw it. The billowing thick, dark grey and brown wall coming in the distance. It was spectacular with a well-defined edge, in no way resembling dust but more like a very thick wall of smoke or an upside-down dark storm cloud. I got out of my car and took a picture of it, having just enough battery life left.

I assumed I would have plenty of time to get to the bakery before it hit, but as I drove down my street, the dust wall was approaching much faster than I anticipated. Only halfway to the bakery, the force of the storm hit with a vengeance and quickly turned the atmosphere opaque brown, reducing visibility and creating ultra-hazardous driving conditions. There's never much traffic on Main Street and the bakery was just up ahead, so I slowed down and kept driving instead of finding a place to pull over to wait for the dust to clear.

I was only a few blocks away from work when a large, black and white Great Dane darted out into the street right in front of my car. If it had been even a few feet farther in front, I wouldn't have been able to see it. I made a sharp swerve to the right and successfully avoided hitting the terrified dog; however, I felt a thump at the front of my car. Oh, please no. Was there another dog? I would never be able to forgive myself if I hit a dog, even if it wasn't my fault. I put the car in park and got out, covering my face as best I could to avoid breathing in the dirt in the air. Then, I braved the elements to walk around the front of the car, anticipating the worst.

I braced myself, imagining I'd find an injured or dead dog in front of my car, but it was much worse than I'd imagined it would be. It wasn't a dog. Laying partly on the brick road with his head and chest face down on the sidewalk curb was a man. He wasn't moving. I looked around for somebody who could help, but all I could see was brown air.

Panicked, my heart raced as I hurried over and crouched next to him, patting him on the back, trying to remember the steps from the CPR class I took years ago. "Sir! Sir, are you ok?" *Please don't be dead, please do not be dead*, I thought. What if he has a family! And also, I can't go to prison! I was driving slow; could that little thump even kill him? Surely not. But he's just lying there...

I let out the breath I'd been holding as he finally started moving and put his hand over his face to keep the dirt out of it while he tried to get up. Thank God! I didn't commit vehicular manslaughter. His shirt was pulled up a little, exposing his tanned and toned midriff, not that it was even remotely appropriate to notice something like that in this situation. "I'm alive. The curb broke my fall," he said flatly in a voice that although muffled, sounded strangely familiar.

"I'm so sorry, sir! I was trying to avoid hitting a dog and I didn't see you. I'm really sorry. Do you need any help?" The wind and dirt were beating down on us as I tried to cover my face with one arm to try to help the man up with my other.

"Peewee! Where did she go?" Suddenly panicked, his eyes grew large, darting around, looking for his lost dog. We couldn't see much with all the dust, so she was going to be hard to locate.

"She ran across the street. She's yours?"

"Yes! The wind blew part of my fence down while she was in the backyard. I was trying to catch her when you hit me!" He had to raise his voice to be heard over the wind and through his shirt which was now covering his face. It stung a little when he said I hit him, as if I'd been recklessly driving, which I wasn't.

"I'm sorry! I'll help you find her. Get in my car!" This poor guy was trying to catch his dog and here I was, running him over with my car. Accidentally, of course. The least I could do was find his poor dog, who was lost somewhere in this dense fog of dirt.

As he got up off the ground and grabbed hold of a bench to pull himself up on, he stopped quickly and held onto his left arm as if realizing that it was injured. Still holding onto his arm, he climbed into the passenger seat and pulled his shirt down off his face.

"Your arm! Are you hurt? I really am sorry..." I stopped short. OMG. His face was no longer covered, and I remembered where I'd heard his voice before. I opened my mouth, but then closed it again, at a loss for words.

He looked at me for a couple of seconds, wiped the dirt off his forehead, and shook his head. "Please try to not kill us both with your driving."

"I promise. Um... Officer..." This can't be happening; I've hit a police officer with my car. Is there jail time for this?

"Just call me Kade."

Chapter 4

Kade

I hit my arm on the curb when I fell, but I tried to play it off. She already felt bad about hitting me, and I didn't want her worrying about my arm and wasting any more time in finding Peewee.

When I pulled her over last week, I wasn't exactly Mr. Friendly, but in my defense, I thought she might have been drinking, and I don't have any tolerance for drinking and driving. Turned out, she simply isn't good at driving with yogurt spilling on her lap. But then again, she also just hit me with her car so maybe she isn't a good driver, period.

My truck was parked at my house, a few blocks away, so I didn't see any other choice but to let this woman drive me around to find Peewee, even though she'd already proven twice in a matter of days that riding with her isn't the wisest thing a person could do.

I may give off the vibe of being tough and insensitive, but the thought of something happening to Peewee was just unbearable. She is the only thing I have right now. I got Peewee 7 years ago when she was just 8 weeks old. My ex-wife and I picked her out of the litter before her eyes were even open. She ended up being the worst puppy I've ever had in my entire life. She made me miserable, and every day I regretted bringing her home. Fortunately, I held out hope that she would make a miraculous turnaround. To my surprise, she eventually grew out of her horrendous puppy stage and turned into the best dog I've ever had. Right now, Peewee is my best friend, my only friend, unless you count Liam. But that's another story.

"We are going to find her! I'll call some people and have them be on the lookout." She picked up her phone and frowned. "Oh no. I knew I should have charged my phone before I left! It's dead. Maybe you should call some people and tell them to look for her."

"I don't have any people. I just moved here, and I don't really have any friends yet." I looked down at my phone, which was cracked, and the screen was black and wouldn't turn on. "Besides, I don't think my phone survived the accident." Add breaking my phone to the list of what this girl has been able to accomplish in the past few days.

Eyes beginning to water, she looked defeated. “I broke your phone too... I really am sooo sorry. I can’t believe this. I’m really not a bad person, please believe me. I’ll replace your phone. I feel just awful about this.” Crap. I couldn’t be mad at her. She’s obviously accident prone, but she feels bad enough about it as it is. Plus, she’s not bad to look at.

I couldn’t remember her name. Something to do with a flower. Rose, or maybe Jasmine? “Look, um... sorry, I don’t remember your name.”

“It’s Lilly.” Ah, yes. The name fits her.

“Lilly, I’ll worry about my phone later. Can we just go try to find Peewee before something happens to her? She’s an inside dog and has no idea what to do with herself out in the world.”

“Ok, sorry. I’ll look to the left, you look to the right,” she said as she started driving. The visibility was still not great, but better than it had been a few minutes ago. I’d never seen anything like this. In Austin, where I lived before moving here, dust storms were rare and definitely never anything like this.

“You focus on driving; I’ll do the looking.” I’d seen enough to know that she had no business doing anything at all other than concentrating on the road, especially in these conditions. With her skill level, she probably doesn’t even need to have music on when she drives.

We drove up and down Main Street, at a snail's pace. No Peewee. Then we crept along the neighborhood streets for about half an hour until I spotted her, crouched under a porch swing, looking as though she was scared out of her mind. For such a big dog, people would think she was tougher than she is, but Peewee is afraid of almost everything.

"There she is!" I shouted. Lilly stopped the car, and Peewee ran to me as soon as she saw me get out, all fear diminishing and not a trace of guilt for running off in the first place. As relieved as I was to find her, I couldn't even be upset at her for running away from me. It was the first time she'd ever done that.

"We can put her in the backseat!" Lilly offered, opening up the back door for Peewee to get in. She graciously accepted the offer, taking up the entire back seat.

"Oh, my goodness! Look at you, you sweet little thing!" Lilly's voice, suddenly high pitched, squealed, petting Peewee on the head. Little? I've always wondered why women call everything "little." Peewee is anything but little. Great Danes are large dogs, but Peewee is a hefty size for a female, weighing in at 150 pounds.

"Do you mind dropping us off at my house? It's just a couple blocks away, on Maple Road."

"Of course not! I was already planning on it," she said as she put her seatbelt on and started driving. "Your dog is adorable. I've always loved Great Danes. My house is just a little small to be able to have one." She looked over at me and smiled. "I'm so glad we found her."

"Me too. Thanks for your help."

Now that the commotion of being run over and trying to find Peewee was over, I finally took the time to get a good look at Lilly. Her long blonde hair was all over the place from the wind, much different from the way it was the other night when I pulled her over. Her eyes had been the first thing I'd noticed last week though, the green was striking and stood out against her light complexion. Near her right elbow was a tattoo of a simple smiley face which suited her perfectly even though I wasn't much of a fan of tattoos.

Putting my own seatbelt on, the movement sent a slight twinge, and she noticed me wince.

"Your arm... What if I broke your arm?" She stared wide eyed at my arm.

"Eyes on the road please. My arm is fine." It was definitely not broken; I could move it just fine. It just banged up a little.

"Ok, I hope not. Oh, and I can ask my brother, Will, to come look at your fence, he used to build fences for a living."

"I can probably take care of it, but thanks," I told her, sure that I could manage repairing my fence on my own.

"Well, I'm sure he wouldn't mind helping if you change your mind. Also, I own a bakery, Lilly's Bakery, right down the street on Main Street. Come in and get some free pastries for breakfast anytime. It's the least I can do for you since you didn't arrest me for running over you..." I couldn't help but smirk. I couldn't even imagine arresting this girl.

She paused and stared at me seriously. "I am in the clear on that, right?"

She was just too fun to mess with. I looked at her with a straight face. "You helped me find Peewee, so we're even. But you might want to look into taking a driving course. I think you could use a refresher."

She pursed her lips. "I think you may be overreacting just a tad on my driving skills, but thank you for your understanding on the little mishap."

"No problem. And if my arm *is* broken, and we go to trial, I'll ask for leniency for you. You'd probably just get a few months to a year in the state jail." I kept a straight face.

"What? There's jail time if I broke your arm? Seriously?" she shrieked with her emerald eyes suddenly huge.

I swallowed my laughter. "No, sorry. I couldn't help it." She was a gullible one. Cute, but definitely gullible. That may possibly be the first time I'd wanted to laugh at anything in quite a while.

"Freako." She shook her head and rolled her eyes with the slightest bit of a smile.

The haboob was dissipating some more, and the air was still brown, but the visibility was much better. I didn't research the weather before moving here, but apparently, I should have. If this was the norm around here, then I may have made a terrible mistake.

"There's my house, right there." I pointed to my modest, brown brick home as Lilly pulled over to the side of the street.

"Do you live here by yourself, or do you have a family here, too?"

"It's just me since my divorce. Thanks again for your help," I told her as I got out and opened the back door, grabbing Peewee with a firm grip on her collar.

"You are very welcome! I'm glad we found your sweet dog. And, again, I'm sorry for running over you... and for breaking your phone," she apologized again with a pitiful, but sincere expression on her face.

I interrupted her. "Seriously, it's fine. I'll see you around, Lilly." I closed the door and watched as she waved and drove away.

I live on a cul-de-sac on a quiet road. At 34, I'm the youngest person on my street; my neighbors are all probably in their early fifties and up, but most are most likely closer to 70. It's the kind of street where everyone keeps their yards fertilized and mowed, and their flowerbeds carefully stocked with flowers, plants, and an occasional small water fountain. The men in the neighborhood tend to gather in each other's front yards to discuss the need for rain, which ant killer is working best for them, and whether or not the people on the corner are ever going to cut down their dead shrubs.

A couple of the neighborhood women have approached me and let me know how happy they are to have a police officer on the street; although, I highly doubt there is ever much need for law enforcement in this neighborhood. But if it makes them feel safe, that's fine with me.

I took Peewee inside and pulled my sleeve up to get a look at my arm. I was going to have an ugly bruise, but that would be the worst of it. My phone was another story.

I sat down and looked at the neatly stacked unpacked boxes still lined along the living room wall. I'd been here a month and still hadn't unpacked most of my things. I don't like to have a lot of things; I just like to stick to what I need and love instead of having a lot of excess clutter to deal with. My house is a little larger than my former house. Even though it has three bedrooms, I can't imagine that I'd ever need a guest room. I didn't see any sense in wasting its potential just to put a bed in one of the rooms that nobody would ever sleep on. I use one bedroom for a workout room. The other bedroom has a very large, south-facing window that gets amazing sunlight. I plan to turn that into a reading room and fill it with plants and books; the things that make me feel most at peace. My best friend, Liam, used to make fun of me for that. He said men are supposed to relax with beer and football, not plants and books. In my defense, I do enjoy a cold beer while I'm watching a game. A man can have more than one hobby.

The backyard is the real reason I bought this house. It seems one of the perks of living in a small town is the yards are bigger. Certainly, bigger than the tiny yard that I had in Austin. I've been working on making a garden. It's a little late in the year to get started, but I tilled up a large section and planted some fast-growing vegetable plants; carefully sectioned it off so that Peewee doesn't trample the plants. It's therapeutic for me, and I'm looking forward to gathering fresh vegetables and fruit that I grew myself. There's nothing like fresh, fried okra or zucchini that came straight from your own garden. I even plan to learn to can my own salsa and sauces next year when I'm able to grow more.

Maybe I'd unpack just one box, and if there's anything I don't want, I'll donate it or trash it. I reached over and grabbed the box nearest to me and opened it up. Right on top were some of the things I'd kept from the marine corp. Under those were the framed photos that I used to have hanging in my hallway. I pulled them out and laid them on the floor, unsure if I wanted to hang them back up. A spider scurried out of the box, making me cringe and jump back. I took my shoe off and smacked it. Once I was sure it was dead, I went back to the photos. The first photo was of my parents, back when they were young and happy, as if everything was good in their world. The picture was taken right after they got married. Little did they know they would spend the rest of their marriage fighting and acting like they couldn't stand the sight of each other. It was probably the only photo I even had where my mom was smiling like that.

The next was a photo of Liam and I, a few months before he was shot. We'd gone on a camping trip in Colorado for Memorial Day weekend. We'd rented ATVs and went up in the mountains, I thought he was going to kill us when he almost drove us over a cliff on the way up, so I kicked him out of the driver's seat and drove us back down. That night we sat on the porch of our cabin laughing and talking, almost until the sun came back up the next morning. It was one of the best trips I'd ever been on, and I'd do anything to be able to do it again.

My method lately has been that if it doesn't make me happy to look at it, then I don't want it out where I can see it. I put the photo of Liam and I aside to hang on the wall, even though happy doesn't really describe what I feel when I see that picture anymore. I put the photo of my parents back in the box along with most of the other photos that I'd pulled out. These photos are just a cruel reminder of some of the things I'd rather forget. I put them back in the box and decided I'd wait until another day to work on unpacking. Right now, though, I needed a new phone. And possibly a pastry.

Chapter 5

Lilly

Apology via sourdough...

I opened the door to the bakery and was practically run down by Kennedy, my most observant employee.

"Where have you been? We've been calling you and everyone has been worried. You should have been here at 1:00. It is 2:43 PM. I thought you might have been impaled in the neck by flying debris." She stood there looking sternly at me, eyebrows raised, one hand on her hip and the other holding a broom.

I have three employees. First is my assistant manager, Caitlyn, of course. Then, I have Javier. He is a baker and an exceptional decorator. I've had him take over most of the decorating classes. He is a bit eccentric, extremely friendly, and the classes have increased in popularity since he started teaching them. Then last, but certainly not least, is my newest hire, Kennedy.

Kennedy is Will's sister-in-law. She has autism and has not had the best experiences with the other jobs that she tried in the past. When I met her, I just had this feeling that she would fit in perfectly at my bakery and she certainly did not disappoint. She simply needed to find the right place, a place where she could fit in and that could meet her unique needs. My bakery has been just the right place for her, and she has thrived here.

Kennedy is fixated on things that involve medical care, diseases, and sanitation. Originally, she was hired as Cleaning Captain; a new position that I created just for her. However, due to her unwavering devotion to her position and to the prevention of food born illness, I've given her the new, more prestigious title of Director of Sanitation and Infection Control. It's basically the same job duties, but I did give her a well-deserved raise with her title. Kennedy is as cute as she can be. She doesn't wear any makeup or jewelry and keeps her dark blonde hair in a neat bun which she insists on covering with a hair net even though I've told her repeatedly that she isn't required to wear one. She runs a tight ship and vows that there will be no violations of sanitation or food safety under her watch.

"My phone was dead, and I hit..." I started to explain, but then Caitlyn and Javier walked in from the back and saw me.

"Lilly! We've been worried sick! You went out to watch the haboob and then got stranded, didn't you. We knew it!" Caitlyn started in as soon as she saw me. She and Kennedy both looked at each other disapprovingly, shaking their heads then turned back to me.

"Well, I was on my way..."

"Lillian Scott, you are going to be the death of us, you know," Javier chimed in, pointing a flour sifter at me. Javier was 62 but could pass easily for 45 even though his hair was completely grey. He always wore the trendiest clothes, had regular manicures and facials, and abided by a strict fitness routine. Plus, he was vegan. He'd been resourceful in coming up with the few vegan options that we offer now.

Nobody would ever guess that I am the owner of this establishment by the way every one of my employees was talking to me as if they were all my parents.

Frustrated, I finally got a word in. "Would you all settle down and let me talk?"

All three looked taken aback and stared at me, waiting for my explanation for my tardiness to my own bakery.

I took a deep breath and finally was given the opportunity to tell my story. "I was on my way to work, and I thought I was going to have time to get here before the haboob hit. But it got here before I made it to work, and a dog ran out in front of me. I swerved to miss the dog but ended up hitting a police officer. Then we had to go search for his dog, and when we found the dog, I took them back home and now I'm here."

"Uh huh..." Caitlyn looked side eyed at Javier and then at Kennedy, none of which appeared to believe me.

"And you didn't answer your phone because...?" Javier questioned, skeptically. Why did I feel like I was on the witness stand?

"Because my phone was dead! Don't you think I would have let you all know if I was going to be late?"

"If you hit a police officer, then why aren't you in jail? And did you administer CPR and first aid? Did he need a tracheotomy?" Kennedy questioned, then added. "I know how to do a tracheotomy with a straw." I hoped none of us were ever unconscious; we could fall victim to Kennedy's first straw tracheotomy procedure.

"He was fine. And it was an accident; he wasn't even mad about it." I looked at the other two. "Any more questions?" They were making this into a bigger deal than it was.

Caitlyn looked at me puzzled. "Wait. So, this actually happened? You didn't go out somewhere to watch the haboob against everyone's orders?"

"No! The whole thing is 100% true! It's nice to know I have such a comforting support system for the trauma I just went through." I looked at my three interrogators, now with sorrowful expressions. "Now, if you will all excuse me, I'm going to go wash the dirt off myself and charge my phone," I snapped and headed off to the restroom.

From the reflection in the mirror, I looked homeless. My hair looked like it hadn't been brushed in weeks, and my skin was splotchy with brown, visible dirt all over me. I washed my face in the sink and wiped the rest of my body down with wet paper towels. Then I freshened up my hair and makeup with the bag of toiletries that I keep in my office.

"Knock, knock." I heard Caitlyn say as she opened the door. "I brought you an ice-cold cucumber lemonade, your favorite." She handed me the drink. "I'm sorry we were so insensitive. We just thought..."

"I know. It's ok," I said, taking a huge, refreshing gulp. We have a large variety of lemonades that we have perfected, and this one is my current favorite.

"So, is he cute? The officer?" she asked. "I mean, since the hardware store isn't working out, I guess running over men is an interesting approach." She giggled.

I couldn't help but laugh. "I was so worried about him and his dog and the haboob that I really didn't pay that much attention." He wasn't bad looking. Not at all. Of course, I noticed how attractive he was from the moment I first saw him, but I didn't want her driving me crazy with questions. It's his personality that hasn't won me over. "He said he just moved here recently."

"So, you know where he lives now, right? Maybe you could get all sexied up in a cute little dress and take him a pie as an 'I'm sorry' gift? As they say, the way to a man's heart is through his stomach."

"What? No. I already told him he is welcome to come in anytime for some free food. I'm not about to go taking any pies to him, especially not all *sexied up*... he would think I'm some kind of freak."

"Ok, well, don't come crying to me when he meets somebody else, and you lost your chance."

"I'm pretty sure he is not even the slightest bit interested in me. At all... He pulled me over last week and gave me a sobriety test. I hadn't even been drinking."

Caitlyn nearly aspirated on her lemonade with that comment.

"And he wasn't very friendly either. He kept criticizing my driving skills." I wouldn't say I'm a bad driver, even if Kade thinks otherwise. I trust my driving completely. Isn't it better to be totally comfortable in your own driving skills than to be nervous? I've always heard that nervous drivers are the most dangerous.

After Caitlyn returned to the counter, I turned on my phone and checked my messages after it had a chance to charge a little. I had four missed calls and six texts, all from my mother. I looked them over and sighed. I made one bad decision with a haboob a year ago, then the next time we have one, the entire town of Willow Creek is on high alert, monitoring my whereabouts and assuming I'm out doing something stupid if I'm not answering my phone. I texted her back, telling her my phone was just dead and I'm safe and secure at the bakery. I wasn't going to go into any detail about what went on before I got to work. I have to admit that I have given people enough reasons in the past to make them worry when I'm not where I'm supposed to be, especially when I don't answer my phone, but it can be annoying.

I went up to the front and found Kennedy, wearing a mask, vigorously sweeping the floor.

"Did you notice how much dirt was on the floor? I almost have it all cleaned up now, but we are all still at risk of pneumonia, bronchitis, and acute respiratory failure because of our lungs filling up with dirt." She was full of medical facts. Sometimes, I googled them to see if she was correct, surprised at how often she was accurate, although usually on the more extreme end.

"Well, I sure hope we don't get any of that! But the floor looks great. Thanks, Kennedy."

I went over to the class sign up board. Usually, we only offer decorating classes, teaching techniques for decorating cookies and cakes. However, I'd had some requests lately for some baking classes and decided to offer a few bread and muffin classes. I was thinking of a few beginner classes for zucchini bread, cinnamon rolls, pumpkin bread, and carrot cake. But I wanted to focus more on some specialty sourdough classes. I put them all on the calendar and asked Caitlyn to update the website with the new information.

We close at 5:00 PM, but I'm usually the only one that stays that late. Business fades by late afternoon. Kennedy doesn't drive and is usually picked up by about 3:30. I am flexible with her schedule and let her work according to when she has rides to and from work.

Before I headed out the door, I noticed the loaves of jalapeno cheddar sourdough bread that were left over from the day. Most people like sourdough bread, right? I mean of course they do since it's one of our top sellers. Men, perhaps… seem to like jalapeno cheddar sourdough bread? It's just that it would be a shame to waste a loaf when there are people who might want it, people who are new to the neighborhood. People who may have injured arms and might not want to fix themselves something to eat. Such a shame to waste this.

Ok, enough. I'm not going to take him any bread. That's a ridiculous idea. He probably thinks I'm a psychopath as it is by the way our last two unintentional meetings went. And since when did I get any idea in my head that I was going to pursue Kade? He wasn't even all that nice. I left the loaf on the counter, locked up, and went to my car.

Maybe not pursue him... maybe apologize for the accidental vehicular assault. I thought about how I ran him over with my car, hurting his arm, and breaking his phone. Maybe his lack of personality was due to being run over and needing to find his dog.

I went back inside the bakery and returned to my car with a loaf of jalapeno cheddar sourdough bread.

Chapter 6

Kade

It was sourdough…

That haboob was no joke. I felt like every inch of me, including my teeth, had been sand blasted and was coated with a gritty layer of dirt. Lilly seemed fairly unfazed by it which was concerning. I hoped that this wasn't the usual around here since it's not something I could ever get used to. I took a shower and rinsed all the dirt off me, surprised at the amount of dirt swirling around in the bottom of the tub.

Afterwards, I put Peewee on a leash to take her out since the fence was broken and I couldn't let her loose in the yard. She'd proven that she couldn't be trusted. Fixing the fence was the next thing on my list and I'd have to make a trip to the hardware store sooner than later. It wasn't anything I couldn't handle on my own even though Lilly was gracious enough to offer her brother's services without his consent.

I needed to find a phone store and get my phone looked at, hopefully repaired rather than having to deal with a new phone. I would rather have my armpit hair waxed than even think about getting a new phone. If I could, I'd gladly keep the same phone until the day I died instead of deal with the inconveniences that came with a new phone.

An hour later, Chad from the phone store broke the news that my phone was a total loss. Fortunately, he was able to work a type of magic that only phone store employees can do and retrieved all of my information, which was a plus. I had two missed calls from my mother and about eight texts from her. I tensed up just seeing her name on the screen. She was in one of her moods again, and as usual, found a reason to be mad at me. She's never upset with my sister, Haleigh, just me. Today, she was upset because her new TV still needs to be mounted on the wall and if I had visited her more often, I could have mounted it by now.

3:03 PM: When are you coming to visit?

3:04 PM: My birthday is coming up. It would be nice to see you, but I'm sure you are too busy.

3:10 PM: Never mind.

3:23 PM: My TV still hasn't been mounted.

3:32 PM: Forget it.

3:48 PM: I've been asking you to come visit for a long time and you never have time for me. My neighbor's son came to see her last week. He put up a ceiling fan for her.

4:12 PM: Forget I said anything.

4:37 PM: I can just keep watching it on the floor.

I ran my hand through my hair and groaned outloud to myself. I used to visit her weekly. I took care of her yard, household repairs, maintenance on her car, programing her thermostat, anything she needed. She never actually appreciated it; it was more of an expectation, and she usually complained that I didn't do it right. I would have mounted her TV if it weren't for the fact that she moved seven hours away about three years ago, making it a little difficult for me to visit often enough to take care of things like that. She'd seen a property for sale in Oklahoma and had to have it. She sold her house that she'd lived in since before I was born and off she went, not wanting to listen to any unsolicited advice from me or my sister. The problem is she seems to have forgotten that I have a full-time job and can't travel for seven hours to mount her TV. The best I can do is visit a few times a year and take care of what needs to be done during those visits.

My mom and I never had a great relationship, not even when I was little. Of my parents, the one that was actually proud of me was my dad, but my relationship with my dad carried a different set of difficulties. Unfortunately, he passed away five years ago from cirrhosis of the liver, after many years of alcoholism. By the time he admitted he had a problem and was willing to get help with his drinking, it was too late, and the damage was too severe. He didn't drink during the weekday. He successfully held down a job as an accountant for twenty-five years. He drank during the weekends and at night when he came home from work, opening his first drink as soon as he set his keys down. He didn't go out to bars or drink heavily at restaurants when we went out to eat; however, we only went out to eat for special celebrations which consisted mainly of birthdays. Fortunately, we never had to worry about him drinking and driving because once he opened the first drink, he stayed home. As much as I didn't like the drinking, I appreciated him not putting himself and others in harm's way. He was a loving dad, even when he was drinking. He had a great sense of humor, and he used to make jokes about my mother that would have probably landed him a slap across the face if she'd ever heard them. I wish we had been able to have more quality time together, just me and him, but he wasn't very present in my life because the only time he was sober was when he was working. I wasn't able to have a normal father-son relationship with him. He and my mother were at each other's throats for as long as I can remember. It seems they only stopped fighting when he was on hospice, confined to a bed and too weak to argue with her anymore.

Unlike my dad, my mother wasn't loving. She didn't seem to enjoy being a mother; we were always a disruption to whatever she wanted to do, and even now, she doesn't seem to actually like me very much. I'm more of a handyman to her. She certainly never approved of me being a police officer. "You won't get rich doing that," she'd said. I used to think my mother's grumpiness was due to my dad and his drinking, But she is just as grouchy now as she ever was when he was alive, maybe even more so. Apparently, she's just an unhappy person. She's one of those people who will never be happy, no matter what the situation. She is retired now, but she went through numerous jobs. She'd find a job that she was sure she would love, like it for about 6 months, then decide she hated it for one reason or another. It was a cycle that never ended.

After my mom moved, my sister moved to Kentucky to be closer to her husband's family. My sister and I are close, and she understands me more than anyone. She has two kids, both boys, and I used to take them fishing or to the park to play ball. But her husband's mother was having health problems and needed their help. Of course, I understood why they needed to move, but I missed having them around.

A few years ago, I went through a series of events that left me just numb. I tried to make things work in Austin, but I had to get out and start fresh somewhere new, which is how I landed here in Willow Creek. I'd been passing through town and stopped for gas and lunch. I liked the small-town vibe, which was much different from what I was used to. It has everything you need, but on a smaller scale. The people are friendly, the crime rate is low, and you can get from one end of town to the other in just a few minutes. I was able to find a job and a house, and it all fell into place like it was meant to be.

All that reminiscing about the past made me want something sweet to take my mind off it. Would it be weird to show up at the bakery the same day as the whole dramatic haboob incident? Maybe, but Lilly didn't strike me as one who cared if something was weird, which was a quality that I was finding oddly endearing.

I found Lilly's bakery, but the sign showed they closed at 5:00, just a few minutes late. Disappointed, I drove on home. When I pulled into my driveway, I immediately noticed a large, pink foreign object stuck to my front door. On closer inspection, I realized it was an entire loaf of bread, wrapped in pink plastic and taped firmly to the glass, definitely an unexpected and peculiar sight. A note was taped next to it. '***I rang the bell but there was no answer. I hope you like jalapeño cheddar sourdough bread.***' The note wasn't signed, but I had a feeling this was Lilly's doing; although I was baffled that she just happened to have a roll of tape handy in her car.

Is this what happens in small towns? People tape loaves of bread to front doors? This proved my theory. Lilly didn't care if things were weird. I peeled the excessive amount of tape off the door, took the loaf inside, and put Peewee's leash on for her walk.

"I noticed you had something stuck to your door earlier. Couldn't quite figure out what that was!" my next-door neighbor, Leonna, hollered at me from her yard as we walked outside. Leonna looked to be in her late 70s and always wore the kind of leisure suit that had matching pants and a bold patterned jacket. Her white hair hit just below her chin and curled under in perfect symmetry all the way around her head. She was a sweet lady, but a little hard of hearing.

I waved at her. "Yes, it was a loaf of bread." I hollered back at her, realizing how ridiculous that sounded after I said it.

"It was what?" she yelled, holding a water hose over her potted, red geraniums.

"Bread! It was a loaf of bread," I responded loudly.

"It was a what?!" she shouted back, again. I plastered a smile on my face and walked over to her instead of continuing yelling back and forth over our yards.

"Hi, Leonna, I was trying to say it was a loaf of bread. On my door, it was bread."

She looked puzzled. "Now, why on earth would anyone do that instead of just hanging it in a bag on your doorknob?"

"I was wondering the same thing, ma'am. Have a nice evening." I waved and walked Peewee back to the sidewalk while she stared after me, still seeming deep in thought about the bread mystery.

Back inside after Peewee's walk, I stared at the bread for a minute, thinking of Lilly. She had gotten her pretty little self stuck in my head all afternoon, so it was a pleasant surprise to find this little gem taped to my front door. I don't know any of my neighbors very well, and I suspect they would have simply come back when I was home rather than wasting what had to be an entire roll of tape. Or like Leonna suggested, they might have simply placed it in a bag and hung it on my doorknob like normal civilized people often do.

I opened up my laptop and looked up Lilly's Bakery. She had an impressive website going. There was a photo of her on the home page, wearing a pink dress with a baker's hat and apron, flour or powdered sugar on her face. She was laughing and holding out a plate of cream cheese Danishes. Damn, she is gorgeous.

I hadn't dated much since my divorce, a few dates here and there, but they never went anywhere. Maybe my ex, Bethany, ruined things for me. I can't say that I blame her, though. I thought we had a perfect marriage. I spoiled the crap out of her; she was everything to me. But then, when I went through that traumatic event on duty, it changed me. It changed us. Honestly, it was almost just as traumatic for her, and in the end, she couldn't do it anymore. She couldn't be married to a police officer. I let her have the house and everything in it. I only took Peewee and a few boxes of personal items.

I hadn't been this intrigued by a woman in a long time, but there was something about this girl that caught my attention. For the next several minutes, I continued to creep through Lilly's website like some sort of stalker. I learned their business hours, read the story of how the bakery started, browsed their coffee, tea, and extensive lemonade selection, and researched their list of classes. Apparently, Lilly's Bakery also participates in a Farmer's Market on the last Saturday of every month. It's hard to believe that the same person that owns this successful bakery is the same woman that drives like a drunk driver, hit me with her car, taped an entire loaf of bread to my door, and who I cannot stop thinking about.

Chapter 7

Lilly

A few days later...

If there's one thing about Willow Creek, it's that we do love a Farmer's Market. Even though I have a brick-and-mortar shop now, I still love the vibe of the Farmer's Market. I think it's the wholesome casualness of it. People can just come as they are, bring their dogs, and interact with others in the community. It's the kind of place that makes you crave homemade preserves, local honey, handmade soaps, and fresh picked tomatoes.

The Willow Creek Farmer's Market is opened every Saturday from Spring through Fall, but we only do a booth the last Saturday of the month. Caitlyn and Javier take turns helping with it. Today, Caitlyn was helping, and Kennedy volunteered to come for a few hours as well. Caitlyn is good at keeping the information plastered all over several social media platforms, so we usually have a pretty good turnout.

I'm proud of our set up. The table was decorated in a pale pink tablecloth with an ivory lace runner. Some of the vintage cake stands that I've collected are used for displaying cookies, pastries, and cupcakes. A variety of breads were arranged aesthetically in stained wooden crates with fresh cut flowers sticking out from behind. We've also put together some cookie decorating kits for the kids that contain colored icing bags, sprinkles, and sugar cookies. We always pick three different lemonades to bring, which are always a big hit. Today, we chose watermelon mint, peach, and pomegranate. Being one of the world's biggest lemonade snobs, I like the flavors to be on point.

"So, I wonder how the police officer is doing since you crashed into him?" Caitlyn smiled and asked as she finished setting out the croissants.

"It was more of a bump than a crash, but I'm sure he's fine," I quickly responded and tried to act like he was the least of my worries, even though it was far from the truth. Not so much a worry as it was just not being able to get him out of my head.

"Did you at least listen to my advice and take him a pie as an apology gift?" She raised her eyebrow, staring straight at me. As much as I love Caitlyn, she could be very persistent, especially when it came to my love life... or lack thereof.

“No, I didn’t take him a pie, I took...” I started, then hesitated, not necessarily wanting to tell the tale of what actually transpired.

“Wait, what? You really went to his house? Tell me everything and leave nothing to my imagination.” She clapped her hands together and waited anxiously like she was going to explode with anticipation.

“Settle down. He wasn’t even home when I got there. I just took him a loaf of bread.”

Caitlyn looked disappointed and dropped her hands to her sides. “So, what did you do with the bread? Does he even know you stopped by?”

I could feel my face turning red, this was the part that I had been worried about. He was going to think I’m some sort of lunatic. “You don’t want to know.”

“Oh no. What did you do...”

“I kind of taped it to his door,” I blurted out, knowing how stupid it sounded.

With a total look of disbelief, Caitlyn’s eyes were huge. “Excuse me, what?”

“Well, I mean, he wasn’t home, and I didn’t want any dogs or cats to get it. I happened to have some tape in my car so I just kind of taped it really good to the glass door...” Saying it out loud like that sounded way worse than I anticipated.

She interrupted, still completely perplexed. "So, Mr. Police Officer comes home to find an entire loaf of bread *taped* to his front door? Did you ever think of just putting it in a bag and hanging it somewhere for him? Did you at least leave a note?"

"His name is Kade... and it was wrapped in plastic, so it wasn't like I taped it directly to the bread. And I taped a note next to the bread, but I forgot to sign my name." This wasn't sounding any better. I honestly was just trying to come up with a way to keep the bread safe and I didn't have a bag. Looking back at it now, it would have made way more sense to do basically anything other than what I actually did. There is no way he doesn't think I'm a total and complete idiot.

She looked at me for a second with a blank look on her face. "I can't understand you sometimes," she shook her head and poured herself some lemonade.

Just in time to break up this conversation, Kennedy and her mom, Lynette, showed up. Lynette has always been extremely friendly with us and expresses her gratitude to me often for hiring Kennedy. Apparently, she tried everything to help Kennedy get a job, utilizing all the right services available, but nothing seemed to work out for Kennedy until the bakery. Kennedy usually looks annoyed with her mother and today was no different.

"Hi there! The booth looks amazing as usual!" Lynette looked over the goods, picking up a package of tea cakes.

"I'll get a package of these; they are my favorite of all time," she said, pulling some dollar bills out of her purse.

"No, no, Lynette. You can have them. Now, go enjoy your teacakes and we'll see you later!" She always tried to pay me, but there was no way I was taking money from Kennedy's mother for just a few teacakes. The way I saw it, the bakery could afford to give away a few cookies to the parents of our staff.

"Thank you! You girls have fun today." She waved. Kennedy rolled her eyes at her mother and didn't say goodbye to her. Lynette was clearly used to this as it didn't seem to faze her at all, but I had a feeling she needed a break from Kennedy just as much as Kennedy appeared to want a break from her.

After Lynette left, Kennedy stood with her arms folded across her chest and a disapproving look on her face, looking toward one of the produce stands.

"What's the matter, Kennedy?" I asked her, already sure that she was going to complain about a food safety issue. She could do well as a food safety inspector one day; except she would probably have even the best restaurants shut down due to too many critical violations.

"I'm pretty sure they are cross contaminating at that produce stand."

"Well, let's just worry about our own stand. Would you like to be in charge of the samples?" I knew this would get her attention. She quickly snapped out of her disapproving stance and went to get a pair of gloves from the supply box.

Caitlyn left the booth for a few minutes to get both our dogs some treats at the pet supply booth. She returned excitedly.

"Lilly! You should have seen this dog at the dog treat booth! She's a Great Dane and she is huge and the sweetest thing ever! I could barely tear myself away from her. And her owner was H.O.T. by the way. Seriously, you wouldn't believe."

Kade and Peewee. It had to be them. I'd never seen another dog like that around here. I couldn't let him see me; I was too embarrassed about the bread incident. What I thought made sense at the time, now just sounds ridiculous. I mean, what kind of self-respecting woman goes around taping bread to men's front doors? I have a way of doing random things and then realizing way too late that it was dumb, but that's neither here nor there at this point.

Without making eye contact, for fear that she would be able to read my mind, I made an excuse to get myself out of sight. The Farmer's Market didn't actually have a restroom; however, the convenience store next to it did. "I'm going to run to the restroom. I'll be back in a few minutes."

Once I was at a safe distance, I turned around and scanned the crowd. Sure enough, I spotted Peewee first.

Then, holding her leash was Kade, looking even hotter than he was last time. He shouldn't be allowed to have that kind of body when he doesn't have the personality to match it.

I'd wandered around the convenience store, chatted with the store owner, and freshened up in the restroom when Caitlyn texted me. **Are you ok? You've been gone forever.**

On my way. Apparently, I had stalled for long enough. If I had any luck at all, he was already gone.

I slowly made my way back to our booth, glancing around, and didn't see any sign of Kade or Peewee. Kennedy was already running out of samples, so I busied myself with helping her get some more ready.

"Oh, there's that cute little puppy again!" Caitlyn squealed. Oh, please no. I looked up from the tea cake pieces to find none other than Kade and Peewee standing right in the middle of our booth. "Lilly, look at this dog! She is the absolute sweetest!"

"They've actually already met," Kade said, looking right at me with his eyebrows raised and a slight smirk on his face. "Hello again, Lilly." The way he said my name in his low voice was almost criminal.

Why did he have to be looking like that with his athletic shorts and his T-shirt that fit him just tight enough that his chest muscles showed through the material? His arms looked rock solid; like he obviously works out regularly.

Not just cardio either, this guy lifts some weights. And those eyes? Even under the brim of his red baseball cap, the blue in his eyes still popped.

Caitlyn stopped petting Peewee and stared back and forth at Kade and I as if she was waiting for an explanation.

She turned her attention back to Kade. "Wait. You two know each other? You wouldn't happen to be a police officer, would you?" she asked, eyes wide.

I shot her a look. "Caitlyn, let's not question our customers on their occupations," I tried to intervene.

Kennedy walked over to Kade and looked at his arm. Sure enough, a large bruise could be seen above his elbow, partly covered by his sleeve. "I think we've found the victim," she announced firmly and nodded to Caitlyn. "Officer, have you been checked for deep vein thrombosis or tetanus? Because you *will* end up hospitalized if that is the case."

Kade's forehead wrinkled as he replied, "Um... no?"

"Kennedy, I don't think he has either of those conditions. Why don't you get back to the samples?" I told her as Kade watched her, curiously. I looked back at him. "Is there something in particular you are looking for? We have some samples of our teacakes here if you would like to try some." I motioned to the platter that Kennedy was re-stocking, trying to steer the conversation away from anything that could lead to more embarrassment on my part.

"Actually, I'm here to get some more of that jalapeño cheddar sourdough bread. The last loaf I had was delicious, but it's already gone, and I figure it would be easier to get it myself rather than have to pull all the tape off." And there it was... exactly what I was trying to avoid. He said this so calmly and expressionlessly that I couldn't tell if he was being sarcastic, funny, or just matter of fact.

I felt my face turn hot and beet red just as an audible giggle came out of Caitlyn. I glared at her out of the corner of my eye. Doing my best to act oblivious to his remark about the tape, I picked up a loaf and placed it in a bag for him.

"Here you go, Officer. Have a nice day and enjoy the bread." I had no intention of discussing the taped bread incident ever again, especially not with him. I'm usually fairly confident, but I definitely made an error in judgement on that one.

"I will. You do the same... Lilly." He nodded to me with the slightest hint of a grin and walked away.

"Lilly, you didn't tell me the police officer looked like *that*! Here you have been frequenting K&A's Hardware and turning up with nothing, then you freaking run your vehicle into *that* non wedding ring wearing specimen of a man?" Caitlyn exclaimed animatedly.

"It would appear so, yes."

"If he looks that good in shorts and a T-shirt, I can't even begin to imagine what he looks like in his police uniform."

"Hot. He looks freaking hot in his uniform. However, I'm not interested. I like gentlemanly men, not butt heads, not even if they look like he does."

Chapter 8

Kade

I went into the hardware store to get some supplies to repair the fence where it blew down. Normally, I worked the early shift, but I'd agreed to change shifts for the day with another officer today, so I'd go in this afternoon. I wanted to get the fence fixed before work though, because I wasn't able to tolerate one more day of Peewee not being able to run in the backyard. She'd been getting way too hyper inside the house, even with multiple walks a day, and she'd already completely knocked over the couch. I had to move it up against the wall to keep her from knocking it over again.

I had my supplies loaded up on the lumber cart and was on my way to grab a post hole digger when I saw dark blonde hair, the color and length of Lilly's. I turned the corner and walked up to her. "Lilly?" She turned around.

"Oh! Um, hi there! We meet again!" She nervously looked around at the boxes of screws she'd been examining.

"Are you working on a project?"

"Yep, just needed to get some screws. A cabinet door at the bakery fell out of the hinge and I didn't have any screws." She picked up a box of one-inch screws. Way too long for a cabinet door.

"The front hinge or the side?"

"It's the front, the part the door sticks onto."

"You don't want those. They're too long, it will go straight through the cabinet and stick out the other side." I picked up a box of 5/8th inch screws and handed them to her.

"Here, get these."

"Thanks!" She smiled and looked at me as if she wanted to say something else but didn't.

"No problem... Do you need help with your cabinet door?"

Her eyes lit up for a second as if she was going to take me up on it, but instead she declined. "Oh, no. I can do it... But thanks! See you later, Officer."

"It's Kade, remember?"

Her face flushed. "Sorry. See you later, Kade." She smiled and walked off toward the self-checkout.

.....

"Need any help over there?" my neighbor across the alley yelled over at me as I worked on the fence.

"Thanks, but I think I've got it, sir." I should have gotten started earlier on it before it got so hot, but it was already miserable. The temps lately have been consistently in the low 100s. It was dry heat and combined with the never-ending wind, it usually felt like being blasted by a hair dryer.

The next thing I knew, he was standing next to me, surveying my situation.

"Larry Friedman, but you can call me Mr. Friedman," he announced, holding his hand out. I couldn't tell if he was serious or if this was some of the small-town humor I'd experienced in the past few weeks. Larry Friedman was round in the middle but thin everywhere else, his grey hair was parted neatly on the side, and he sported a full mustache. He wore a short sleeve button-up plaid shirt with a pencil, pen, folded paper, and eyeglasses stored neatly in the front pocket. His appearance reminded me of an older version of my own dad as he used to have a closet full of shirts just like Larry's and he too stocked his front pockets with the same items as Larry did.

I hesitated for a second, unsure of how he really wanted to be addressed.

"Nah, I'm just joking with you. Please... call me Larry. I see you're new to the neighborhood. Where'd you come from?"

"I moved here from Austin a few weeks ago. My name's Kade, Kade Wayland," I replied, shaking his hand.

"Quite a storm we had here, wasn't it? I bet you hadn't seen anything quite like that in Austin. Fortunately, we don't get haboobs like that too often. It was unexpected because we usually don't get them in the summer, normally just springtime." He looked around at the tools I had laying out on the ground and picked up my post hole digger. "Your post hole digger looks a little bent, I've got a brand new one if you want to borrow it. As hard as the ground is, you need a good one."

Seeing Lilly at the hardware store had distracted me enough that I'd forgotten to get the post hole digger.

"Sure, I'd appreciate that." I hadn't seen any rain since I moved to Willow Creek, and the ground was hard and dry; might as well be attempting to dig into concrete. I followed Larry across the alley into his garage.

Larry's backyard looked like it came straight out of a gardening magazine. The dark green grass resembled carpet. The flowerbeds were neatly manicured with various shrubs, flowers, and vines. A water fountain trickled in the corner next to a firepit. The opposite corner featured a birdhouse surrounded by a bird bath, hummingbird feeder, and a metal bird with wings that moved in the air like a pinwheel.

Larry's garage was the complete opposite of his yard. It was cluttered, unkept, and in dire need of cleaning. He had more tools and gadgets than I'd ever seen in one garage. Just the number of clamps he had all lined neatly along one wall was unbelievable and surely unnecessary unless you were in the clamp selling business, which I suspected was not the case with him. There didn't seem to be much thought put into organization in Larry's garage; things just seemed to be stuck where there was a place to put them. The workbench by the door contained everything from empty relish jars to a stack of model car kits. Under the bench was a pile of at least 20 empty wine boxes, the box-o-wine kind that has a spout for pouring directly from a box. That also reminded me of my dad, except his stack was empty twelve packs of beer boxes and empty whisky bottles.

As Larry was getting his post hole digger from behind a vast assortment of fishing poles, a woman emerged from the house carrying two to-go cups of what appeared to be lemonade.

"Here's your lemonade, Larry. They were out of your strawberry flavor, but I got you the regular kind." She saw me and stopped. "Oh, I'm sorry! I didn't know we had company."

"Alana, this is Kade, he just moved into the Crawford's old house across the alley. The wind got his fence last week so I'm letting him use my new post hole digger," he introduced us as he took his lemonade and took a huge gulp out of it. "Kade, this is my wife, Alana."

Alana was probably about 15 years younger than Larry. She was very stylish and was probably around 60 years old, but he had to be in his late 70s or early 80s. They were an odd-looking couple; Alana with a classy, stylish look paired with a man who is quite the opposite. I couldn't help but wonder how she ended up with a man like Larry, but that's really none of my concern.

"Kade, it's nice to meet you. If I had known, I would have brought you a lemonade also."

"Oh, that's ok. I'm not much of a lemonade guy and I need to get back to my fence, anyway. It was nice meeting you both and I'll bring this back as soon as I'm finished." I waved and carried Larry's post hole digger back to my own yard, wondering how I was ever going to fit into this exceedingly neighborly neighborhood.

It didn't take long for me to get the fence fixed and good as new. The hardest part was getting the ground wet enough to dig the hole for the post. Even Larry's brand-new post hole digger wasn't a match for this rock-hard ground. But finally, for the first time in a few days, I was able to let Peewee free in the backyard to play.

.....

Although I haven't necessarily become close friends with any of my coworkers yet, I get along with them and I like how everyone works as a team. I've taught myself that it's easier to not get attached to people. Anybody that I get close to either dies, or moves away, or divorces me, or gets shot. So, it's safer to keep my interactions at work strictly professional rather than becoming good friends with the other officers.

It's a small police force and the crime rate is low compared to larger cities. It's been a nice change of pace for sure with the majority of my time being spent handling occasional traffic stops, minor drug offenses, and some property crime with teenagers being the main culprit. I haven't had to restrain anyone, there hasn't been a need to pull out my gun, and the citizens have mostly been very respectful and easy to deal with. The most interesting traffic stop I've had so far was pulling over Lilly.

I'd stopped for an iced tea at a gas station and when I went back to my car, I noticed smoke billowing into the air from a neighborhood, not far from where I was. Once I got there, I found the structure in question was a one-story corner house which had smoke coming from the roof above the garage, most likely an attic fire. An older woman wearing a patriotic, red, white, and blue outfit waved frantically as she saw me approach.

"Help! Officer, there's a couple inside!" she yelled, hurrying toward me as I got out of the car.

I grabbed the fire extinguisher out of my car and picked up my radio. "372 to dispatch." When they responded, I continued, "Request fire and EMS. People inside burning house."

"10-4 requesting fire and EMS now."

The house wasn't engulfed in flames; I felt certain I could get them out myself. "10-4. I'm going to enter the residence."

The front door was locked, so I gave it two strong kicks. Once it opened, I covered my face and entered the home. I ran toward the northwest side of the home, which is where the garage is located and where the smoke appeared to be coming from.

"Hello! Anyone here?" I yelled.

"Help! We're in the garage!" I heard a woman yell followed by coughing.

In the garage, I found an older man lying on the floor and a woman trying to pull him up, gasping for air. I tried the garage door opener on the wall, but it didn't work. The fire was in the attic, but it was burning through the ceiling, causing debris to fall into the garage.

"Something fell on him!" she cried.

"Ma'am, I need you to go outside and stand on the sidewalk where it's safe. I'll get him out. The fire department and EMS are on their way."

The woman did as I instructed. I grabbed the gentleman and dragged him out of the house, then placed him on the ground in the front yard just as I heard the sirens. He was unconscious but breathing. The woman was lying on the ground at this point, surrounded by a growing crowd of concerned neighbors.

Some of the crowd was getting too close to the house, trying to see the fire and coming up with their own assessments as to the source. I ushered them away from the house to the sidewalk and cleared them away from the victims as EMS and fire arrived.

EMS took over with the medical care of both the woman and man while firefighters entered the home and extinguished the fire. The woman, now with an oxygen mask, appeared to be struggling more than she was when she was inside the house. The man, also on oxygen, was still not conscious. His shirt had been removed and there was an obvious injury to his collar bone.

"We're going to have to intubate him," the EMT shouted at his partner.

"Officer! Will they be ok?" The woman in the patriotic outfit came up to me, a panicked look on her face. "I saw the smoke coming out of the house and I tried to call them, and then I tried to go inside but the door was locked."

"Do you know their names?" I asked, taking out my notebook.

"Oh, yes. They are Leonard and Barbara Scott. They've lived in this house for about 30 years. Barbara's in my crochet club. They're the nicest people you'll ever meet. Are they going to be ok?"

"I hope so, ma'am, but I can't give you an answer on that. Do you happen to know of any family members we can contact?"

"They have three children. One of them lives in New Mexico and I don't have his number. They also have two kids that live here in town, Will and Lilly. I don't know either of their phone numbers, though."

I froze. "Does Lilly happen to own a bakery?"

"Yes! The one on Main Street."

Chapter 9

Lilly

I'd given up on scoping out dates at the hardware stores. But honestly, it wasn't even that I'd given up on it. I hadn't wanted to go since I met Kade, even though I was trying to convince myself I wasn't interested in him. When I went to Mike's Lumber, I was legitimately looking for screws for the cabinet, not for men. Is it a coincidence that I happened to run into Kade? At the hardware store of all places? These accidental meetings were adding up. Even in a small town, it's strange to keep running into the same person so often.

I felt fine in the morning, but by lunchtime, I was feeling awful and had to come home early. It might have been from being out in the heat at the Farmer's Market on Saturday. I don't know, but I was tired, weak, and everything from my hair to my bones hurt. I didn't think I was sick; although, it's hard to tell sometimes. This kind of thing happens to me far too often and it's one of the things I don't talk about to almost anyone other than Jo and Caitlyn.

Immediately after I got home, I changed into my comfy clothes: a pair of black leggings, a T-shirt that read 'Employee of the Month' which I bought thinking it was hilarious since I'm the owner, and blue fuzzy socks with a hole so big my entire heel stuck through it. I'd fallen asleep on the couch and couldn't manage to get up after that. I'd planned to stop at the pet store today for crickets for Penny, but she could wait until tomorrow. The rest of the day was going to consist only of staying right where I was, rotting on the couch. I didn't even feel like reading my current romcom.

Originally, I'd planned to start going over some ideas for Kip and Leanne's wedding and groom's cake today, but that was going to have to wait until I felt better; we still had plenty of time to sort out the details. Besides, Leanne and I needed to break the news to Kip that he did not, in fact, need a red velvet cake shaped like a hog. The last thing their guests needed was to see a mutilated animal on the table next to a gorgeous, white wedding cake.

My dad texted me early this morning asking if I wanted to stop by for lunch today. We normally have monthly lunch dates at his favorite restaurant, Loonie's Lunchbox. We both always order the same thing, sizzling chicken and shrimp, but they are closed for remodeling for a few days. He wanted me to give him some ideas for a new window display for the shop. My parents own a vintage toy store called Back in Time, and they seem to think that owning a bakery also qualifies me as an expert in toy store marketing. He said he would even ask my mom to make her famous squash casserole that I love so much. As much as I hated telling him no, I didn't have the energy for it. He tried to hide his disappointment, but I could tell. I promised him we would have lunch together later this week and I'd bring his favorite chocolate pie for dessert.

The TV stayed on the food network all day, but that only made me hungry. Another thing I wasn't going to do today was fix anything to eat and I didn't have anything to heat up in the microwave. I placed a delivery order at my go-to sandwich shop, Annie's Deli. If there was a fan club for their Thanksgiving Sandwich, I would run for president of it. It has made it to my Best Foods Ever Consumed list with the most magnificent combination of turkey, dressing, cranberry sauce, and gravy all on the most perfectly toasted bread. Originally, it was only offered seasonally until word spread about this spectacular sandwich and it became their top seller. I don't want to take the credit, but I may have pushed that sandwich on basically everyone I met. Now it can be enjoyed all year long. The manager, Laurie, always puts extra cranberry sauce on mine and doesn't even need to be asked anymore. She sees my name, she knows what I'm going to order.

After my sandwich arrived, I ate it on the couch and let Beatrice have the little bit that I didn't finish. Then I must have fallen asleep again because I was woken up by my doorbell, followed by Beatrice' barking. There was no way I was opening the door looking like I did. It was probably just a salesperson even though I had two no soliciting signs; one on the front of my door and another right over my doorbell. The doorbell rang a second time. I finally got up off the couch and looked through the peep hole.

It was Kade. In uniform, looking like he'd stepped out of a sexy police officer calendar. Here I was looking like I'd been in solitary confinement for thirty days. I couldn't answer the door looking like this, and how did he even know where I lived, anyway? Second of all, why is he even here? Or maybe he was at the wrong house and wasn't even here to see me at all.

"Lilly, open the door. I know you're looking through the peephole." Ok, maybe he was at the right house.

"I can't. I'm sick."

"Open the door."

I mean, sure, I was curious about why uniformed Kade was standing at my front door, but the very last thing that needed to happen was him seeing me looking homeless and definitely lacking a shower and clean clothes. I looked down at my outfit and noticed some cranberry sauce on the front of my cherished employee of the month shirt where my sandwich dripped earlier.

"Why, is this official police business? You can't prove it was me with the taped bread incident."

"Lilly, there's been a fire at your parents' house and they're both in the hospital."

My heart stopped and, in an instant, it no longer mattered what I looked like or how I felt. I swung the door open, my lips trembling.

"What? That's impossible. What happened? Why didn't anyone call me?" I cried, panicked. This didn't seem real.

"Your phone goes straight to voicemail," he said calmly. I picked my phone up off the coffee table. Dead. I hadn't been great at keeping my phone charged lately, but I didn't think I could forgive myself for it this time. What if they'd tried to call me?

"Are they ok? What happened?" Tears were streaming down my face, thinking of how scared they must have been.

"The fire started in the attic, possibly due to a short in the wiring. The fire burned through the garage ceiling and your dad was hit by falling debris. Your mother was trying to get him up when I arrived."

"But they are ok now, right?" They had to be. If it was just in the attic then surely it wouldn't have been bad enough to cause any real problems.

"They are both being treated for smoke inhalation. Your mom is doing much better now." He paused and hesitated.

I froze; my throat felt constricted. "And my dad?"

"Your dad was inhaling the smoke for longer than your mom was. He was unconscious when I arrived. He's been intubated and he'll be moved to ICU. I'm sorry, that's all the information I have right now."

I stood staring at Kade, waiting to find out that this was all a misunderstanding. But he didn't say anything else. He stood there looking at me seriously. "No, no, no. This can't be happening. He wanted me to have lunch with him today. If I'd had lunch with him then maybe this wouldn't have happened. I could have helped. I could have..." I could have prevented this. I might have smelled smoke. I could have done something. What if he doesn't make it? No, I couldn't let myself think that.

Kade interrupted me. "Lilly, stop. It isn't your fault." I was only half listening to him. I looked around trying to find my shoes, my purse, and my keys. Why wasn't anything where it was supposed to be?

"I have to get to the hospital. Where are my stupid keys!" I cried. This was not the time to lose my keys.

Kade picked up my tennis shoes from off the floor. "Here, put these on. I'll give you a ride." He also found my keys that were on the end table right next to my purse where they always are. "And here's your phone charger and your phone."

As Kade pulled the patrol car out of my driveway, I asked, "how did you know where I live?"

"I tried the bakery first, but they said you went home sick today and gave me your address."

"What about my brothers? Did my mom call them? Do they know about Dad?" I figured if Will knew, he would have come to get me if he couldn't reach me by phone.

"Yes, they have both been notified. Will went to the hospital, and I volunteered to come tell you since your phone seemed to be turned off or dead."

"Thank you," I said quietly, staring out the window while tears streamed down my face. Kade reached into his console and handed me a package of tissues, then we rode the rest of the way in silence.

Of both my parents, I was closest to my dad. I'm close to my mom too, but my dad and I have a special kind of bond. He's always been proud of me, no matter what I did. He was the one that sent me flowers at school when I won student council vice-president in elementary school. He was the one that cried giving a speech at my college graduation party. He's the one that still shows my picture to practically everyone he meets as if I was just born yesterday.

We pulled into the hospital parking lot. "Thanks for the ride, Kade. I really appreciate it."

"I've already gotten my report from your mom, but I can go in with you if you would like," He looked at me with the most caring eyes, something I hadn't really noticed in him before.

We walked into the hospital and were informed at the front desk that Dad was in the ER still, waiting to be moved to ICU. When we got to his room, my mom was in a wheelchair with oxygen on. Will was in there too. He saw me and walked out into the hallway.

Will's eyes were red and watery. "They only allow two visitors at a time in here, so I'll go out in the waiting room with Sydney. He doesn't look good, Lilly. He also has a broken collar bone, but that's the least of the worries. He was unconscious when they pulled him out of the house, and he's been intubated."

I walked in and stopped just as I entered the room, suddenly very aware of the sounds of the machines, the lighted numbers and graphs going up and down on the monitor screen, and the tube that was sticking out of my dad's mouth while he just lay there, seemingly oblivious to what was happening. How could that be when I just talked to him earlier and he was perfectly fine, completely unaware of the pending fire in his attic. And if I'd just gone to have lunch with him today, maybe none of this would have happened.

I was afraid to talk to him or touch him; I didn't want him to wake up and panic with that tube in his throat. That happened to Will once and I don't want that for anyone.

I looked at my mom, sitting in a wheelchair with a portable oxygen tank next to the bed. "Is he going to be ok?" I felt like a little girl again, imagining that nothing bad can happen to him because I love him and need him to be ok, as if that makes a difference.

"Oh, of course he is, just give him a little time to get perked back up and he'll be out of here in no time," she said, but I knew she was only saying that to make me feel better. She looked over at Kade, who was standing in the doorway, and her eyes lit up with gratitude.

"We would probably both be dead if that officer there hadn't come in and saved us. As hard as I tried to get Leonard up, I just wasn't strong enough and I wasn't going to leave the house without him. We're just so blessed that he saw the smoke and kicked the door in to save us before the firemen even got there." Her eyes teared up as she looked back over at Kade. "I don't even know how to thank you, Officer." Kade saved them? I had no idea it was him. I thought he was just the one to tell me about it.

"I'm glad I was able to help, and I hope your husband recovers quickly." Kade nodded at my mom. "I'm going to get out of your way now, please let me know if there is anything else I can do for any of you." He looked toward me with a soft, empathetic gaze, as if he'd experienced something similar himself.

I followed him out into the hallway and without even thinking about it, I threw my arms around him and gave him the tightest hug I've ever given anyone. He saved my parents' lives. Kade did. Of all the people that it could have been, it was Kade that saved their lives.

Chapter 10

Kade

There's one food that makes every recipe just a little bit better. Bacon. Of course, I put bacon in my peach cobbler. I opened the smoker and took a peek at my cobblers, which were just about ready. I'm not a great cook, I do ok, but I'm not going to win any awards for my kitchen skills. However, I can make a mean brisket, a mouthwatering pulled pork, and I haven't had any complaints so far about my bacon peach cobbler. Back in Austin, I'd taken a two-day barbecue class, and I learned tricks that have made all the difference. Though I've seen other somewhat similar recipes, I've tweaked my smoked peach and bacon cobbler until it's about as good as I could get it and it's one of my go-to dishes when I'm forced into attending events where people are required to take food.

I'm terrible at social gatherings and avoid them by any means necessary. I don't want to engage in small talk, or games, or the awkward getting to know each other thing. There's nothing I hate more than those ice breaker games they make people play at some of the trainings I've been to. Staying home alone with Peewee would suit me fine; however, I'd been talked into going to a barbecue with some of the other officers and a few guys from the fire department. They caught me in a moment of weakness and once I'd very hesitantly agreed, I couldn't find a way out without coming off as a jackass. We were all supposed to bring something that would go along with hamburgers and hot dogs but all the obvious things like buns and chips were already signed up for, so I was in charge of dessert. I made two cobblers, but only one was for the barbecue.

It had been four days since the fire at Lilly's parents' house. I'd heard from another officer that her mom had been released from the hospital that same day. Her dad, although still in the hospital, was doing much better as well. The image of Lilly's mom trying unsuccessfully to move her unconscious husband to safety had not left my mind. At the hospital, she'd said she wouldn't have left the house without him. I'm glad I saw the smoke when I did or it's possible neither one of them would have made it out.

I don't know Lilly very well, but I wish I did. I've really only even seen her a few times and one of those times was a traffic stop so it doesn't really count. What I saw the other day after the fire was a girl who has so much love for her parents, and it would have broken my heart to have to tell her that one or both of them had not made it. Telling people that they have lost a loved one is the worst part of my job.

I was seventeen years old, standing next to my dad the day he was told that his parents both died in a house fire. My granddad used to smoke in bed and had fallen asleep with a cigarette in his hand more than once. Everyone used to warn him that it was a matter of time before he burned the house down, but he was too stubborn to listen to any of us. And then it happened. The bedroom caught fire during the night. My grandmother was found only a few feet from the front door; my granddad was still in bed.

That night after we found out about my grandparents, my dad didn't bother with beer. He went straight for the whiskey and drank it straight out of the bottle and didn't try to disguise it by mixing with soda in a red plastic cup. I never understood why he always did that; it isn't like we didn't know what was in that red cup. He'd gotten so drunk that he'd fallen on the floor in the hallway, and I'd had to help my mom get him up off the floor and into bed. It's the only night that I remember not being angry at him for getting so drunk.

.....

I probably come off as a jerk. I don't mean to, but I won't deny that my people skills aren't necessarily my strongest trait. I do care about people, which is why I became a police officer, to help others. For the last few years, it's been easier for me to keep a distance, not get too involved with others, but that kind of personality doesn't go over well in a small town like this. Lilly unknowingly weaseled her way into my head, and I can't seem to get her out of it. Now that I've met her mom, I'm finding myself even worrying about her, and how she and Lilly's dad are doing as well. Today, I wanted to check on Lilly's family and see for myself they are doing ok after the fire. I had some time to spare before the barbecue, so I picked up my extra cobbler and headed to the bakery.

The bell on the door rang when I walked inside, and I spotted the girl that had inspected my bruised arm at the Farmer's Market. She was organizing some shakers of colorful sprinkles.

"Welcome to Lilly's Bakery," she said without looking up, then returned her attention to the sprinkles.

"Hi there, is Lilly here?" I asked her, looking around but seeing nobody else there.

"No," she responded, not going into any further detail. Was she the only one working?

"Ok, is she going to be here today?" I looked at her nametag and remembered that her name was Kennedy.

"I don't know." She looked up at me. "Oh, you're the guy that likes Lilly. Are you here to ask her out on a date or something?" Kennedy asked, staring at the foil container I was holding. Wow, that caught me off guard. First of all, how was she under the impression that I liked Lilly. Second of all, I wasn't sure how a covered foil pan would indicate that I had intentions of asking her on a date. Is that how they do it around here?

"Um... that's not what..." I stammered, uncomfortably.

"Oh, hi there! Sorry, I was in the back." Caitlynn, Lilly's assistant, walked in. "Can I help you with something?" She looked at the pan I was holding. Suddenly, I was incredibly self-conscious about holding this damn cobbler.

"I was just looking for Lilly, but Kennedy let me know she isn't here."

"Oh, yea, she's been out all week. Probably won't be back until next week." She nodded toward the cobbler. "Did you bring something for her?"

"I thought she and her mom might like a cobbler."

She stared at me wide-eyed for a couple of seconds before asking, "You made her a cobbler?" She said it very slowly as if it weren't even believable. Ok, now I definitely was regretting the cobbler idea. I thought this was a nice gesture but quickly second guessing my decisions based on Caitlyn's response.

"Well, yes." I shifted uncomfortably, feeling like an idiot. "I'm going to a barbecue, so I made an extra one for her and her mom. Thought they might like it, and I wanted to check to see if they were doing ok since the fire and her dad being in the hospital." Why was she looking at me like I'd said something completely outlandish?

"Huh... well, I happen to know she is at home right now so maybe you could take it to her there?" Was she being serious?

"To her house? She isn't going to mind me just popping by unannounced?" Most people don't really love unannounced visitors, me being one of those people. Plus, Lilly wasn't even willing to open the door for me last time I was there, until I told her the purpose for my visit.

"Nope. Sure won't," she replied with confidence.

I started out the door and turned back around to Caitlynn, who was still watching me. "Be honest, is it dumb that I'm taking her a cobbler?"

She smirked a little and then softened. "You are a man, not a bad looking one either, checking on a girl's parents, holding a homemade cobbler. It's a lot of things, but dumb isn't one of them."

A few minutes later I was standing on Lilly's front porch, cobbler in hand, feeling more confident after Caitlynn's remark; however, still quite awkward. In my line of work, it's not uncommon to deal with people who have been in fires, accidents, or other disasters, and this is the first time I've ever felt inclined to show up to any of their homes with a homemade dessert. I also stopped at the grocery store on my way over to get some vanilla ice cream to go with it.

The last time I stood here, I hadn't paid any attention to what the porch looked like. It had her personality all over it. On the red front door hung a large floral letter S. Next to the door was a blue, antique hand water pump with a bucket of potted pink petunias hanging from it. There were also two vintage-looking red concrete pots with a colorful mix of flowers planted in them on either side of the front door. I looked up and stared curiously at the item hanging over her door. Lilly is the only person I've ever known that had a crystal chandelier outside on the porch. It didn't appear to be hooked up to any electricity, just hung there as decoration.

Her dog immediately started barking as soon as I rang the doorbell. A few seconds later, there was Lilly, standing in her doorway with her blonde hair in a messy bun, pieces of it falling out around her face. She was in black shorts and a red tank top that was cut just low enough that I had to force myself to pretend I didn't notice. Even though it was scorching hot outside, her feet were clad in warm fuzzy socks, the kind that women like to wear in the dead of winter except these even had pictures of sloths wearing Santa hats on them.

"Oh! Um... hi! Is there..." she fumbled, obviously baffled about why I was standing on her doorstep and holding a covered foil pan at that.

“I hope you don’t mind me popping by. I tried the bakery first, but Caitlyn said you’d be out all week and that I should bring this to your house.” I handed the pan and bag to her. “I heard that your dad was doing better and that your mom was staying with you. I thought you and her might like a cobbler and ice cream.”

Her eyebrows raised up, wrinkling her forehead. “You... you made it?” she asked, clearly in disbelief as she took the items from me.

“I made the cobbler. But you can’t eat cobbler without ice cream, so I bought that at the store. It’s my own recipe, peach and bacon. I cooked it on the smoker.” I didn’t even recognize myself at that moment. I’m never so... friendly. Lilly’s family was bringing out a side of me that I hadn’t seen in years.

She continued to stare at me with wide eyes. “Kade, I don’t even know what to say. This is so sweet.” She stepped aside and opened the door wider. “Please, come in.”

Her house smelled of something sweet, like lemons. “It smells good in here, are you baking something?” I asked, looking around.

“No, no. It’s just my candle. Lemon Cupcake, I think. I may have a bit of a candle addiction.” She smiled as she pointed to a shelf completely filled with unused candles, waiting to be burned.

Her homely dog came up to smell me. The last time I was standing in his room, I'd been too preoccupied to notice just how unfortunate looking it is. The word 'homely' didn't do it justice. It was hideous in every sense of the word. I've always thought that some dogs can be so ugly they're cute, but this poor little thing wasn't one of them. Even its tongue was sticking out the side of its mouth. I shuddered just thinking of it possibly sleeping in Lilly's bed with her. On the fireplace mantel was the proof that I wasn't wrong about this dog. It seems she had earned an award for her looks, Willow Creek's Ugliest Dog. An award that Lilly apparently wasn't ashamed of.

I walked over to Lilly's mom, who was coming into the living room from the kitchen. I was relieved to see that she looked good, much better than she did the other day. "Hello, ma'am. You probably don't recognize me without my uniform, but I'm the officer from the other day, Kade Wayland. I wanted to come check on you and I brought you and Lilly a cobbler and ice cream."

"Oh my goodness! Thank you so much! Yes, I'm doing just fine, and Leonard is in a regular room now. I think he's going to be discharged in a day or two. Even his collar bone is going to be ok. Dr. Ramos said it just needed a sling, and he would be good as new in no time."

"Wonderful news, ma'am. Like I said the other day, if there's anything I can do for you, please don't hesitate to call me." I took a card out of my wallet and handed it to her. “I don’t think I left my card with you last time. Here’s my number.”

“Oh, please call me Barbara! Why don’t you sit down, and I’ll fix us all a bowl of cobbler and ice cream? I already have on my stretchy pants so it’s perfect timing.” She laughed and pulled on the elastic of her knit pants.

I would have much rather stayed and had cobbler with Lilly and her mom, but I’d already committed myself to going to the barbecue with the guys. “I’m sorry, Barbara, I can’t. I’m on my way to a barbecue with some people from work. But I hope you two enjoy it.”

I talked with Lilly and her mom for a few more minutes and then headed out to my truck. Lilly followed me.

“Thanks again for everything, Kade. It means a lot to me and my mom,” she said, looking up at me. “I can’t wait to dig into that cobbler. I mean, bacon and peach? A combo like that has to be good.”

“I hope you like it. People sometimes make a face when they find out there’s bacon in it, but trust me, it belongs there.”

She laughed. “So, I was thinking. You obviously like barbecue as much as I do. There happens to be a barbecue cook-off next weekend. I’ve got two tickets already. Do you think you might want to go with me? It’s a lot of fun and I go every year.” Standing there in her tank top and shorts paired with her fuzzy Christmas socks, she exuded a sense of confidence that I envied. I also found it incredibly attractive.

"I just so happen to be off duty next weekend."

Chapter 11

Lilly

Tiger lillies...

My mom was able to move back to her house two days earlier and my dad was discharged from the hospital; life was returning back to normal. Not that I didn't like having my mom at my house, but she could be a lot to handle. She'd brought her crochet over and she still worked at the toy store during the day, but she's too set in her ways to handle being in somebody else's house for very long. She let me know that I didn't have the right kind of waffle iron, my fabric softener made her itch, and my shower would be cleaner if I'd spray it down after every use like she does. She also took everything out of my pantry, cleaned it, re-organized it, and put it back the way she organizes her own pantry. I almost gave up trying to find my taco seasoning until I realized she had all my seasoning packets carefully organized in a wicker basket.

The cobbler that Kade brought over a few days ago was mouthwateringly delicious. My mom and I both even ate it for breakfast one day. He could easily win a contest with it. Men that can cook hold a soft spot in my heart. Sexy men that can cook and bring women unexpected cobblers? That's kind of a rare find. It also helped that his personality was coming through, and I liked what I'd been seeing.

Today was the day that Kade and I were going to the barbecue cookoff. I don't know if this was going to be a date or just a friendly welcome to town kind of thing. But I'd gone and invited Kade without putting any thought into it first, so I guess we'd have to just see what the vibe turned into.

It was the beginning of August, so it would be in the upper 90s by the time the cookoff started. I slathered myself in SPF 50 then tried on almost everything in my closet; finally settled on a sundress with a sunflower print on it along with a pair of brand new simple white sneakers. I like a balance of dressy and casual, that way I'm covered no matter what the theme is wherever I go.

Kade agreed to pick me up at my house at 1:00 PM. Right on schedule, the doorbell rang at 12:54 PM. Add promptness to his list of good qualities. When I opened the door, Kade was standing there in navy shorts and a white buttoned up shirt, looking totally gorgeous as usual. He smiled when he saw me, a genuine smile that made his blue eyes sparkle. I hadn't had the pleasure of seeing him do that very often.

"Wow, you look incredible, Lilly," he said, then bent down and picked up one of the two long boxes that were on the porch next to him. "I brought these for you. I was planting some of these in my yard and thought you might like some for your yard too. I noticed you like flowers."

I looked into the box and found several containers of beautiful, bright orange flowers. "Oh, wow! Thank you, Kade!" What did I do to deserve all this? First cobbler and now flowers?

"They're tiger lilies. They're perennials so they will come back every year. They're my favorite and I had a whole flowerbed full of them back at my other house. I hope you like them, plus it fits with your name." This was a first for me. Usually, men would bring a bouquet of flowers that die in a few days. This was a whole other level of bringing flowers, and probably one of the sweetest things any man had ever brought me. I also loved it because it was a type of lily, and he picked them with my name in mind. It made it much more special.

"Oh, Kade, I love them! I can't wait to plant them!" I knew just the place for them too, right in front of the porch. It was hard to believe that the man standing there, offering me his favorite flowers, was the same one I had thought was a jerk just a few weeks ago for making me do a field sobriety test.

He opened the passenger door for me to climb into. Kade kept his red and black truck extremely clean; it looked like he'd just driven it off the showroom. He even had a cute little trash can in one of the cup holders and a red and black football helmet shaped air freshener hanging from the rearview mirror. There was literally not one spec of dust to be found; unlike my own vehicle which I rarely ever cleaned out. Now that he'd already been in my own car, I wondered what he'd thought about the condition of it being nowhere comparable to his standard of cleanliness.

"Is this a brand-new truck? It's really... clean," I asked him, still scanning the area for any dust particles or maybe a stray dog hair somewhere.

"No, it's three years old." He chuckled a little. "I just like to keep it clean." I wondered what his house looked like inside, and I had a feeling it was most likely spotless as well. I liked that trait in a man. Harrison didn't keep his truck or his house clean; they were both trashed almost 100% of the time. I used to have to throw things into the backseat to just get in the front seat of his truck at all.

The barbecue event was held at the fairgrounds and the smell of all the food being cooked was intense. After handing our tickets in at the gate, we walked around and scoped out the various options. Smokers and barbecue grills with smoke billowing out were arranged in a semi-circle surrounding an area of picnic tables placed in the middle. One booth even had a griddle, making bacon pancakes. Kade and I loaded up on an assortment of pulled pork, brisket, ribs, and chicken along with potato salad, and slices of bread. I opted for one pancake also.

Sitting across the table from Kade, I watched him start working on a sauce-covered rib and wondered how his clean, white shirt would ever survive this. Not wanting to witness the certain death of his shirt, I got up and walked over to one of the booths and returned, smiling, with two plastic red and white checkered bibs that read 'I like pork butts' across a picture of a pig.

"Here you go, put this on." I handed him the bib as I put mine on.

"A bib?" The skeptical look on his face was priceless.

"Of course! You can't go to a barbecue cookoff and not wear a bib. It's all part of the experience." Had he never been to a cookoff? It's standard procedure.

"I don't see anyone else wearing one," he said as he scanned the area for other bib wearing patrons, finding none. Just as he said that, a drip from his rib fell onto the front of his white shirt.

I laughed loudly, pointing to the proof of bib necessity. "I rest my case."

He rolled his eyes in defeat and attached the plastic bib to his neck, as a smile crept across his face.

The large stack of napkins on our table was barely enough and I laughed at the pile of them, now crumpled around our plates. I took out my phone and took a picture of the two of us in our matching bibs, both smiling, holding our messy barbecue over plates piled high. The relaxed, happy, bib wearing Kade was truly the opposite of my first couple of impressions of him and not a sight that I ever imagined I would see.

"How was the pancake?"

"It was good, I'll rate it a 7 on the pancake scale. The best pancake ever is a couple hours from here at a little place called the Bald Egg. Their sweet cream pancakes are to die for. I'm not even joking. I'd seriously drive there just for the pancakes and then come back home."

"I think they need to hire you for their commercials. I'll have to try them someday," Kade said, then eyed the cobbler stand. "I'm stuffed, but I want to try the cobbler. Do you have room for dessert?"

"I always have room for dessert," I said, as he got up.

He returned with two bowls of cherry cobbler, topped with vanilla ice cream. It was delicious, but it was no match for his homemade peach and bacon cobbler.

"This is amazing, but I think your cobbler has ruined me on cobbler because it's the best I've ever had. I'm not just saying that to make you feel good either. Even my mom said it's her new favorite and she's more of a cobbler snob than I am." This was true. She's the pickier about cobbler than anyone else I've known. "It's all in the crust," she always says.

He beamed at that news. "I'm glad you liked it. I'll have to make another one sometime. But I can also make a fairly edible pecan pie if you want to try that."

"Fairly edible? Heck yea, I definitely want one of those. And I love the sheer bravery of offering a fairly edible pecan pie to a bakery owner." I laughed.

A band had been setting up on the small stage at the end of the eating area. When they started to play, a few people gathered in front of the stage and began dancing. I really wanted to dance, but I didn't picture Kade as the dancing type. Instead of suggesting we join them, I watched the group as they spun around. However, Kade was full of surprises.

Kade picked up his iced tea and gulped down the last of it and then stood up. "Come on." He held out his hand. Did he want to dance? I took his hand and sure enough, he led me toward the group of dancing couples.

"You dance?" Kade dancing wasn't something I could even picture in my mind.

"I mean, I'll probably suck at it, it's been a few years, so I apologize in advance. But I saw the way you were watching everyone dancing and I'm willing to risk it if you are."

He took my hand and wrapped his other hand around my waist, and we fit together perfectly. His hands were large and rough, and he smelled like cologne mixed with brisket. He was a little rigid at first, but he loosened up by the second song. By the third song we were still dancing, both sweating in the summer heat, trying to stay near the water misters and fans.

I don't know what I was expecting when that slow song came on, but Kade pulled me in close to him, surprising me completely. Both his hands rested on my lower back as we began to sway to the music. Kade was quite a bit taller than me, but I linked my hands behind his neck and looked up at him, searching his face for a hint of what he was thinking. And when he looked back at me, it was no secret. This absolutely gorgeous man was attracted to me, and it showed. Being pressed up against him I could feel his solid ab muscles and the curves of his biceps. There was the smallest amount of hair peeking out through the opening of his shirt and I couldn't help wondering what he'd look like without that shirt on.

The song ended and I started to pull away to sit back down, but he pulled me back to him and locked his eyes with mine. Was he going to kiss me? I felt weak in my knees. Officer Kade Wayland was going to kiss me.

Just at the worst possible time ever, somebody bumped into us, ruining the moment.

"Oops, sorry," a familiar voice said. "Oh, Lilly, I didn't notice you!" It was Sydney. She'd been dancing with Will right next to us and I didn't even notice them. But at this point, noticing them meant Kade and I were not going to be kissing, at least not at that moment.

"Hey there!" I said, trying to not sound like they'd just ruined my hopes and dreams for the moment. "Kade, this is my brother, Will, and his wife, Sydney."

"Oh, yea, you're the officer that saved my parents in the fire! Thank you so much for that," Will said as he shook Kade's hand.

"You're very welcome. I'm glad I was in the right place at the right time."

"Lilly, I need to tell you something real quick," Sydney said and pulled me away from the men, far enough that they couldn't hear our conversation. "What is going on here? Hmmm?"

"What do you mean?" I knew what she meant, but I played innocent.

"You and Officer Kade over there looking all cozy and romantic? Is this a date and when did this start? Details, Lilly. I need details."

"I invited him to the cookout with me and that's about it! We're just here having fun. Now, let's get back over there. Kade isn't great at small talk."

We'd been talking with Will and Sydney for a few minutes when I started to feel a little bit queasy and clammy. "I need to sit down for a minute, I think the heat is getting to me. Will and Sydney, I'll see y'all later, ok?" I waved at them and headed back to the table.

Kade held my arm on the way to the table, looking concerned. "Let me go get you some ice water. Maybe that will help."

When he returned with the water, I sipped it and did not feel better. "Kade, I think I'm going to need to go home. I'm sorry, maybe something I ate doesn't quite agree with me." How could this happen at a time like this when we were having so much fun? We were going to kiss!

On the ride home, every bump and turn made me feel even more nauseous. My head was spinning, I felt chilled but was sweating at the same time, and I wanted to lie down more than anything. I was fine just a little while ago, and now I felt like I could puke at any moment. Please not in Kade's immaculately clean truck. Anything but that; I'd never be able to deal with that kind of embarrassment.

Instead, what I did was even worse.

So much worse.

As I got out my key to open my front door, the moment came. I could not hold it and to my absolute shock and horror, I threw up. Projectile vomited, to be exact. Everything happened so fast that I couldn't process it. Then, I looked up and Kade's white shirt was covered in my regurgitated barbecue lunch.

"Ohhhh, no. Please, no, this isn't happening." What does one do when something like this happens? It isn't like I could hand him a napkin. His shirt was soiled in my vomit. He was never going to want to go out with me again, probably too disgusted to even look at me again.

"It's ok. Let's get you in the house." He calmly ushered me in as if he was totally used to being thrown up on. "Here, lie down on the couch and I'll get you all fixed up. Mind if I take my shirt off?" he said as he went ahead and peeled it off. No, I definitely don't mind if he takes his shirt off. I just wish it wasn't on account of what I just did to it.

Shirtless, he began maneuvering about my house without me having to ask for anything at all. First, he let Beatrice outside to potty. Then, he found a bag under the kitchen sink to put his dirty shirt in. He set a trashcan at the side of the couch and covered me up with a lightweight blanket. He went to the kitchen and returned with a cup of ice water, a sleeve of saltine crackers, and a wet, folded washcloth which he placed gently across my forehead. Then, as if he already knew me so well, he brought me the book from my reading chair. This half naked specimen of a man just did all that for me without me even having to request anything.

"I'd be happy to stay for a while if you need my help," he said, his eyes sincere.

"It's ok, but thanks. I'm just going to go to sleep."

"Ok. Maybe after you get some sleep, you'll feel better." He picked up the bag containing his shirt and opened the front door. “I had a good time today, Lilly,” he said sweetly.

I could feel myself falling asleep, but muttered, “Thank you, Kade, I had fun too. Sorry about the throw up.”

I woke up about three hours later, still feeling nauseous but able to get up off the couch. I opened the front door and couldn’t believe my eyes. The tiger lilies were planted. Right where I had wanted to plant them, in front of the porch.

Chapter 12

Kade

She's a ten, but she likes spiders...

The stack of boxes that had been neatly lined up against my living room wall was slowly diminishing, and my house was starting to look like somebody actually lived in it. So far, the reading room was by far my favorite room in the house. The large, south facing picture window lets in the perfect amount of sun for my growing collection of plants and has a view of the tiger lilies I planted in the backyard. There's a built-in bench seat which I never sit on because it isn't comfortable enough for reading; however, Peewee has made it her official spot which is evidenced by the white and black hair covering the cushion.

I'm no decorator, but I'd impressed myself with what I'd done in this room. I built a bookshelf out of a tree from the backyard, inspired by a photo I saw online. I'd removed the bark, cut the branches, and arranged them on the wall with wooden shelves. It extended to the length of one wall. An assortment of cacti, succulents, and vining plants sit on the shelves, mixed in with my ever-growing collection of hardback books. The end result looked even better than the photo I was using for my inspiration.

My black, leather reading chair and ottoman is positioned in a corner of the room, surrounded by more plants. It's peaceful in this room. It's where I come to drink my coffee in the morning and unwind with a beer at night. Sometimes I just sit and do nothing but stare out the window for an hour or more, letting my mind wander. And lately, I find myself staring at the pages of my current read, thinking of Lilly instead of reading the words.

In the few days that had passed since the barbecue cookoff, Lilly and I had texted each other a few times a day. I'd never been much on texting. Actually, I'd never been much on calling or socializing much at all. Her contact photo was the selfie that we took with our bibs on. We were both laughing. I couldn't even remember the last time I'd laughed but I felt sure that it had been years. Lilly brought out something in me that I'd kept hidden down in the dark corners of myself since Bethany and I divorced. It's like I'd been afraid to even make any attempt at happiness again after having my heart shattered the way it had.

I also danced for the first time in years. The way Lilly had been watching the others that were spinning around the makeshift dance floor, I knew she wanted to be out there too. I had a feeling Lilly was the kind of person that could be the only one out on the dance floor and not have the slightest bit of insecurity. Letting myself unwind was exhilarating. It was like the rubber band that had been wrapped around me for years had been released and there was a newfound sense of fresh starts that I'd not allowed myself to explore until now.

I have no doubt that Lilly did not think about it very long before she invited me to the barbecue cookoff. She's kind of a spur of the moment kind of girl, very opposite of myself, but I found myself liking that. And if I'm guessing, I'd say she didn't even know if she wanted it to be a date or not. I didn't know what it was either until we were halfway through eating, then it was obvious. It was a date, and we both wanted it that way. If her brother hadn't bumped into us, I would have kissed her. I wanted to kiss her so badly, and I didn't care that it was in the middle of a crowd of strangers.

Lilly's stomach had other plans, and it didn't involve any romance. As much as Lilly probably wishes I would forget the projectile vomit that landed all over the front of my shirt, I'm certain I'll always remember that ending to our first date. It wasn't the first time I'd been covered in another person's barf, and it definitely wasn't going to be the last. Usually, it's in the midst of dealing with intoxicated or drug overdosed individuals while I'm on duty. As difficult as it always is, I have to maintain my professionalism and certainly can't be awarded the luxury of taking off my soiled uniform. Though still not overly pleasant and her aim could definitely have been much better, but I knew how embarrassed she was. I was more concerned about making sure she was alright than I was about being covered in her vomited barbecue feast. And even though she didn't feel good, I noticed her expression when I took off my shirt and I pretended to not notice that she seemed to like what she saw.

I needed to see her again. I picked up my phone off the table.

Me: **What's your favorite food?**

Lilly: **Thanksgiving sandwich from Annie's Deli.**

Me: **What a coincidence, I was going there tonight for dinner.** I'd actually never heard of Annie's Deli, but that's beside the point.

Lilly: **Hmmm. It is a coincidence because I was also planning to go there tonight.**

Me: **Carpool? I'll pick you up at 6:00.**

....

Lilly opened the front door looking as gorgeous as ever even though she was dressed casually in jeans and a floral T-shirt. She would look good in literally anything she put on.

"Hi there!" She smiled and gave me a hug, and I noticed she smelled fresh like lavender. "Can you help me with these cupcakes? I just need to drop them off at Wacky Wednesday on our way to eat. I volunteered to take them." I looked at the counter and there were two boxes full of brightly colored cupcakes.

I took the boxes and put them in the back seat of the truck, wondering what Wacky Wednesday was. It sounded like it might be a children's event.

Once we got on the road, I finally asked. "What is Wacky Wednesday?"

"Oh, sorry. I should have explained. It's an event that is put on by a nonprofit, Shell's Place, on the last Wednesday of every month. It's for adults with intellectual and developmental disabilities. My brother, Will, volunteers there."

The event was put on at the Willow Creek Baptist Church. Once inside, we were shown where to place the cupcakes by an older woman whose nametag let us know her name is Hazel.

After putting the cupcakes down on the counter, Lilly looked around, then pointed across the room. "Oh, there's Kennedy! Let's go say hi to her real quick before we go." Lilly grabbed my hand and led me over to Kennedy, who was wearing gloves and a hairnet, passing out pieces of pizza. Her straight posture and stern expression indicated she was not one to be messed with during her pizza duties.

She didn't hand the pizza out politely either, she slapped the pizza on the paper plates with a splat, as if she were working on the serving line in a prison.

"Hi, Kennedy! Where's Will?" Lilly asked, looking around.

"He's over there with Xavier." She motioned over to where Will was standing with a very tall individual who was clearly agitated.

"Tomorrow is Thursday!" the man, whom I assumed was Xavier, yelled loudly. I watched closely in case I needed to intervene.

Hazel from the front counter hurried into the room, her face red. With a raised voice, she said, "Xavier! What is your problem? Sit down and eat your pizza." That was clearly not what Xavier wanted to hear, and he immediately picked up a chair and threw it off to the side, hitting the wall. I made my way across the room to him.

"Tomorrow is Thursday! It's Thursday!" he screamed and picked up another chair. When he saw me approaching him, he became more upset and lifted the chair off the floor.

"Please get everyone out of the room," Will calmly instructed to Hazel. She and Lilly, along with the other volunteers, began ushering everyone to the front desk area.

Will turned toward me. "Kade, I think I can handle this. He just needs to be left alone for a minute to calm down.

I'll explain in a minute." I backed up and as I did, Xavier put the chair back down. Will sat down in a chair and Xavier sat down in the one he was holding and began to cry.

I watched Will and Xavier from the doorway in case things ramped back up. Will took his cell phone out of his pocket, dialed a number, and gave it to Xavier. After a few minutes, Xavier handed him his phone back, picked up the chair he threw, and placed it gently back under the table.

Will gave Xavier a pat on the back, walked back into the front area, and gave the go ahead for everyone to go back to their pizza and activities. "He's fine now. He was upset because he always goes home with his parents on Thursdays, but his parents are out of town, so he wasn't going to be able to go tomorrow. Apparently, he found out about this right before he was dropped off here, not really the best timing. It didn't help matters when Hazel talked to him the way she did, it just made him more agitated. Once he talked to his parents, he felt better."

The training I'd had involving disabilities and mental health was not quite enough, in my opinion, and I would not have de-escalated it as well as Will did. I was impressed with the way Will handled the situation. He apparently had a good rapport with Xavier and understood his needs, far better than I would or even Hazel as it seemed. If Will hadn't been there, things could have easily escalated, possibly resulting in somebody being injured, or worse, Xavier being arrested.

After saying goodbye to Kennedy and Will, Lilly and I went on to dinner. When our food arrived, Lilly did a happy little jig in her seat as she unwrapped her sandwich.

"Kade, you have to take a bite of this. No other sandwich even comes close to comparison. Trust me, I even have it on my Best Foods Ever Consumed List." She pulled the top off the sandwich to show me, but nothing about that sandwich looked appealing to me. It reminded me of something my grandmother might have put together with leftovers that she didn't want to throw away. She used to call them leftover medley sandwiches, and they were rarely edible.

"Oh no, I'm good with my club sandwich." I smiled as she rolled her eyes at me.

"Suit yourself, but you don't know what you're missing." She bit into the sandwich, closed her eyes, and smiled dreamily as she savored the bite. "The manager, Laurie, made this a year-round sandwich instead of just a seasonal special. I like to think I had a little something to do with it. It's their top seller now."

"Between the sweet cream pancakes at the Bald Egg and this sandwich here, you certainly do your part to promote business. You should be on the payroll." I laughed.

"I have to keep them in business!" she exclaimed, covering her mouth, which was full of thanksgiving sandwich.

"So, tell me more about the Wacky Wednesday? I guess I didn't realize Kennedy volunteered there too."

"Oh, no. Kennedy doesn't volunteer there. She's one of the participants. She attends there every month. She likes to help pass out the pizza and they've let that be her thing. She's very particular about it."

"I knew there was something a little different about Kennedy, but I hadn't figured out what that was."

"Kennedy has autism. She's on the higher end of the spectrum, but she still needs quite a bit of support. She's one of those that kind of falls through the cracks because her skill level is quite high; however, not high enough to drive a car, live independently, work in certain environments, that sort of thing. When I met her, I just knew she was a great fit for the bakery, and she has done exceptionally well."

"That's great that you saw something in her and gave her a chance. It looks like it works out great for both of you."

She nodded excitedly. "Sure did. I can't even imagine the bakery without her now. And the customers love her."

We sat in the booth at Annie's Deli for two hours. This was the first time we'd ever really sat and had a long conversation together. She was everything and more than

I thought she was. She likes to read all genres, and we share some favorite books. I told her about my reading room, which she eagerly requested a tour of. I also learned that she is somewhat of a thrill seeker, loves adventure, and wants to explore the world.

"My best friend, Jo, and I are going to Germany in a few months. I can't wait! I have a plan to randomly point to something on the menu and just eat whatever it is. I won't be able to read the menu anyway if it's in German." That's brave, I could never do that, but from my experience, she may not even get to.

"I have some bad news for you. When I went to Germany, most of the menus had both English and German... but maybe you'll get lucky. I was in Frankfurt in the more touristy areas, so maybe try a different area."

She frowned. "What the flapjack! That was going to be my favorite thing to do. Eating foods that I've never had before is the highlight of any vacation for me."

"Easy now, that's a strong use of the word flapjack." I laughed.

"Sydney is always saying that, and it's rubbed off on me." She smiled and took a sip of her sweet tea.

We sat for a few minutes, finishing off our drinks. Then Lilly spoke up again, "So, what made you decide to become a police officer?"

"My sister had a best friend, Layla. They'd been best friends since the 3rd grade. She was like a sister to me too.

After she graduated from high school, she moved in with her boyfriend and ended up having a baby. We didn't know that he had been beating her. She never said a word about it. Then she finally did speak up after he beat the crap out of her one night. She took the baby and ran to our house. We called the cops, and she pressed charges and got a restraining order. Of course, he didn't stay in jail long and he came out pissed off. She moved in with her dad for protection, but just a few nights later, he broke into a window at her dad's house in the middle of the night; he shot both her and her dad and ran off with the baby. He's in prison now, but that doesn't bring Layla or her dad back. And now her daughter is having to grow up without knowing either one of her parents. I've always wondered if there was something I could have done to save her, and I'll never be able to get that thought out of my head. That's when I decided to become a police officer. I want to be able to help people, keep them safe."

"Oh, Kade. I'm so sorry, that is terrible."

"So, what made you decide to become a bakery owner? Surely, it's a happier story than mine."

She smiled and sat up straighter, seeming happy to have been asked. "Well, my degree is in psychology, and I used that for a career in a kind of a social services type field for a while. I did love the idea of the position, but I couldn't seem to find a way to separate my home life from work. I was working all the time, even when I was on vacation or when I was sick because we had to use our personal cell phones for work, they didn't give us work phones. It seemed like everyone on the planet had my phone number. I gave up reading, going to the movies, going on vacation, just about everything. I didn't see any point in even trying when I knew that I would most likely end up working. I wanted to be able to put my family first and work second, but that seemed impossible with that type of job. I started doing my bakery as a food truck and then as it became more successful, I was able to move it into a building. It was the best decision I ever made, and it's done wonders for my mental health. I have Caitlyn to handle things when I'm not there and I don't even have to think about the bakery when it's closed." She was beaming, and I could tell she had made the best decision for herself with her bakery.

We talked about everything from her favorite scent, which happened to be honeysuckle, to my fear of spiders, which isn't something I tell just anyone. I've found that once they find out about the spider fear, they will do everything they can to freak me out with them on a regular basis, sometimes using the excuse that they are doing exposure therapy with me. My arachnophobia is extreme. Just seeing pictures of spiders can be more than I can handle and my sister used to use her evil ways to torture me with spiders when she was younger, still does sometimes.

"You're afraid of spiders?" She raised her eyebrows. "I'm sorry, it's just that I love them..."

"You can't possibly."

"I may or may not have a pet tarantula," she confessed.

I almost spit out my tea. Just when everything was going great, she drops this kind of a bomb? I didn't see a tarantula when I was there. I felt my skin crawl just thinking of it.

I coughed, nearly aspirating on my drink. "Please, tell me you're joking."

She laughed at my reaction. "Her name is Penny, and she lives in my bedroom. She's really sweet and she likes to be held." She's got to be kidding. I was blown away with just the thought of sleeping with that beast in there. I shuddered thinking of it.

"I can't even process this information. This is horrific. A freaking tarantula? In your bedroom? No. Just no. I'm surprised at you." I shook my head in utter disbelief.

Lilly shrugged and smiled, then raised her right hand. "I solemnly swear to never get her out of her cage when you are there." So, she wanted me back at her house again. Can I do that knowing about the beast lurks in her bedroom?

Even with unsettling new information about the tarantula, I found myself becoming more and more attracted to this woman. She was not only beautiful with a body that won't quit, she had great personality, a sense of humor, a good heart, and she was also intelligent. She also seemed to be very genuine and didn't put on a show to impress anyone. If it weren't for being a spider enthusiast, she'd be perfect.

When I drove Lilly to her house, it was pitch dark on her front porch. I wasn't going to miss this chance again. I looked down into her eyes and lowered my voice. "Lilly, just so you know. I'm going to have to kiss you right now."

She looked up at me, smiled, and wrapped her arms around my waist. "Just so you know, I was hoping you would."

Chapter 13

Lilly

Maybe it was fate that brought Kade and I together. I'd been looking in the wrong places, trying too hard to meet men. Clearly, the hardware store strategy wasn't doing it. And then out of nowhere, there was Kade, when I least expected it. My feelings took me by surprise, considering I wasn't his biggest fan in the beginning.

At first, Kade was just Officer Wayland, the asshole-ish officer who wrongly assumed I was driving under the influence and provided me with my first ever field sobriety test. He wasn't even swayed by my attempts to charm him with my winning personality. Then, at our second unplanned meeting, he was equally critical of my driving skills, this time with the added proof of also being unintentionally physically harmed by me. But somewhere along the line, this hard core, non-smiling, driving critic of a police officer turned a complete one-eighty. Was it something I did that caused the turnaround? Perhaps it was the sourdough bread peace offering that I taped to his door that started it all.

I'm not sure when my feelings for Kade started, but by the time he showed up at my door with a cobbler, it was pretty clear to me that there was more to Kade Wayland than I originally thought. That kiss, though. It was everything. It's all I could think about the past few days. I needed to share the details with my best friend.

Jo and I had plans for breakfast at the Crunchy Chicken, which we did at least once a month. We hadn't had much time to catch up with each other the last couple of weeks because she'd been busy working on a big project at work and hadn't had much time to chat. After receiving our food and sitting down in a booth, we got down to business with discussing our Germany plans. But first, I had to update her on the advancements in my dating life.

"So, first order of business. I went on a date," I announced, taking her by surprise.

"Date? You met someone?" she asked with huge eyes and stopped stirring the granola into her yogurt parfait.

"Kade, the police officer."

"Excuse me, what? Isn't he a jerk?"

"Well, I mean, he was at first. But it turns out he's so sweet, Jo. He just didn't come off that way at first."

"Ok... Tell me everything, and do not leave anything out." She had a death stare into my eyes. Jo could give the most intense stare. She had long, wavy hair that was dark enough that it was almost black. And her deep brown eyes bore a hole in me, waiting patiently for as much info as I'd give her. Jo was a human resource manager, but I always thought she should have been an interrogator.

I'd already told her about getting pulled over. I'd also told her about running into Kade with my car during the haboob and Kade pulling my parents out of their burning house. So, she had some background info, just didn't know anything had gone further than that.

Jo had good reason for being skeptical, which she likely was. I hadn't had the best track record with men. She'd seen right through Harrison. She's also been there through the other boyfriends before that, which may have included one ex-convict. I wasn't aware of his criminal history until Jo did her own private investigation.

"So, after the fire, Kade came to check on my mom. And he brought a homemade cobbler... that he made himself. He made it himself, Jo. With ice cream." I'd tried to call her to tell her about the cobbler, but she'd been so busy with work that I hadn't been able to get a hold of her.

That got her attention, and she put her spoon down. "Go on."

"We went to the barbecue cookoff together and he brought me tiger lilies. Tiger lilies, Jo. He planted them himself in my flowerbed without me even knowing he was doing it. And he took care of me and put a cold washrag on my face after I threw up on his shirt."

"You didn't," she asked, straight faced.

"Oh, I did. Projectile. But he didn't get mad about it. And he's really nice; he has a good heart, he's just new to town and he doesn't know anyone. I think that's why he was a little rigid at first. But he's great. I think you'll love him." I stopped for a minute and then added quickly, "And he kisses like you wouldn't even believe."

She smiled and shook her head. "Welp! I hope things work out! The hardware store wasn't really the best method anyway, vehicular assault seems to work better for you." She laughed and started eating again.

After we got the Kade conversation out of the way, we made some plans for Germany. Everything had already been purchased: plane, train, and Airbnb. We decided to stay in Wiesbaden, the town I'd seen when we first started talking about Germany. I just had to figure out the fun things to do. We had a good itinerary planned based on videos we found online. She was still not sold on the idea of just picking random things off a menu that we couldn't read, so I eased her mind with what Kade had told me about the menus. I'd never been more excited about a vacation than this one. My bucket list was drinking a local German beer out of a beer stein even though I didn't actually like beer, but when in Germany... I also wanted to buy a cuckoo clock because I just thought it would be cute in my house. We'd be making our rounds to all the German bakeries too, because you can't not go to a German bakery. Our phones were going to be put to the test with the number of photos we were going to be taking and therefore, our social media friends were going to be sick of us.

……

The bakery is closed on Sundays, but I'd offered to use the classroom to host a wedding favor making party for Leanne. Her and Kip's wedding was coming up in just two weeks. I'd met with them recently and they'd decided on the flavors and designs of their cakes, lemon and raspberry. We'd been successful in talking Kip out of the realistic hog shaped, red velvet cake. Actually, it wasn't a matter of talking him out of it. We just told him it wasn't going to happen. There would be no dead animal cakes gracing the tables of this classy wedding event.

Aside from myself and Leanne, the group consisted of Sydney, Kennedy, Leanne's sister Ashley, and their friend Jamie. I already knew everyone through Sydney. Leanne and Kip actually met at Sydney and Will's rehearsal dinner.

The classroom was decorated with Sydney and Kip's wedding colors, sage green, ivory, and blush. Kennedy had done an exceptional job of making sure the room was clean and free of all safety or sanitation hazards, as usual.

I'd set out wooden boards with all the good snack foods: cheeses, dips, crackers, fruits, and chocolate were all present and accounted for. Of course, I'd also put together a platter of assorted pastries and cookies. Ashley brought a floral arrangement that she put together for the table centerpiece. It all came out beautifully.

Leanne passed out the supplies, and we decided to go in an assembly line fashion. She couldn't decide on just one wedding favor; so, the guests would have their choice between a handmade aromatherapy candle, a homemade lavender scented bar of soap, or a mini succulent. All were decorated with twine and a sprig of greenery attached to a tag that read 'Thank you for celebrating with us, Kip and Leanne.'

"So, Lilly, how are things going with the guy from the barbecue cookoff? Kade, right?" Sydney asked, carefully pouring melted wax into a jar.

"Guy? What guy?" Ashley inquired, her eyes becoming rounder. Kade was weaseling his way into all my social interactions today, it seemed.

"I didn't know there was a guy? Was he one of your hardware store finds?" Jamie stopped working on her candles and stared at me, anxiously waiting for the juicy gossip.

I looked around at my audience, all eagerly waiting. "I didn't find him at the hardware store. He's a police officer and he kind of pulled me over for drunk driving a few weeks ago. But I wasn't."

Everyone started talking at once, not giving me a chance to finish my sentence. I instantly regretted my life choices in re-telling that story.

"Drunk driving?!" Sydney shrieked; her mouth fell open. "I knew I shouldn't have gotten you started on peach wine!"

"So, did you get arrested? What was it like on the inside, did you have to shank anyone?" Leanne laughed, knowing I didn't really get arrested.

"No, I didn't get arrested or make any shanks or any of that. I hadn't even been drinking. But I ran over the curb and then I accidentally almost hit his car, and there was yogurt everywhere. It was just a whole thing. He made me do a sobriety test and everything." There was a roar of laughter at my expense.

"I can't even imagine you doing a field sobriety test. I just wish we could have all been there to witness it," Sydney said, still laughing, tears rolling down her cheeks.

"We need to see a picture of this guy," Jamie insisted as the laughter faded. Everyone enthusiastically agreed and started making their way over to me.

I pulled up the picture of Kade and I at the barbecue cookoff with our bibs on. That was followed by a chorus of 'ooohs' and 'awwws.' "Here's a better picture of him, though." I found his social media profile and showed them a full body photo of him in a t-shirt and jeans. That got their attention; although, a little weird with all of them ogling over the guy I was dating.

"Woah, he's hot. Like... damn!" Jamie nodded her head as the others all looked at each other in approval.

"I know who he is! He was at a cookout with me and Antonio a few weeks ago. He brought a cobbler... one that he made himself!" Ashley exclaimed, jubilantly. "He was a little quiet, but I think it's because he didn't really know many of us. But his cobbler was a huge hit. And yes, he's really good looking."

Kennedy, who had been quiet this whole time, suddenly decided it was the perfect time to bring up another bit of information that could have been left untold. "She hit him with her car." Lovely. Good ole' Kennedy, always there to help.

"Some things don't need to be told," I started to tell her, but knowing that these girls weren't going to let this story go untold.

"Excuse me, what the actual fajita meat?" Sydney questioned, loudly. I guess she'd moved on from flapjack to fajita meat now.

I groaned out loud and sat back down in my chair. "Ok, yes. I kind of hit him with my car. But in my defense, it was during the haboob, and I couldn't see him... and it was fine. He wasn't even hurt that bad."

“He had an injury to the arm; I saw the contusion myself,” Kennedy announced, really on a role all of the sudden.

“Anywhooo, let’s get back to talking about the wedding. Have y’all got everything ready?” I tried to change the subject because this event was for Leanne, after all, and not to discuss my personal life.

“Oh! I think it would be fun if we all did beauty treatments the day before the wedding! I can set up all my stuff,” Ashley volunteered.

Sydney spoke up quickly. “Hold on, Ashley. First of all, let the record show that there should be no hair chemicals used in this event. Remember my white hair the day before my wedding?”

“Honestly, even skin care treatments are risky the day before the wedding. Remember my half eyebrow the day before Easter last year?” Leanne laughed. “How about just some face masks?”

“Fine, fine. Face masks it is but that’s not as much fun.” Ashley gave in, disappointed.

“Pretty much everything else is ready, except for one thing. Lilly, will Kade be your plus one?” Leanne, still smiling, asked.

Chapter 14

Kade

People are jerks...

I never realized how great it would be to have a dumpster in my alley. I didn't have this luxury in Austin; we had trash cans that we had to take out to the street every Tuesday. It's funny how a dumpster can make me feel so free, but somehow it does. A stack of broken-down boxes had accumulated by the back door from some unpacking I'd done the night before. When I took them to the trash, Larry was out there trying to heave a large box into the dumpster, but it seemed to be too heavy for him to lift high enough to get it in.

"Hold on there, Larry, let me help," I hollered at him and dropped my boxes on the ground as I rushed over.

"Thanks, Kade, I don't know why I thought I could lift this in there by myself!"

"What do you have in here anyway?" I asked as I hoisted the box into the dumpster.

"Oh, just a dead body," he said and started chuckling. "Actually, it's a bunch of junk that I finally decided to get rid of from the garage. Alana has been nagging me all month to get some of my crap out of there, so I finally got tired of hearing it. Come see what I've done in there." He motioned for me to follow him back to his garage. I had a feeling that I was going to be spending more time over at Larry's garage than I ever imagined I would, and I didn't mind that either.

He'd made a dramatic transformation from the way it was the last time I saw it. At this rate, he might even be able to get one vehicle into this two-car garage. Even the wine boxes were cleared off the floor. The train table took up enough room that it would be impossible to get two cars in. It was quite large and had a whole town of miniature houses, buildings, little lakes and scenes set up. I don't know how I missed seeing that the last time I was here, but there were so many things to see that it must have just gotten lost in the clutter.

"I'm sure Alana is happy with what you've done! Looks great, Larry," I praised him.

"It's an improvement." Larry picked up a cup and took a few big gulps out of it and licked his lips. "Gotta love this lemonade. This watermelon mint is my favorite. We've been buying it by the gallon from Lilly's. And if I'm feeling fancy, I mix in a little vodka. Want me to make you one? It's 5:00 somewhere." These people sure do love their lemonade. They were drinking it the last time I was here, too.

"Oh no, but thank you anyway."

"Have you been to the bakery yet? It's the best one in town. Alana took a cake decorating class there and she's been making so many cakes I've probably put on 15 pounds." He patted his basketball shaped gut.

"Yes, I've been there. I've actually gotten to know Lilly a little bit." I'd like to know her a lot more than just a little bit, but that's news that I'd rather not share with Larry.

"I've known Lilly since she was this tall," he said, gesturing with his hand at waist level. "Great family, everyone in Willow Creek knows them. Lilly, though, she's something else. You should have been here when she got her driver's license. The whole town was on high alert." He laughed, shaking his head. I laughed out loud at that, too. I could just imagine what she was like back then considering everything I'd already witnessed with her driving. We talked for a few minutes more and then I walked back across the alley to my own house.

All that talk about Lilly just made me want to see her. I was off work and had the time to spare. I knew she was at work this morning, but I could go for a pastry. I took a quick shower and headed over to the bakery.

The bakery smelled of vanilla and bread dough as usual. I didn't see Lilly, just Kennedy. She was wiping down the counters, talking to a customer that appeared to be 17 years old or so. His body language reminded me of one of those kids that was used to getting whatever he wanted. One of those who got a participation trophy for everything he's ever done in his short life, but never actually had to work for it. I stood off to the side to wait.

"Hey, get me two cheese Danishes and a chocolate croissant," the kid told her, in more of a command than a request. I didn't like his tone; it reinforced my theory about him. Hearing him talk confirmed that he was one of those entitled kids that thinks everyone owes them something.

Kennedy stopped wiping the counters. "I have to get my boss," she told him, putting her rag down.

"Your boss? It's just some pastries; it isn't rocket science. Just ring it up real quick, I'm in a hurry." This kid was an ass. I stepped closer to the counter to intervene.

Kennedy's face flushed and she didn't seem to know what to say. "I don't know how use the cash register, though," she said, looking down at the counter.

"I've got cash, so just hand me some change real quick." He put some dollar bills on the counter.

Kennedy looked at the money on the counter and stammered, seeming to be unsure what to do with it. "I...

I don't know... I can't count money," she finally said, looking down, her face turning red.

"Kennedy, it's ok, I'm going to find Lilly for you." I started to walk off to find her until I heard what the kid said next.

He looked at Kennedy like she'd said something totally inconceivable. "What do you mean, you don't know how to count money? What are you, some kind of idiot? How can you even have a job?" Ok, that was enough.

I walked up to him. "Look, kid, there is no need to act that way to her. I think you need to leave." I looked toward Kennedy, her face was beat red now and her eyes were beginning to water. "Kennedy, go on to the back and get Lilly. I'll stay here and handle this."

Arrogantly, he jutted his chin and thrust out his chest. "Who the hell do you think you are? You can't tell me to leave, dumbass. I'm not leaving without my damn breakfast."

Lilly rushed to the counter, followed by Kennedy, who I'd hoped would stay in the back. "What is going on in here?" Lilly demanded, looking back and forth between me and the customer.

"I believe this man was about to leave." I took my badge out, but the kid didn't notice it yet.

"Oh, the boss lady. I just needed my order, and your little employee doesn't even know how to count money, so

I'm not sure why she even works here. Then this dude thinks he can tell me to leave." He pointed at me.

"Please leave my bakery and you are not welcome back. I will not have my employees disrespected," Lilly firmly instructed him, her face stern but professional.

"That's fine. The food isn't even that good anyway and your staff are apparently a bunch of freaks." He strutted toward the door, then flipped us all off on his way out.

Kennedy picked her cleaning rag back up and resumed scrubbing the counter with vengeance, her face dark red. I walked over to her. "Kennedy, are you ok?" She didn't look ok at all.

"Yes," she replied shortly, not looking up from the counter.

Lilly, still fuming, walked over to me and put her hands on her hips. "Kade, what the hell happened just now? I was stuck in the back on the phone with a customer and couldn't get up to the front."

"That kid came in and tried to get Kennedy to ring up his order. Kennedy tried to go to the back to get you, and the kid started getting pushy and she ended up telling him she couldn't count money. Then, it went downhill from there."

She winced and walked over to Kennedy, putting her arm around her shoulder. "Oh, Kennedy, I'm so sorry. Are you ok? You can go home early if you want to, you've earned a day off anyway."

Kennedy stiffened, clearly not wanting to be touched. “No. I don’t want to leave. I need to use the restroom,” she said and briskly walked away, avoiding eye contact with either of us.

Lilly’s eyes began to water. “Thanks, Kade. I guess I need to make sure one of us is always at the front. Usually, Kennedy just goes to get us if somebody comes in. We’ve never had an issue until today. Javier was in the classroom teaching a class, and Caitlyn isn’t here today.”

I thought for a moment about how this could have been prevented. “I know Kennedy’s job duties don’t include using the cash register, but could she be trained on it just to help out occasionally? Some extra help with counting money?”

She let out a deep breath and seemed to try to form the right words. “Kade, Kennedy really can’t count money. Her parents have tried so hard to teach her, but she can’t figure it out. Trust me, we’ve all tried to help her. She has a significant learning disability along with her autism. She can read, but she is severely limited in math, money, things like that. It’s part of why she had had such a hard time finding a job until she started working here. She was able to do things like sack groceries, but even that stressed her out during busy times.” The look in Lilly’s eyes showed just how much she truly cared about Kennedy. “Why are people so mean? How could anyone treat Kennedy like that when she’s such a good person?”

The restroom door opened, and Kennedy returned with a blotchy face and red eyes. She said nothing to either of us, still avoided eye contact, then picked up where she left off with her cleaning.

Lilly lowered her voice and said to me, “Can you stay here for a minute? I’m going to go in the back and call her mom to let her know what happened. I have a feeling Kennedy is going to let it all out when she gets home this afternoon, Lynette might want to be prepared.”

After Lilly walked off to the back I watched Kennedy, still aggressively taking her anger out on that counter. She looked like she was going to completely explode at any second.

I moved closer to her, hoping to somehow calm her down. “Kennedy, you know the things that jerk said about you aren’t true. You know that, right?”

“Yes,” she quietly murmured, slowing down on her scrubbing.

“Sometimes people are mean because they aren’t happy with themselves, and they take it out on other people. You handled that very well, I’m proud of you.”

She put down her rag and thought for a moment. “I don’t know how to count money, that’s why he was mad.”

“I think he was going to be mad even if you did know how. He’s just that kind of guy. Honestly, I think he’s just jealous of you.”

"Nobody is jealous of me." The way she said it broke my heart.

I looked at her nametag which stated her position. "Kennedy, you are the director of sanitation and infection control at the town's finest bakery. And from what I'm hearing, you are the best of the best in this town. You should be very proud."

"He said I'm an idiot, but I'm not."

"No, you're sure not."

I didn't know Lilly was behind us, hearing the conversation. "Kennedy, I think you could use a break. Why don't you fix yourself some lemonade and whatever you'd like to eat and take it in the back for a while."

I watched Kennedy take a cup and then pour a mixture of a little of every flavor of lemonade into her cup. Back in school, I remember the kids doing that with fountain drinks. We used to call it a 'suicide' and we drank it knowing it didn't even taste good. She picked up a couple of teacakes and headed to the back with her snack.

After Kennedy was out of sight, Lilly turned to me and smiled almost seductively. "I heard what you said to Kennedy."

"I thought you were going to be on the phone. Why were you spying on us?" I grinned.

"Her mom didn't answer, I'll have to try again later. But you said some really nice things to Kennedy. I think it really helped her."

"I just told her the truth."

"My brother's best friend is getting married next weekend. I'm making the cakes. You don't happen to want to go to a wedding with me, do you?"

"A wedding? Oh, yea. I'm definitely down for that. Weddings are my favorite," I teased. Weddings are not my favorite, more like least favorite.

"Your favorite, huh?"

"Not particularly, but I'm all in, for anywhere you want to go, even to a wedding."

Chapter 15

Lilly

Everyone thinks I'm crazy for my obsession with haboobs, but this last one proved my theory. Haboobs can be horrific and dangerous; there's no doubt about that. I don't like that they cause pile ups on the highway or that they blow down fences and roofs. And as Kennedy would say, we could do without the respiratory illnesses that follow. Sometimes they are so intense that you can't even see a few feet in front of you. Then, the dust eases up and you can see what was there, sometimes it's something that you didn't know was there before. Like Kade, who seemed to blow in with the wind, right in front of my car.

Over the years, I've dated plenty of guys, but I've never felt the way I do with Kade. None of them would have baked me a homemade cobbler or planted flowers in my yard, and not one of them would have taken the time to talk to Kennedy the way Kade had today. The simple fact that Kennedy opened up to him was astonishing. I think he's one of the good ones, for sure.

I'd finally been able to talk to Lynette and fill her in on the details of what went on with Kennedy. There was no mistaking the anger she felt, and the sad thing is that she's had to deal with situations like this more times than anyone should. One time would have been too many times.

I decided to call Sydney before it got too late. She's one of those early to bed, early to rise kinds of people whom I'll never quite understand. She hadn't spoken with her mom yet and didn't know what happened. Once I got the story out, she did not hold back like her mother did.

"I'm sorry, what the hell did that punk ass kid say to my sister?" she questioned, becoming totally unhinged.

"I'm so sorry, Sydney. It was awful. I felt so bad for Kennedy. But she handled it with more class than most people would have."

"First of all, who does this little prick think he is going in there and talking to her like he's somehow better than she is, which he definitely isn't. Second of all, he was bent out of shape because she can't use a cash register? Not every single person uses a cash register with their job! I don't know how to use a freaking cash register either because that's not what my job is! Why are people so stupid!" I am pretty sure Sydney hadn't inhaled one single time.

"I..." I started to reply, but Sydney was on a roll.

"And furthermore, he probably doesn't even have a job! He's probably one of those little spoiled rich kids that has never worked a day in his life, spends his whole day making YouTube videos about video games, and uses his daddy's credit card for lavender lattes and pedicures! Then he goes waltzing into your bakery and thinks he's entitled to whatever he damn well wants and belittles my sister because his own dumb ass needs to feel better about himself!" Her voice was shaky and if I know Sydney, her face was beat red and her eyes had turned from blue to turquoise as they do when she's fired up about something.

"You're probably right. He was dressed the part. That had been the first thing I'd noticed about him. But she told him she can't count money and that's really what did it for him."

Sydney, who was typically very sweet and wholesome, wasn't one to be reckoned with when it came to anyone hurting those she loved. She was fierce when it came to her kids or with Kennedy. She sounded out of breath. I knew exactly what she was doing as I heard what sounded like cabinets closing and water running. She was in full force rage cleaning; probably would give herself an asthma attack in the process.

She continued on. "Well, crap! And you know what gets me the most? Kennedy is so innocent. She's so pure and genuine with more integrity than anyone else on the face of the earth. She's never hurt anyone, and she doesn't expect people to hurt her. She's just there doing her job and doing it with so much pride in her work than I'd ever dreamed she would have; then this kid comes in and treats her like she's less than him? He's making fun of her because she can't count money, but I bet he can't either. Plus, that's not even her job! Does he expect the janitor at the grocery store to ring up his groceries?! How can a person be so mean? That's the stupidest thing I've ever heard of! Something has to be done about this. People can't go around treating others this way."

"I know. She responded very well to Kade. I was very surprised, she opened up to him a little bit," I said, calmer, trying to de-escalate Sydney.

She relaxed a little. "Aww... I'm glad. She doesn't do that with very many people. At all."

"Speaking of Kade, I'm taking Kade as my plus one to Kip and Leanne's wedding," I added, veering to a happier topic.

This seemed to do the trick with Sydney. "Oh? You know, this may work out perfectly. We need to set him, Will, and Kip up on a man's play date so they can be friends. It's a win win situation for all of us." She laughed. We needed to get them all together, but probably need to not call it a play date... Kade could use some guys to hang out with.

....

The sound of the phone woke me from a deep sleep. The clock showed 5:03 AM. Who the heck would be calling this early?

"Lilly, I'm sorry to wake you up, but something happened at the bakery." It was Javier. He always gets to the bakery early to get things baked and ready for the day.

"What happened, Javier?" I asked, trying to come out of my sleep coma.

"I think you need to come up here." He hesitated and took a deep breath. "Somebody vandalized the bakery." What? I'd never had so much as a trashcan tipped over, much less vandalism.

"I'll be right there." I sat up straight and threw the blanket off. That kid from yesterday. It had to be.

It only took me a few minutes to get dressed and drive to the bakery. I pulled into the parking spot right in front and was disgusted with what I saw. My beautiful bakery, which was pristine and flawless just yesterday was now spray painted with red paint randomly all over the otherwise flawless, grey brick. A large rock had been thrown through the giant picture window. Pieces of torn up flowers were sprinkled through the shattered remains of the three overturned flowerpots, scattered over the porch.

"Who would do this?" Javier threw his hands up in the air, almost as upset about it as I was.

"I know exactly who did it. We had a situation yesterday while you were in the classroom. Some teenage kid came in and he was horrible to Kennedy. Kade and I kicked him out. I told him he wasn't welcome back here." Javier had missed out on the drama because he had been in the back teaching a class.

Javier shook his head. "I can't imagine anyone treating our Kennedy that way."

"I'm calling Kade. I can't remember what time he gets to work, but I know he's supposed to work this morning." I took out my cell and dialed his number. Fortunately, he was already on duty.

"My bakery was vandalized, Kade! I bet it was that kid from yesterday."

"Dammit. I'm so sorry, Lilly. Will you call the non-emergency number at the station and make a report? I'm not in the area, but I'm going to call my supervisor and ask permission to go to the bakery."

It wasn't but a few minutes after I called the police station that Kade pulled up in front of the bakery in his patrol car. This is the first time I'd seen him in uniform since he came to my house the day my parents' house caught on fire. I've always had a weakness for men in uniform, basically any uniform. But Kade in uniform was a sight to behold, and for a moment, I forgot why he was even here as my eyes took a moment to appreciate the image they were seeing.

He stepped up onto the porch and gave me a hug. “Are you ok?” Kade just being here did help me feel better, especially since he was also the officer that was going to take care of it.

“Not really. Why would anyone do this? I’ve worked so hard on this bakery and now look at it!” I looked around, my eyes tearing up. The good thing was they didn’t break into the bakery, they only vandalized the outside.

Javier spoke up, “Lilly, do we need to close for the day? Get this cleaned up?” My first instinct was to close for the day and get this place back in shape, but I had a better idea.

“Oh, heck no. No way is he getting the satisfaction of thinking we lost business for the day because of him. We’re going to open at the same time as we always do. And you know what? We’ll have our first ever Vandalism Special! A red theme to match the red spray paint. Maybe buy one get one free on all red velvet items! Or free red thumb print cookies with any purchase! I’ll let you decide, Javier.”

Javier looked at Kade, shook his head and chuckled. “That’s our Lilly for you,” he said, seeming to agree with my idea, then walked to the back to start getting things ready for the day.

"Vandalism Special?" A slight smile crept over Kade's lips.

"Well? I mean, I've got to make the best of the situation, right? Anyway, what do we do now?" I asked, picking a rock up off the middle of the floor that had been thrown through the window.

"Don't touch any of that. I need to take pictures before anything gets cleaned up." He took pictures of the front of the shop, the porch, the shattered pots, and the broken window.

"I have a security camera. Do you want to see the video? I haven't even looked at it yet." I'd almost forgotten I even had it. I never have a reason to use it. Kade nodded and as we watched the video, there was no denying that it was the same kid from yesterday, along with two of his friends. He was on spray paint duty while one of his friends handled the window and flowerpot destruction. The third juvenile delinquent was the lookout.

"I knew it! So now that we know who it is, are you going to go cuff him and stuff him?"

"Well, it isn't that easy, Lilly. First of all, I don't know where to find these kids. We will need to do an investigation first. He looked to be somewhere around seventeen years old or so, give or take a year. Seventeen is considered an adult, but chances are, they might get booked but would most likely get off quickly. Honestly, they'd probably do restitution and community service."

"Seriously? That's it? For doing all this? It's going to cost me a fortune to get this fixed. The whole front of the building has to be repainted!"

"I know. It sucks. But your insurance will most likely cover it. Look, if there's anything I can do to help, just let me know. Whatever you need, just say the word."

Moments like this are what bring out the best ideas. Out of nowhere and without so much as a second of hesitation I blurted out with a furrowed brow, "I know what I want to do. I'm going on the news. That sorry S.O.B. didn't hurt me like he wanted to, and I'll be damned if he hurts Kennedy again."

"Okay, but what's this about the news?"

"I figured out what needs to happen, and it doesn't even directly have anything to do with that kid. But people who have disabilities deserve to have jobs, and they should be treated respectfully at their workplace. They have a purpose in the world just as much as everyone else does. I've known what an asset Kennedy is to us, but I don't think I ever realized the full extent of the difference my bakery has made to Kennedy."

"Ok, what are you thinking?"

"I want to start a public awareness campaign. Something to encourage businesses to give people like Kennedy a chance; hire them, empower them with job skills and confidence. And I think Kennedy would be a great spokesperson if she's willing to do it with me."

Chapter 16

Kade

I've never been big on phone calls or texting, but I found myself looking forward to Lilly's calls and texts. She was always sending me videos she'd found of things she wanted to do in Germany with her friend, Jo, or she'd send me videos or memes. Sometimes I'd barely even be out of bed, and my phone would ding with a random fact. Once it was to tell me that the word 'mellifluous' means a sound that is pleasingly smooth and musical to hear. She was a hot mess, but I couldn't get enough of her.

She had calmed down from the vandalism incident, and she hadn't been kidding when she suggested the Vandalism Special, either. She'd stuck a big sign up outside the door, offering buy one get one free red velvet items plus a free red thumbprint cookie with any drink.

Caitlyn put it all over social media, too. She had customers lined up out the door, but it wasn't just for the Vandalism Special, it was because the community loved her and her bakery and wanted to show their support for her.

On my list of things I do not enjoy, attending a wedding was near the top. But attending a wedding as Lilly's date is the exception to the rule. The wedding was tomorrow, and she would be busy all day today getting the cakes done. I was off work and decided to use the day to dive into a project.

One of the things I missed about my house in Austin was the firepit in the backyard. Sometimes, Bethany and I would roast marshmallows and make smores in the fall. But mostly, I enjoyed sitting in the peacefulness of the night. There is something strangely therapeutic about watching a fire crackle and listening to the popping sounds of the wood as it burns. It was a way for me to think and clear my head of the tiny demons that tried to live inside my brain.

The back corner near the cherry blossom tree was the perfect spot to build my firepit. I unloaded the flagstone, rocks, and bricks from the bed of the truck. I also bought two wooden Adirondack chairs and a wooden bench; not that I've ever needed that much seating, but it would look nice.

I'd unloaded most of the supplies when I heard Larry's panicked yelling coming from across the alley. "Help! Help me!"

I dropped the brick I was holding and ran through the back gate to Larry's backyard. His gate was locked, so I climbed over the fence which was built with the rough side to the alley, providing a ladder for me to climb over. I'd never understood people building their fences that way. It was prettier from inside the yard, but it was much more dangerous in a way of providing easier access for criminals.

Larry was on the ground next to his truck. I assumed he had fallen. I knelt down next to him to help him up.

"I can't get up! The truck is on my hand!" Then I saw it. The truck tire was literally on top of Larry's left hand. From the looks of it, he'd been working on the truck and it had fallen off the jack.

"Ok, I'm going to put it in neutral and push it off." The keys were in the ignition; I turned it, put it in neutral, then gave the truck a push until it rolled a few inches.

"Ok, I'm out!" Larry said, pulling his hand away and trying to get himself up. I put the truck in park and helped him stand up.

"Let me see that hand." Larry's hand was swelling, and his entire thumb was already turning purple. "I think you need to have this looked at."

"Alana is out of town on a work trip, and she is going to kill me when she gets home. She told me to take it into the repair shop, but I've been changing my own brakes all my life and I'm not willing to stop now just because she thinks I'm too old to do it anymore. I'm old, I'm not dumb." I felt bad for the old guy. He was the kind of man that spent his entire life learning how to fix things himself instead of relying on others to help him; he doesn't want to lose his independence or his pride.

"She might be mad, but I doubt she'll resort to homicide. Either way, we need to have this looked at, I have a feeling it's broken. Let me drive you to the ER."

About an hour later, Larry was called to an exam room. "Kade, you come back here with me to keep me company," he told me. You learn a lot about a person when you go into an exam room with them. I hadn't been too far off on my guess for his age. He was 77 years old. I learned he has a pacemaker, he's a cancer survivor, had two knee replacements, and he had shoulder surgery after a "freak golf cart accident." By freak accident, he admitted that he had been driving recklessly on a hill and the golf cart rolled, throwing him out.

"Well, well, well. Mr. Friedman! I thought we weren't going to keep meeting this way!" The doctor walked in, smiling. She couldn't be more than five feet tall, and even though she was smiling, she had the kind of face that indicated she didn't put up with any bull crap. She looked at me and stuck out her hand. "I'm Dr. Ramos. Nice to meet you, sir. I've done a few surgeries on this guy." She nodded toward Larry as she shook my hand. "His wife's in my archery club."

Larry took one look at her and sighed, rolling his eyes. "Dr. Ramos, there's a logical explanation for this. I was cleaning the tire and it rolled over on top of my hand." Dr. Ramos and I exchanged a look at his ridiculous attempt to twist the truth.

"Gosh, I just hate it when vehicles suddenly start rolling when we least expect it. If I had a nickel for every time that happened." She finally cracked a smile. "So basically, you were fixing your brakes against your wife's instructions, it fell off the jack and landed on top of your hand. The nurse already told me. Does Alana know about this?"

"No, she's out of town. I haven't called her yet because, well... I'm terrified of her. Is it broken?"

"You're very fortunate. The only thing that's broken is your thumb and I'm just going to put it in a cast. You're lucky your friend here was able to help you before you had a much bigger problem."

We finished up at the ER and walked back to the truck. "Kade, you don't happen to be hungry, do you? I thought we could get a bite to eat at Annie's Deli, my treat." I wasn't hungry, but there was no way I was going to say no to this guy, especially after he'd had a truck sitting on his hand.

"I'm starving," I lied and headed to the deli.

The bell on the front door jingled as we walked inside the deli. "Good afternoon, Larry! The usual for you?" the woman behind the counter asked as we approached the counter.

"Yes indeed, Laurie. I wouldn't have it any other way!" He looked back at me. "What'll you have, Kade? You should get the thanksgiving sandwich, it's won awards." What is it with this sandwich? It's the same thing that Lilly was raving about when we came here.

I ordered the club sandwich, instead, and chuckled at the way both Larry and Laurie looked taken aback when I didn't want the Thanksgiving sandwich.

We settled into a booth and ate our sandwiches. Larry struggled with holding his food due to the new cast, so I cut it into fourths for him to make it easier. He was a talker and carried on most of the conversation on his own. He told me that he owned a furniture store for thirty years. He and his three employees built the furniture themselves which explained the abundance of wood clamps in his garage that I'd been curious about. Apparently, the store was very successful at one time until the bigger furniture chains started popping up, offering lower prices, but also cheaper quality products. With the way things have been for the last several years, people have wanted to pay less, and they didn't care as much about quality anymore. Unable to compete with that, he could no longer afford to stay in business and had no choice but to retire. I could see it in his eyes; he would still be working today if he could have.

Alana and Larry didn't have any kids together; she'd been unable to get pregnant. He had two sons from a previous marriage; however, neither of them had anything to do with him anymore. They'd formed a close bond with their stepdad when they were young, and Larry had taken a back seat to him almost immediately. They both lived far across the continent, rarely even calling him. He had grandkids that he'd never even met. He said he didn't know what he did to make them not want anything to do with him. He tried; he called them, sent cards and gifts, even money. But they seemed to have their own lives and didn't see a need for him to be in them. Larry is a great man, I didn't understand how his kids could treat him that way and it made me furious with them.

Once I got Larry home, I went back to my firepit project. Spending time with Larry today made me miss my own dad. We didn't really spend a lot of quality time together because the majority of the time that he was home, he was drunk. I couldn't take anything that he said very seriously because he most likely wouldn't even remember it the next day. But the few good times we had when he was completely sober were amazing, like the times we went fishing at the lake on his boat. We always went early in the morning before the sun came up; he said that was the best time to catch fish. Those times will live forever in my head. Then there is Larry, alive and well, and his kids don't even want to talk to him, much less spend any time with him.

I worked on the firepit for a few hours, immersed in my thoughts, before quitting for the day, then sat down on my new bench to call Lilly. She didn't know it yet, but I'd already planned a surprise for her for next weekend.

"Hello?" she answered. There's not a better sound than the sound of her cheerful voice. I could picture her sitting there with powdered sugar and icing all over herself and her hair piled haphazardly up on top of her head. It didn't matter what she did; it was impossible for her not to be gorgeous.

"That's the most *mellifluous* sound I've heard all day," I replied, then smiled as I heard her laugh.

Chapter 17

Lilly

Wedding date...

I'd gone shopping with Sydney and Ashley the weekend before and chose the most stunning blush pink chiffon dress and a pair of strappy stilettos to wear with it. After I finished the cakes yesterday, I'd gone to the salon with the girls, and we'd gotten mani-pedis. The color I chose worked perfectly with the dress and shoes. The others got facials also, but I'd been having something going on with my lips and the skin around my eyes, so I opted out of that for fear it would make it worse.

Skipping the facial didn't seem to matter though, because it did get worse. I woke up to a burning, swollen sensation on my face, worse than it had been the last few days. It started out as some mild irritation and burning but continued to worsen over the past few days. I'd tried a variety of home remedies that I'd found online, but nothing was working very well and if anything, may have made it worse. I climbed out of bed and padded to the bathroom to look in the mirror, then gasped in horror at the image looking back at me under the bright lights. It was worse than I thought it would be. So much worse. My eyelids and the skin surrounding my eyes were red, flaky, and quite swollen with a rough sand papery texture. My lips were even worse: swollen, red, and chapped to the point they almost reminded me of cornflakes. I couldn't go out in public like this; I looked like I'd put on costume makeup for Halloween! And I was supposed to be Kade's date!

I used my app to find a virtual doctor and was on a video chat with him in only five minutes. Gotta love technology. The doctor was very friendly, I had to keep a straight face while talking with him because my lips were literally cracking just from trying to smile. He prescribed medication but informed me that even if I started taking it now, it likely wouldn't make too much of a difference in time for the wedding tonight. He did, however, tell me what I could put on them to prevent them from cracking. With any luck, I would at least be able to smile at the wedding.

......

Leanne wanted the cakes delivered to the venue by 2:00 PM to give her time to set the tables up before she started getting ready. I put on dark sunglasses to hide my eyes, but my lips couldn't be covered up. Already thin, the extreme chapping made my lips appear to cinch up even more, looking like a ninety-year-old that had been smoking a pack a day since she was twelve years old.

The cakes are quite heavy and require two people to deliver them. Caitlyn went with me to set them up and noticed my misfortune immediately. "Um, do you need some chapstick? Your lips are practically bleeding," she asked, looking closer at my lips.

How the heck was I going to attend a wedding looking like this when she noticed immediately. "I've tried. I've tried everything, but anything I put on just makes it worse. I have a prescription, but it isn't going to make any difference in time for the wedding. But wait, it gets better." I took off my sunglasses and looked at her.

Her eyes grew huge. "Oh..."

"Yea..."

"What happened? I mean, is it an allergic reaction or something?" she asked.

"The doctor said it probably has something to do with Lupus. But no matter what it's from, I can't go around looking like this. And I can't miss the wedding, I mean, it's Kip and Leanne!" Nothing was going to make me miss that wedding, Kip has been like a brother to me for years.

"No, you can't miss the wedding. You're going to do what you do best. Just own it. Just like you did with the

Vandalism Special. I mean, that's really all you can do, right?" Easier said than done, but she was right.

Kip walked over to us as we were setting up the cakes. "The cakes look amazing! I still wish I had the red velvet hog, but this works too." He laughed and gave me a hug. "Leanne had to run back home to get something, she'll be back in a minute."

"That's ok, I'll see her tonight. I can't believe you're getting married! And to the most amazing person to ever live, too! I can't tell you how happy I am for both of you." I looked up at him and took off my sunglasses. "But I'm going to look like a freak, so just beware."

Being the gentleman that he is, he looked worried instead of horrified. "Are you ok? That looks painful," he asked, examining my eyes.

"It actually does hurt kind of bad, but it'll get better after the med kicks in. I wish I could look a little more presentable for your wedding, but Cailyn says I need to just own it and have fun."

"Caitlyn has good advice. We don't care what you look like, just as long as you're here." He smiled and gave me another hug. "See you tonight and save a dance for me!"

I texted Kade when I got home. **Please be aware that your date tonight will not be very attractive.**

Kade: **Not possible.**

Me: **Here's a sneak peek of what you are in for.** I texted him a photo of half of one eye. **I totally**

understand if you suddenly have plans and need to back out.

Kade: **Oh, yea. I forgot I have to be somewhere tonight.**

Me: **You're kidding, right?**

Kade: **You're beautiful, no matter what you think. I'll see you tonight.**

.....

I inspected myself in the mirror one last time. I'd left my hair down, styled it my favorite way, using the curling wand to create loose waves. My face was the struggle. I couldn't use any eye products other than mascara. Obviously, lipstick was out of the question, but I did put the oil on my lips that the doctor recommended. I was able to put on some blush and do a little contouring, which I never do, but at least it was something. Finally, I'd thrown up my hands and said to myself, "It is what it is," and gave up on it. There wasn't much I could do other than take Caitlyn's advice and just own it.

Beatrice started barking before the doorbell even rang. Standing on the porch was Kade looking like the first photo that would come up if you simply googled 'sexy man.' He had on khaki pants and a navy blue, linen button-down shirt that was fitted just tight enough that the definition of his chest and arm muscles showed through. Damn. Just, damn. He looks good in everything he puts on.

“Wow, Lilly, you look amazing,” he said, his eyes trailed down taking in everything from my hair to my shoes.

“Even with the face?” I laughed.

“Even with the face.” He reached out and touched my waist. “And that dress is… damn hot.” The way he said that made my face flush.

The pink gift bag he was holding caught my eye. “What do you have there? You do realize you aren’t required to bring gifts with every date, right?”

“Yes, but I like to bring things. So, hopefully you don’t think this is dumb. But I found it online and I thought it would be perfect for you. I know you like to try new foods, especially foods from other countries. So, I got you a subscription to this snack box that has snacks from other countries. It will be a different country every month.” Seriously, the coolest thing I’ve ever heard of, plus the sweetest.

“Are you kidding me! I’ve never heard of anything like this!” There was no time to waste. Tearing into it I found that this month’s items were from Colombia! “Officer Wayland, who knew you would be such a thoughtful gift giver?” First, the cobbler. Then, the tiger lilies, and now this? Most guys just give you the standard issue bouquet of flowers, if even that, and move on.

“I’m glad you like it. I wasn’t sure if you’d think it was stupid.”

This was anything but stupid and probably the best invention ever. I live for things like this, and now I'd have a surprise every month to look forward to.

.....

The wedding was like none other I'd ever seen. Truly breathtaking. Ashley had outdone herself with the phenomenal floral arrangements. Arranged on a wooden display among lit candles and twinkling lights were the wedding favors we'd made. The cakes were set up in a similar fashion, which I approved of 100%.

Will sang during the wedding. My brother has one of the best voices I have ever heard, and I'm not just biased because he is my brother, either. He sang during his own wedding also, a surprise to Sydney.

Once the vows were repeated and the happy couple were pronounced husband and wife, we found Sydney and Will talking with Kennedy and Lynette.

I already knew I would not be able to get through the evening without a medical evaluation from Kennedy. And just as I expected, she approached, her eyes fixed on my eyes and lips. "Whoa," she said, not trying to make light of it at all.

"I know. I have a prescription for it." I glanced over at Kade who had a smirk on his face. We'd already debated on how long it would take Kennedy to form a diagnosis.

"I believe you may have a flesh-eating parasite, and I hate to tell this, but it probably *will* kill you." She was off her game.

"Anywho..." Sydney interrupted her sister. "Your dress is absolutely fabulous, Lilly. I'm glad you picked that one." Sydney also looked stunning in the sage green dress she had on.

"Kade, they have an open bar. Do you want to go grab a beer with me?" Will asked him.

"Sure, I could use a beer. Lilly, do you want something?"

"Maybe a glass of champagne. Thanks!" After they walked off together, Sydney got serious. "Ok, let's get down to business. So, tell me everything before they get back. How serious is it between you two?" Sydney had her blue eyes in a death stare at me.

I laughed at her. "Well, I mean, we haven't known each other very long, so not too serious, I guess."

"Must I remind you that Will and I were literally married three months after our first date? So that means nothing to me. Now, go on."

I let out a deep breath. "Well, I mean, I'm not wanting to date anyone else, and I don't think he is. We've been out a few times, nothing major. And we text and talk daily."

"Ok, so you really like him. He seems like a good guy. Any red flags at all?" Sydney has an internal radar to spot any and all potential issues with men. Her first husband was an jerk, and she still has some lingering effects of that.

"None at all. All green flags so far. He's divorced and he hasn't really dated much since his ex-wife. He didn't have much of a personality when I first met him during the sobriety test... but after we started talking more, he really came out of his shell. He's thoughtful, different from the other guys I've dated. And I don't have to mention what he looks like. Did you notice how that shirt and pants fit him?"

Kade and Will returned with the drinks, then we all mingled for a while until Leanne and Kip made their grand entrance. Once the first dances were completed, the dancefloor started filling up. I danced with Kip, Will, and of course, with Kade. I watched as Kade made his way over to Kennedy and asked her to dance, surprised that she was willing to, then even more surprised that she smiled and laughed while he taught her how. Aside from Kennedy, nobody else mentioned my eyes and lips. All everyone cared about was having a good time and it was the most fun I'd had in a while.

After we saw Leanne and Kip off in Kip's decorated truck, everyone began leaving. We weren't ready for the night to end and headed to a little cocktail bar near my house.

I ordered my favorite drink, a chilton. It seems like it's a Texas thing because I've been to bars in other states that don't know what that is, or else they don't make it quite like they make it here. Kade ordered a local beer.

"I don't really go to bars much, but I really like this one. It's quiet and kind of classy. And they make a perfect chilton."

Kade looked around and agreed. "This is a nice place. I don't really go to bars either, but I could handle coming back here."

"Not a big drinker?"

"I just don't like to be around people who are drunk." He took a drink of his beer. "My dad was an alcoholic."

"Oh, I'm sorry."

"No, really, it's ok. He died about five years ago from cirrhosis of the liver. He drank since I was born, so that's all I ever knew. I've kind of made a rule for myself to not drink enough that I get drunk. I always felt like by me not drinking as much, it somehow counteracted my dad's drinking. It probably sounds stupid, but I've always thought that maybe his drinking was supposed to be a lesson or something. Anytime I've had more than a couple of beers, I just felt guilty. I know it doesn't make any sense, but to me it kind of does."

"I think it makes perfect sense. Thank you for telling me that story." I was glad to know a little about Kade's history, to get to know where he came from and what makes him who he is. "So, changing the subject, I have a random fact about Germany. Did you know that on the autobahn, there is no speed limit? So basically, if I rent a car there, I can drive as fast as I want and I won't get pulled over."

Kade took another drink and seemed to mull that fact over in his head. "Lilly, please tell me that you are not going to rent a car."

I burst out laughing and had to get my oil out, so my lips didn't crack open. Kade had already made known what he thought about my driving skills, so the thought of me driving with no speed limit was surely more than he could fathom. Pretty soon, he was laughing too. We paid our tab and as we opened the door to walk out, a tall brunette stood on the other side. Kade's smile immediately faded, and he came to a dead halt when he saw her.

"Kade," the woman said and then shifted her eyes over to me. They knew each other?

"Bethany. What the hell are you doing here?"

Chapter 18

Kade

Bad memories...

Trigger warning: This chapter involves a memory of a police involved shooting. Content may be triggering for some readers.

"Your mom told me where to find you. Can we talk?" Bethany looked over at Lilly, then back at me. "In private? Please?"

"Hold on," I cocked my head. "My mom doesn't know I'm here, at this bar. Have you been following me?"

Bethany looked away, clearly guilty. What was my mom thinking? I didn't give her permission to tell her where I was. If I'd wanted her to know, I would have told her myself.

Lilly looked back and forth between Bethany and I. The thoughts racing through her head right now couldn't be good. Taking Lilly aside, out of earshot from Bethany, I handed her the truck keys. "Here's my truck keys. There's nothing to worry about. I'm going to talk to her for just a second, and I'll be right back if you want to wait for me in the truck."

"Who is that?" she asked, taking the keys.

"My ex-wife."

After Lilly walked away, I went back over to Bethany, who was still standing on the sidewalk. How could she think she could waltz over here and expect me to not be infuriated with her.

"You've got five minutes. Start talking," I told her, impatiently. I could feel the veins twitching in my neck.

"Look, Kade, I just..." Her eyes started watering, and she took a deep breath, her voice shaky. "I was wrong. I realize I made a mistake. I hate that I hurt you and I never should have done that to you. It's just that, after what happened with Liam... I was trying to protect myself because I couldn't stand the thought of the same thing happening to you, or worse." She wiped the tears that were rolling down her face.

"Five years later? Five years, Bethany! It took you that long to figure this out? Seriously?" I snapped, refusing to be swayed by her sorrowful tears.

"I'm sorry, I tried to move on. I really did. I dated other people; I even went to counseling. But I just need you back, Kade. I still love you; I never stopped." She had a lot of nerve coming back here like this. I'd worked so hard to start a new life away from everything I was trying to leave in my past, and now here she was, bringing it all back like a re-opened wound.

"So, Liam was shot, my dad had just died, and you left me because it was too hard for you to deal with... Never once even telling me there was a problem until you'd already filed for divorce. Right when I was going through the worst time of my life. And now that I've moved on and built a new life, you want to come back and say you're sorry? And what, I'm supposed to take you back and act like nothing ever happened? No thank you." I turned around toward the truck.

"Kade, please, can we talk about this some more?" she pleaded, grabbing my arm.

I yanked my arm back. "Your five minutes is up." I marched back to the truck, refusing to turn around to look at her. I slammed the door when I got back inside and took a deep breath to try to calm myself down. I didn't want Lilly to see me like this.

Lilly fumbled nervously with her dress, then took her phone out of her purse. "I can call a ride home if you need to talk to her some more," she said quietly.

"No, it's ok. I have no plans of ever talking to her again. I wouldn't have had to tonight if my mom hadn't told her I was living here."

I drove Lilly back to her house, mostly in silence. We tried to make small talk, but Bethany had done an excellent job of ruining our night. When we pulled up in her driveway, I expected Lilly to be in a hurry to get rid of me for the night, but instead, she said, "I'm not tired yet. Want to come in for a while?" I wasn't ready to go home yet either; but some more time with Lilly was exactly what I needed.

"Where's the spider?"

She smiled in an almost protective way. "Penny is in her cage in my bedroom, safe and sound. Don't worry, she can't get out of it." Anyone else would have made a snide remark about it, but Lilly wasn't sarcastic at all. Of all the women I've ever known, why did Lilly have to be the one with the pet spider?

Lilly's pet preferences are simply abnormal. I sat on the couch with the unfortunate looking Beatrice while Lilly got the drinks. As ugly as she is, she was a sweet little thing. She curled up next to me and put her pitiful looking head on my leg, something I never imagined letting her do. Lilly came back with a beer and a lemonade, pleased to see Beatrice and I were getting along.

"I'm going to go change out of this dress. You and Beatrice can hang out here for a second," she said as she walked off towards her bedroom. She returned a few minutes later in leggings and an oversized What Happens in Vegas T-shirt, and fuzzy socks which seem to be her favorite kind of sock. She plopped down on the couch, sideways facing me, and picked up her drink.

"Wanna talk about it?" she asked, her voice soothing as she put her hand on my leg.

Did I want to talk about it? Not really. Did I need to talk about it? Probably. I'd refused counseling, refused any and all help that had been offered to me. This was the first time I'd felt at all inclined to discuss it in a long time.

"She came here to tell me she made a mistake, she feels bad for hurting me, all that crap. I wish she'd never come. I thought I wasn't ever going to have to see her again."

Lilly nodded her head, paying close attention. "So, what happened? Why did the two of you get divorced? Please don't feel like you have to tell me, I totally understand if you would rather not."

I had kept this tied up in my own head for five years. I'd felt like it was better for me to leave it hidden where it was, because letting it out could mean bringing back all the trauma that I tried to cover up for my own sanity.

"She couldn't be married to a police officer anymore," I explained, taking a drink of my beer and setting it down on the coffee table.

"Did something happen to you at work?"

"Yea, it did. Remember when I pulled you over and I was kind of a jerk?"

"I vaguely remember something like that happening," she said and smiled, then reached over to grab her oil for her lips.

"Officers get a lot of calls for possible shots fired in July, but usually they turn out to be fireworks. When I pulled you over that night, I'd had a few of those calls, people using up the leftover fireworks from the 4th. They were just fireworks, but they tend to be triggering for me. It happens to me around the 4th of July and every New Years Eve. I'm sorry I was a jerk to you."

"It's fine, I mean, I probably deserved it. I did run over a curb and then almost hit your car. I'm pretty sure anyone else would have thought I was drunk also." Her face was warm and comforting. "I'm a good listener if you want to talk about it. Sometimes it helps to just get it out if you need to." She was the first and only person I felt I could talk to about this. Anyone else would brush it off, or try to make light of it, as if that's even possible. Lilly wasn't going to do that, I knew she wouldn't.

"Liam and I met in high school and from that day on, we were pretty much inseparable. After graduation, we went into the military together with a Buddy Program. Eventually, we both started working for the police department. It's crazy how everything had worked out for us that way. We were close like brothers. We worked in a smaller town outside of Austin; it was just a small police department so there were times when we didn't have much backup. We didn't work the same shift, but occasionally, we were able to work together.

"I'd started my shift that night at 11:00 PM. On my way to the station for roll call, I'd heard over the radio that another officer was engaging in a pursuit. I was able to assist him in apprehending the subject on foot through an alley, but he was uncooperative and refused to do any type of sobriety test and refused the breathalyzer. We had to take him to the hospital for a blood draw but had to wait for a warrant. Meanwhile, there were a lot of calls coming in for burglaries, domestics, things like that. We didn't have many officers on the streets that night, so Liam offered to help me get the calls caught up.

"After a few hours, we got the calls caught up and the shift under control, then pulled up to the police department to talk about a death report. Some of the other officers were outside the station, talking and smoking cigarettes when dispatch came in and said there were reports of shots fired. Of course, with it being the 4th of July, everyone assumed it was just fireworks. We'd already had a constant stream of reports of shots fired, never amounting to anything besides a few instances of fireworks being shot illegally within the city limits. So, for this particular call, nobody got excited about it either. Something in the pit of my stomach told me this call wasn't related to fireworks. Even though Liam told me he didn't need any backup, I went ahead and followed him. I always trust my gut instinct, and it told me to go."

Lilly sat on the couch motionless, taking in every word.

I took a drink and continued, surprised at how calm I was reliving that night.

"There were four women, mid-fifties, smoking on the front porch. I remember the porch light was on, and one of the women looked like she'd been crying. There was loud music and the sound of other people talking and kids laughing inside the house as if they may have been having a party. Another male, also mid-fifties, was leaning against an old, beat-up travel trailer parked in the driveway. Liam got out of the car and approached the women on the porch, asking if they knew anything about a report of shots fired. None of them were willing to give any information, stating they hadn't heard anything, but we could tell they knew something." I stopped for a moment, took a drink, and re-adjusted myself on the couch. Lilly remained quiet, listening intently.

"But then Liam and I both approached the man and positioned ourselves with me on one side and Liam on the other. Liam walked up to him with his flashlight underneath his armpit and asked if the man heard anything about a report of shots fired. All the man said was, 'Nope.' But as soon as Liam started talking again, the man pulled out his revolver."

"Oh no", Lilly gasped. I swallowed hard, trying not to lose my composure. This was the part that haunted me in my dreams all too often.

"That son of a... he pulled the trigger and shot Liam in the head before either of us had time to react. Liam went down immediately, right in front of me, his blood splattered on the side of the trailer. I'd just finished my active shooter training three weeks prior to that. Freshly trained, something in my head said 'go now' as soon as I heard the pop of the gun. I drew my weapon from my holster, and as the suspect moved toward me, I shot him in the femoral artery and then again in his waist. I later learned that the bullet went through his belt and into his gut. I raised my gun again to shoot center mass, but as I was firing, I heard another shot that wasn't mine. I didn't notice at the time because it was so quick, but the suspect tried to shoot me. He missed only because my bullet hit his fingers and broke the bone in his arm, causing his bullet to hit the ground to the left of me. He was still coming toward me, and I continued to fire, striking him in the nose and chin, then finally in his head. It seemed like everything was moving in slow motion, but finally, I realized the threat was over. I got on my portable mic, reported suspect down, and requested ambulance and to get flight for life ready for Liam."

"The suspect was just twelve inches from my foot and his blood was running down my shoe and into the driveway. I was there by myself, unsure if Liam was even alive. I didn't get a response from dispatch the first time I called out. I called out again, telling them shots fired, officer down, need ambulance and flight for life." I didn't notice I had tears running down my face. Lilly noticed, picked up a tissue, wiped them off my face, and handed me a couple more to hold.

"Liam was on the ground, blood coming out of his head, I didn't know if he was dead or alive. He wasn't moving and I had a growing, angry crowd around me. The women were yelling and screaming at me, kneeling next to the suspect's body. People were starting to come out of their homes and from the home where the suspect lived. They were all yelling at me and becoming uncooperative. We later learned that before we got to the scene, the man had been fighting with his wife. He'd gotten laid off at work and took his anger out on her, even pulled his gun out and threatened to shoot her. Apparently, there'd been a long history of domestic abuse and she'd been afraid to leave him. The whole family was afraid of him, and he'd warned them against calling the police and told them that nobody was going to take it seriously. He'd fired a round into the air which was what was heard when the shots fired call came in from a neighbor."

"Oh, Kade, that's awful. So, this whole time Liam was laying there and you couldn't even help him since you were having to control the situation..." Lilly said, quietly.

"It seemed like a lifetime before backup arrived, but in reality, it was only a few minutes. I later learned that there were twelve shots fired, eleven struck, in a matter of only four seconds but it seemed like so much longer than that. Suddenly there were officers showing up in civilian clothes with their badges and weapons, assisting me in getting the crowd under control while I applied pressure to my best friend's head where blood was coming from. There was no response.

"I'm so sorry, Kade. I can't even begin to imagine what that must have been like," Lilly said, then asked carefully, "Was he dead?"

"I wasn't sure at that time. The ambulance came and loaded him up. The bullet struck him at the right side of his forehead to the back of his right ear. As soon as they got to the hospital, he went straight to the helicopter and was in surgery forty-five minutes later."

"So he made it?"

"Yea, barely. But he was never the same again. The damage was so severe that he was in a coma for a month. Then, his parents moved him to a nursing home in Dallas, to be closer to them."

"I'm sorry," she said softly, grabbing my hand.

We sat in silence for a few moments, then she spoke up again. "So, why did your ex-wife leave you, then? I don't understand."

This was the tricky part. "She never was a fan of me becoming a police officer, but I never knew that. Before we got married, I was a city code enforcer, but I hated it. I mean, nobody loves being a code enforcer. She knew that my dream had been to do something in law enforcement. This hadn't been a secret, I was very open about it with her. When I applied with the police department, she was supportive, and she never gave me any reason to think she wasn't happy about it. I'd always felt a calling toward law enforcement, especially after my sister's best friend was shot and killed by her husband. I wanted to help people. And I believe I did save lives that night. Liam's for one, but anyone in that man's family, particularly his wife, could have been killed that night."

"You were a hero."

"Thank you. But after that night, Bethany was a nervous wreck. She hated seeing me leave for work and she would pace the floor the whole time until I came home safely. She worried every time that I went to work that the chief of police would end up on our porch telling her I'd been killed. The problem was I didn't realize this, she never said anything about it. If she'd just talked to me about it, we could have tried to work things out. I would never blame her for worrying, but she could have talked to me about it. Then one day, only three months after Liam was shot, I came home from work, and she had already filed for divorce without not so much as a word to me about it. It came as a complete shock to me, except she had already told everyone in her family plus my mother about it before she filed. Nobody said a word to me and I was the last to know. And the bad part was my dad had just died right before Liam was shot, and I was dealing with that as well. All of that happened in a time span of four months."

"Wow. That's just unimaginable. So, do you need to talk to her? I mean, do y'all have unfinished business to deal with now?" she asked.

"I do not have any unfinished business to deal with. Our business was finished the day I signed the divorce papers. She's had five years, I don't know why she came looking for me now, but it's too late and I've moved on." I moved Beatrice to the other side of my leg and scooted closer to Lilly, pulling her onto my chest. "And besides, I've found this sexy, spider loving bakery owner that has an ugly dog that I'm getting attached to."

She looked up at me and said, "I'd kiss you right now if my lips weren't defective."

Chapter 19

Lilly

The morning after...

I slept with Kade. It was amazing. By that, I mean we both fell asleep on the couch halfway through an episode of Schitt's Creek. I woke up around 3:00 AM, lying across Kade's chest, with the smell of his cologne still lingering on his shirt. I've always felt safe in my home, but lying there curled up with Kade made me feel like nothing could ever go wrong. Like our little spot on the couch was the safest and most cozy spot in the entire world.

Beatrice was curled up in the crook of his arm, his other arm was wrapped around my back. Ever since Kade came over last night, Beatrice had been all over him and wanted nothing much to do with me; totally out of character for her because she normally doesn't like men at all.

It took me a while to fall back asleep. I liked Kade. Like, *really* liked him. I was in too deep now and I didn't see any way of going back at this point, not that I wanted to. What's not to like? Not only was he drop dead gorgeous, but he was thoughtful and compassionate and had a way of making me feel like I was the most important person in the world. I had no problem with the idea of falling asleep with him many more times and I daydreamed for a while about what that would be like if we were together next year or in five years, waking up together even if it was just after falling asleep watching TV.

The story he shared with me was heartbreaking on so many levels and was an eye-opener of his past, but also his life as it is in the present. I felt honored that he so openly shared his story, when he hadn't wanted to talk about it with anyone else. I couldn't assume that the drama with Bethany was over. She and Kade had shared an entire marriage; he had loved her once. And she apparently still loved him. From what I understood, it wasn't so much that she wasn't happy with Kade, it was that she wasn't happy with his job. She was scared, and she didn't want to be in a situation where she worried every day that he might not come home from work. I don't blame her for that, not one bit. The problem was that she didn't talk to him about it before heading straight to the attorney and then surprising him with a divorce that everyone else already knew about when he was already going through such a difficult time in his life. That five-minute conversation in front of the bar, if you can even call it a conversation, would likely not satisfy her, and I had a feeling she hadn't packed up and headed back home.

Besides the fact that she'd shown up unexpectedly, she's also had the satisfaction of seeing me with my lizard-like lips and eyes, of all the people to meet at a time like that. It's one thing to be around people I already know who don't really care what I look like, but this is an entirely different situation. Bethany looked one hundred percent like a super model. Seriously, she was tall and thin and had the kind of brunette hair that looked like shiny silk; the kind that no matter what brand of hair care or what styling method I have ever tried, is impossible to achieve. Then there I was, barely any makeup, blotchy, flaky, scaly eyes while she had achieved a perfectly seductive, smoky eye look on her own face. My lips had been thin, cracked, rough, and bare, a sharp contrast to her full, perfectly lined, full red lips. Even on a good day when my face had nothing wrong with it, I could never compete with that.

I woke up alone on the couch, covered up with my cozy throw blanket, to the smell of something cooking. Bacon. I sat up, looking for Kade.

"Well, look who finally woke up!" He walked in carrying a spatula, Beatrice following close behind. "Breakfast is almost ready." He had a five o'clock shadow, his hair was messed up, and he had on the white T-shirt that he'd worn under his dress shirt.

"You're cooking?" Kade spent the night and was now cooking in my kitchen. I don't think I remember ever waking up to a man cooking in my kitchen. Harrison sure as heck didn't do that; at the most he would open a granola bar for himself.

"Bacon, eggs, and biscuits and gravy. You didn't really have much in your refrigerator, so I went to the store and got a few things." My gosh, that was a whole feast. I was used to a bowl of cereal for breakfast if I had anything at all.

"It smells amazing. And yea, it's been a while since I've been to the store." I laughed and went off to the restroom to look at myself in the mirror. I'm not the kind of girl who wakes up in the morning looking fresh and beautiful, but combined with the lip and eye thing, I dreaded seeing what I looked like this morning, especially since Kade had already seen me this morning and he still had a fresh reminder of what his ex-wife looked like. It wasn't as bad as I anticipated. The medication the doctor prescribed seemed to be working; my lips and eyes were settling down quite a bit, and I was looking more like myself. I brushed my hair and washed my face before heading back to the kitchen.

"How do you like your eggs? I can do scrambled, poached, baked, hard boiled, soft boiled, sunny side up, over easy, I can go on and on."

"I had no idea you were an egg connoisseur. Scrambled, please." I sat out the plates, poured myself a cup of coffee, and refilled his half empty cup. It felt strangely comfortable and familiar, as if it wasn't the first time we'd had breakfast in my kitchen.

Kade carried our plates to the table then looked down at Beatrice. "Here you go, Beetle Head." He bent down to give Beatrice a piece of bacon.

"Beetle Head?" Beatrice had never had a nickname before other than Bea, which I called her sometimes.

"It's fine, she isn't offended." He chuckled, digging into the feast he prepared.

I dug into my food. Ok, this man can cook. "Oh wow, this is incredible. I was starving too."

"I'm glad you like it!" He looked at me for a minute while he chewed. "Your lips and eyes look better today. What did the doctor say was wrong with them, anyway?" I liked the way he asked.

"He wasn't sure exactly, but he thought it might have something to do with my lupus. I was just diagnosed about a year ago. I'm not supposed to be out in the sun too much, but I was out doing some yardwork without a hat or sunscreen before this happened. He thinks that could have done it, but really, I think a lot of things are just a mystery." I held my breath waiting for his response to this.

"Oh, I'm sorry. My sister actually has lupus, so I know a little about it. She's supposed to not be out in the sun much either." I exhaled, relieved that he was already familiar with it.

"I really don't bring it up too often because my experience has been that it's an immediate turn off to basically everyone other than Jo. I was still with my ex-boyfriend, Harrison, when I found out what it was. I have been to so many different doctors over the years, and nobody ever took anything seriously. He thought I was a hypochondriac. Then finally I found a rheumatologist that actually took me seriously, ran all the right tests, and started me on medication. It was a relief to me to finally have an answer, but it actually seemed to piss Harrison off, like it proved his hypochondriac theory wrong."

"He sounds like an ass."

"Oh, he was. But enough about that... It was perfect timing that your ex-wife got to see me looking so glamorous with my eyes and lips last night. She's probably so jealous that you had such a hot date." I laughed.

"Back up just a second. First of all, it isn't an immediate turnoff. And anytime you want to bring it up, do it. I'm a good listener too, you know." So far, all the right boxes can be checked on Kade. He's a real-life good guy, like he walked straight out of one of my romance books.

I smiled at him, happy that my lips no longer cracked. He was the first guy who had ever told me that or made me feel even the slightest bit comfortable talking about my health. Actually, he may have been the first person ever to say that to me. “Thank you, that’s so sweet of you.”

“And second of all. Anyone would be jealous of my gorgeous date. I mean, did you see how you looked in that dress? Hot, scalding hot.” I felt my face flush. I’ve never thought of myself as ‘hot.’ Medium level attractive maybe, but hot? But here is Kade, of all the eligible men in Willow Creek, thinking exactly that.

I ate every single bite off my plate, something I never do, then took our empty plates to the sink. While I had my back turned to him, Kade came up from behind me and wrapped his arms around my waist, resting his chin on my shoulder. My stomach fluttered like butterflies the instant he touched me. “Thanks for listening to me last night. It helped to get that out, I’ve kept it bottled in for way too long.”

I turned around to face him, curling my finger through his beltloop to pull him closer. “Thank you for trusting me enough to tell it to me.”

“If you don’t have anything else going on next weekend, I have something in mind. But I want it to be a surprise.” He tucked my hair behind my ear and kissed my neck, softly, trailing up to behind my ear, creating goosebumps along my arms.

"I like surprises," I responded, breathlessly. He smiled and, still being cautious of my healing lips, gave me a peck on both cheeks and my forehead before heading out the door, but not before also giving Beatrice a pat on the head. It took a moment to compose myself again after that little tease of Kade's, then I heard my phone ring. It was Jo.

"Forty-two days to Germany!" she blurted out as soon as I answered. "It's down to the wire. You know, I wasn't really too sure about it when we first started planning it, but now I cannot wait!" I was so glad to hear that because I'd been feeling like I was the only one that was excited about it.

"I know! I'm so excited. Jo, you won't believe what happened."

"Ok, start talking." She always wanted to hear the scoop, no matter what it was about.

"So, Kade just left and so much has happened in the last 24 hours. I think we have hit a huge milestone in our relationship. I mean, I think it's an actual relationship now."

"Wait, slow down. He just left? In the morning? Details please."

"Well, it isn't exactly like it sounds... We fell asleep watching Schitt's Creek. But anyway, he made breakfast and everything. And Beatrice likes him so there's that, too."

"Oh... dammit. Ok, go on."

"So, remember when I texted you the pictures of my eyes and lips?" I'd sent her pictures yesterday morning. "Well, they didn't get any better in time for the wedding, and I had to show up looking like that. Anyway, it was fine, and we had a blast at the wedding."

"Okaaay, that doesn't sound very juicy."

"But then we went to the little cocktail bar, and we were leaving when Kade's ex-wife showed up there. She'd driven from Austin to come try to get him to take her back."

"Crap. And she saw you with your face?"

"Yep. And Kade was so livid that she showed up. He only talked to her for a few minutes and that was that."

"Hmm. So, she thought she was going to waltz over to see him unexpectedly and he was just going to lollygag right back to her?"

"Apparently. I'm kind of worried, though. I really don't think that little five-minute chat was going to do much to resolve anything. I mean, Kade said he doesn't want her back, he's moved on and all that. But she didn't look like she was going to give up that easily. At least not from what I witnessed from the truck."

"I'm not trying to be the glass is half empty person, but I would prepare yourself just in case." That's what I was afraid she was going to say.

The past few weeks I'd been happier than I'd been in a long time. It's funny because with all the trips I made to the hardware store to find a date, all it took was a dust storm. Without that haboob, I wouldn't have run into Kade with my car and had all the other events that followed that. Then the next thing you know, Kade is cooking breakfast in my kitchen, giving my dog a nickname, and telling me he thinks I'm hot. I wasn't going to let some ex-wife who changed her mind five years too late mess that up for me.

Chapter 20

Kade

Damn, that girl has done something to me. She hit me with her car, she taped an entire loaf of bread to my front door, she projectile vomited all over my shirt, and still, she's all I can think about.

As I pulled into my driveway, Leonna was outside with her trusty water hose, watering her yard again. Most people use a sprinkler, but not Leonna. She waters the entire yard by hand, the grass, flowerbeds, the whole thing. I suppose it's a way of keeping herself busy and physically active.

"Good morning, Leonna," I hollered over to her as I walked toward my front door.

She put down her water hose and walked over to my yard. I'd noticed that if there was anything about Leonna, she was going to be wearing all matching everything.

Today she sported purple capri pants with a purple T-shirt and a purple visor. Her white orthopedic shoes matched her white life alert necklace. “Hello, Officer. Nice morning, isn’t it? My flowers have been parched with this heat; I decided I’d better water them before they all just kill over.”

“Leonna, it’s Kade. You can call me Kade.”

“Oh! Dave, I like that. I have a nephew named Dave,” she said but quickly continued before I could correct her. “You were gone yesterday evening, but a woman was knocking at your door. Shame you missed her, she was beautiful! Could have even been a magazine model for all I know.” Bethany. My mother gave her my address?

“Thank you for letting me know, Leonna. I think I know who it was. Oh, and it’s Kade, not Dave.”

“Kade? I could have sworn you said Dave. Anyway, I’d imagine a handsome man like you is bound to have pretty women fighting over you all the time.” No, that’s never happened and hopefully it wasn’t going to happen.

Leonna continued talking for several more minutes, updating me on her son-in-law’s new job, her recent podiatrist appointment, and her wall clock that needed new batteries. I walked with her back to her house to change the clock batteries for her. The inside of her house was about what I expected. Tidy as it could be, but with furnishings that she’d probably owned for the last fifty years or more. The first thing that caught my eye was the military flag folded neatly in its triangular display case on top of her piano, I assumed it to be from her husband's funeral.

"Well, I'd better be going, but have a nice day, ma'am," I told her, after setting the time on the clock and hanging it back on the wall, moving the nail lower so she could reach it next time.

"You too, Dave, and thank you!" she shouted after me as I walked out the door. I smiled back at her, accepting the new name.

I could not believe my mother gave out my address without asking me. But on the other hand, it was something she would definitely do. She didn't have a soft spot for many people, including myself it seemed, but she did for Bethany. I'm sure all it took was one quick text from Bethany for my mom to reveal every bit of my private information to her.

After changing into a pair of shorts, I went outside to work on the firepit. The manual labor would be good for letting off steam and thinking about how to address this new situation with Bethany. If I knew my ex-wife, she hadn't gone back to Austin yet, if she even still lived there. I hadn't had any contact with her in almost five years. She was one that didn't stop until she got her way; a trait that I used to admire in her but now found obnoxious.

I heard my phone ding from inside my pocket. Lilly: **You mentioned a surprise? Can I have a hint?**

Me: **Nope.**

Lilly: **Are we getting matching tattoos?**

Me: **Absolutely not. No hints, you like surprises, remember?**

Lilly: **Ok, fine...**

It wasn't ten minutes later that I heard the ding again. Lilly: **Horseback riding?**

I decided to play her at her own game and opened up google. Me: **Fun fact: surprises activate the brain's reward circuitry and release dopamine, creating more memorable experiences and stronger relationships.**

Lilly: **Lol! Ok...**

I shook my head and laughed to myself. For someone who likes surprises, she doesn't have much patience.

I'd been laying flagstone for about an hour when I heard a knock at the gate.

"Larry? Is that you? I'm coming." He'd never knocked on my gate before. Normally, he just yells at me from his own yard. I put down the piece of stone I was holding, wiped the sweat off my forehead, and walked over to unlock and open the gate for him.

It wasn't Larry. Bethany was standing on the other side of the gate. Dammit. I knew she was going to show up here again.

Peewee, who had been laying on the bench watching me work, recognized her immediately and ran over to her for the grand reunion, her entire back end shaking vigorously from side to side.

"Oh, Peewee! You remember me!" Bethany squealed and hugged Peewee around her neck.

I folded my arms across my chest, not wanting to watch Peewee's act of betrayal any longer. "I thought I already made it clear that we have nothing left to discuss, Bethany. And if I'd wanted you to come to my house, I would have invited you. I don't remember doing that." I don't particularly enjoy having company, especially not uninvited guests that basically stabbed me in the back, breaking my heart in a million pieces when I needed their support more than ever.

She inhaled and seemed to hold her breath for almost a minute before letting it back out. "Look, Kade, I know you didn't deserve the way I treated you. I've had five years to punish myself for what I did. If I could take it back, I would. I'm sorry. Can we please just sit down and have a regular conversation? Please."

It wasn't going to change anything on my end, but if that's what it took for her to go back home, maybe I could give her half an hour. I exhaled loudly and ran my hands through my hair in frustration. "Thirty minutes. Let's go inside where it's cool."

Bethany and Peewee both followed me inside. Peewee jumped onto her favorite spot on the couch. Bethany walked around the living room, surveying the furniture and the small amount of décor before finally sitting down next to Peewee.

"I like your house, it's very... you." She smiled nervously, picking the skin around her fingernail.

"Thanks, I like it," I responded, shortly with a straight face. She wasn't going to win me over with compliments.

"So, the woman you were with last night. Is she your... um, girlfriend?"

"Yes, she is." I hadn't said that out loud before. Lilly and I hadn't discussed whether or not we were exclusive, but I sure as hell didn't want to be with anyone else, and I was almost certain she didn't want to either. Even though Lilly was perfectly capable of taking care of herself, I felt protective of her. The mere thought of another man even thinking of putting his hands anywhere near Lilly was enough to piss me off. I was sure Lilly felt the same way about me, or at least I hope she did.

Bethany's awkward smile deflated with that news. She petted Peewee, seeming to psych herself up for what she said next. "Kade, I've thought about what to say for such a long time and it took a lot of courage for me to come here. I knew you wouldn't want to talk to me. But I couldn't just not come either."

"Ok, well, you're here so it's your time to shine I guess," I said, impatiently.

By now the skin around her fingernail was probably close to bleeding from the aggressive picking. She looked at me and finally started talking, her eyes were nervous but sincere. "I knew you always wanted to be a police officer. And I admired you for that, for the reasons behind it and for your bravery, for wanting to protect and help others. I was proud of you for that, I still am. You know how I am though, I'm nervous, I worry about every little thing. After a while, I did get used to it and I relaxed a little. Nothing bad had happened to you, so I began to think nothing ever would. But then Liam was shot while y'all were on duty. In the head, Kade! Not just beat up. He didn't go back home that night and probably won't ever live on his own again. He's so young! And if that man's bullet had hit you like he'd tried to, you could have been killed. After that, I just couldn't do it, Kade. I tried. I went to counseling and didn't tell you about it. I tried talking to other police officer's spouses. I paced all day, couldn't focus on my own job. I watched the front door, waiting for the chief to show up to tell me you were gone. I couldn't eat or sleep. It wasn't healthy. But I didn't tell you about it because I didn't want you to feel guilty. I didn't want you to quit your job because of me. It wouldn't be fair to you. So, I let you go because I couldn't change the way I felt, and I knew you wouldn't feel the same way about me ever again if I gave you an ultimatum of me or your job. So here we are."

"Bethany, I don't really know what to say. You didn't talk to me about it. I had no idea you were going through that. I knew it had to have affected you, but you just kept acting like you were ok. Maybe I should have pushed more to make sure you were ok, but I didn't. What kind of marriage did we have anyway if we couldn't talk about it? You had already filed for divorce before I even knew there was a problem. And right after my dad died, too. But the fact that you had discussed this with your family and even my own mother before telling me about it was the worst part. They all knew we were getting a divorce before I did."

"I know. All I can say is I'm sorry. I thought it was the right thing to do. I really did. And I've struggled with this for such a long time. I've tried to date; I've tried to move on. But I can't move on, Kade. I ruined everything." Tears were rolling down her face, streaking her makeup. I got up to get her a tissue but heard the doorbell ring on my way back to the living room.

My heart skipped a beat when I opened the door, finding Lilly standing there with a cardboard box. "Hey! I just got these in, and I couldn't wait to show you. It's the buttons and bracelets I ordered for the Hire Someone Au-Some campaign I'm starting." If it had been any other time, I'd have been thrilled to see her standing on my porch. She's basically the only person I'd be happy to see standing there.

Even though I was not doing anything wrong, I felt an overwhelming feeling of guilt, like I was keeping a secret from Lilly with Bethany being there. “Those are great, Lilly. You did a great job designing them,” I said, looking into the box.

She looked at me with a puzzled expression. “Can I come in? Or did I catch you at a bad time?”

“I... I kind of have company right now. She popped in while I was working on the firepit. Apparently, my mom was kind enough to give her my address...” Lilly looked past me through the glass door to see Bethany sitting on my couch next to Peewee.

Her face turned red with embarrassment, and she quickly closed the lid on the box. “Oh, well... Um... Ok. I’ll just be going then. I’m sorry to have popped in like this, I should have called first.” She turned and headed back to her car.

I followed her to her car. “Lilly, it’s ok. She wasn’t going to leave until I let her sit down and have a normal conversation with me. She should be leaving in a minute. I’ll call you in a little while, OK?”

All she said was, “Ok, sounds good,” and quickly got into her car without making any eye contact.

I held the car door open before she could close it. “Lilly, wait. Are we ok? Bethany being here doesn’t mean anything. I’m just giving her a chance to talk.”

She had a look on her face and wasn’t mad; it was hurt, disappointed. “It’s fine, really. I need to go, you have company.” I let go of the door and she closed it, smiling slightly at me through the window, but her eyes didn't match the faint smile.

Chapter 21

Lilly

Just when things were going so well...

I drove away from Kade's house feeling like a self-centered jackass, but I couldn't help it. I wasn't even mad at him; he didn't do anything wrong. I guess it's more of disappointment than anything. Bethany showed up just when everything was going so well with Kade and I could feel myself falling in love with him. Who was I kidding, I already loved him; I just hadn't said it out loud yet. But I also couldn't set myself up to be hurt, either. The thing about this situation is that Kade used to love Bethany. He isn't the one that wanted a divorce, she was. If she hadn't filed for divorce, he would probably still be living happily ever after with her. He didn't even know what hit him when she filed, and that devastated him.

So now she's right here in Willow Creek, begging him to forgive her, to take her back. When he saw her last night, he was taken by surprise, and that made him mad at her. And this morning, he still didn't seem to have any intention of entertaining the thought of her. At that time, I saw no reason to be concerned. But then she went to his house again, he let her in, they talked. He didn't seem mad this time. I wanted to give him the opportunity to process this without me being in the way.

About half an hour after I got home, he called. "Hey, I just wanted to check on you. You didn't seem ok when you left."

"I'm fine. Look, I'm not mad. It isn't that," I started.

"Ok, that's good, but what is it then?"

"Well, I mean, don't you think you need some time to think this over?" I wasn't prepared with what to say, and I had that dreaded feeling that I was going to dig myself into a hole that I wouldn't be able to figure out how to get out of.

"Think what over, Lilly? I already told you that there isn't anything to worry about. We're fine. Bethany coming here didn't change that." His voice sounded irritated and I regretted starting it out like that.

Sometimes I just don't know when to stop, so I kept going down the hole I had started digging. "Don't you need some time to think about it, though? She caught you off guard. I mean, you used to love her, Kade. You aren't the one who wanted to end it with her and you'd probably still be married to her if you'd had your way. I… I just need you to know for sure. I don't want to set either one of us up to get hurt." I immediately regretted all the word vomit that came out of my mouth. Saying that out loud didn't sound the same as it had in my mind.

"It sounds to me like you don't trust me. I told you I'm done with her. I didn't ask her to come here; she showed up on her own. What she did to me was inexcusable and unforgiveable, and I have no desire whatsoever, to go through that again. But the fact that you don't seem to trust me, maybe I need to reconsider my relationship with you?"

Dammit. That's what I was afraid he would think. Why can't I just keep my mouth shut sometimes?

"It isn't that, Kade. I just… I want to know that you've really thought about it, and this is really what you want." Why can't I shut up? I was just making it worse, and the rights words weren't coming out.

"Honestly, it sounds like you want me to just go back to Austin with her. Is that what you want? I thought we were going somewhere. I thought we had a future, but I don't know how many times I have to tell you that I don't want her. I don't know if I can be with somebody who can't take my word for it."

"That's not fair, Kade. Can you not see what it looks like from my end? How am I supposed to feel?" I could feel my face turning red, tears welling up along my lower lashes. The last thing I wanted to do was upset him.

"It seems to me like you can't just trust what I say. Why isn't that good enough for you? I have to go. Apparently, I'm supposed to be thinking about what I want. Bye, Lilly." He hung up the phone before I could say anything else.

I stared at the phone in my hand, tears falling down my cheeks. I was blaming myself entirely at first, but this wasn't 100% my fault. He was getting infuriated with me for just wanting to look at it from all angles. It wasn't that I didn't trust him. It wasn't that at all. But if he's not willing to have a conversation about it, then I don't even know what to do anymore. "Dammit!" I yelled and picked up the bottle of lotion from the table and threw it across the room. It hit the TV cabinet before landing on the floor, squirting some out of the opened lid and making Beatrice jump and cower in the corner.

"I'm sorry, Bea." I bent over and picked her up to apologize.

I jumped at the sound of my phone ringing. Kade, maybe he changed his mind and wanted to talk about this. We could fix this. But there was no such luck, it was my mom. I almost didn't answer it, not in the mood to talk to anyone other than Kade.

"Hi dear, Toby and Kayla just got here and I'm going to make dinner for everyone tonight. Your dad wants to play some games too. Oh, and your aunt Harriet is coming, too. I told her you would pick her up. You don't mind, do you?"

I didn't even know Toby was coming. I love how nobody even told me about this, but then they expect me to be available to pick up Harriet for a family dinner with a whole two-hour notice. I love my brother but geez, I wasn't in the mood for all of this, especially not for Harriet. She was one of those people that you have to get your mind straight before being around. I really wanted to just stay home and resolve things with Kade, but I couldn't miss seeing my brother either, I hadn't seen him since Christmas.

"Ok, but it would have been great to have a little more warning. I didn't even know Toby was coming."

"Sorry, dear. Oh, and also, Will's bringing his special potato salad. Can you bring a chocolate pie? You know how your dad loves them." I rolled my eyes and ran my fingers through my hair.

"I guess," I said, not hiding my frustration. At least it works out to have a bakery sometimes because I always have dessert prepared anytime it's needed. I knew I had a couple of chocolate pies at the bakery that were left over yesterday.

"Oh! And bring Kade!" she said, excitedly. I let out an exasperated sigh. I would have loved to have brought Kade...

"He can't come, I think he already has plans today." I wasn't going to tell her he was actually pissed off at me.

.....

Harriet and I showed up at my parents' house to a chaotic scene unfolding. Toby had brought a golf bag for Will, but it had been in his garage, and to my mother's shock and horror, there had been a mouse inside it which jumped out and was running rogue in the living room. My mother and Sydney had found refuge by standing on kitchen chairs while everyone else tried to corral the mouse out the back door. Elsie and Micah, Will and Sydney's kids, were playing basketball with the small, child sized basketball goal on the patio, yelling some sort of gleeful chant that I couldn't quite make out which added to the chaos.

It seemed nobody else was having any luck and I certainly wasn't afraid of a little mouse; I sat the pies down and got the broom and dustpan out of the garage, using them to successfully coax the little guy out of the house. After my mom and Sydney climbed down out of their chairs, we sat down to eat, catching up on the lives of Toby and Kayla.

After everyone was finished eating, I got up and sat out the pies.

"Your face looks so much better, Lilly!" Sydney said, looking closer at my face.

"Yea, it's much better," I said quickly, not wanting to get into a conversation about it.

"Was it because of your lupus?" she went on, not taking the hint that I didn't want to discuss it. Harriet put her fork down and looked curiously at me.

"Probably." I cut a piece of pie. "Who wants pie?"

My dad was the first to stick his plate out for a piece, but before he could say anything, Harriet spoke up. "You know, back in my day, you didn't need to have a disease as an excuse for everything. Just stop using all the fancy skin creams and stick to cold cream at night. That's all it is." Of course, we couldn't get through one whole meal without her saying something offensive to somebody. Usually, she aims her hostility toward Sydney or my mom for some reason, but today was my lucky day. Harriet had single handedly proven my rationale for not talking about my health.

Everyone sat quietly for a while, with only the sounds of forks clanking to plates as pie was eaten. After dinner was cleared off the table, Sydney, Kayla, and I went to sit out on the patio to chat. We always liked to have our talks away from everyone else, partly because we had warped senses of humor that nobody else quite understood. But today, I just wanted to talk to them about what happened with Kade.

"Sorry I brought up the face, Lilly. I didn't expect Harriet to say something like that," Sydney apologized.

"It's fine. We can't care too much about the things she says. Remember what she said to you that time about your divorce?"

Sydney laughed. "Oh, yes. How could I forget!" When Harriet first met Sydney, she had basically told her that she didn't approve of Sydney being divorced and criticized her for not sticking with it. She said marriage is supposed to be till death, not just give up when things get hard. Sydney had been shocked by that; her ex-husband was abusive and she couldn't believe somebody would think she should have suffered with that forever instead of making a better life for her and her kids.

"So, Kayla, let me fill you in on this guy I've been seeing," I started in, changing the subject. Kayla raised her eyebrows and leaned in, ready for the scoop.

"Oooooh, yes... show her a picture, first, Lilly," Sydney instructed. "Get ready, Kayla. He isn't exactly bad looking."

"Oh... my...lanta," Kayla said, smiling approvingly at the photo, but it pained me to see Kade's smiling face on the screen, knowing I might never have the chance to have him smiling at me like that again.

"So, I messed up. I think I've ruined things with him."

"You've got to be kidding. What did you do..." Sydney said, flatly.

"His ex-wife showed up here after the wedding and says she's sorry and wants to work things out with him. She says she made a huge mistake and hasn't been able to get on with her life without him."

"Crap," Kayla said, rolling her eyes.

"So, he told her he isn't interested and that he's moved on and he's through with her."

"I think I'm missing the problem then, Lilly," Sydney wrinkled her brows in confusion.

I exhaled loudly and looked at both of them for a few seconds. "You know how sometimes I speak before I think and just end up getting myself into trouble?" They both nodded. "Well, I may have told him that he needs to think about it for a while to make sure he knows what he wants because I don't want to get hurt." It sounded just as bad saying it the second time.

"You freaking didn't say that. Seriously, Lilly?" Kayla said, not sugar coating her thoughts about it.

"And so now, he thinks I don't trust him, and he's pissed. I tried to explain what I meant, but he wasn't willing to listen anymore, and he hung up. What do I do, now?"

"You fix it. Lilly, no offense, but you haven't had a good track record with men, and you hit the jackpot with Kade in so many ways. You damn sure don't want to let him get away," Sydney said, with a vengeance.

Chapter 22

Kade

A wise man once said...

I'd been sitting in my Adirondack chair at the unfinished firepit for what seemed like forever. Although there was still work to be done on it, it had already become my spot to unwind when I wasn't in my reading room. Peewee snored quietly from her place on the bench. I hadn't eaten dinner yet, but I didn't have an appetite. I'd been holding my phone in my hand the whole time. I'd look at Lilly's name on my phone but couldn't bring myself to call her and I didn't send the texts that I typed. She doesn't trust me. I can't be with somebody who doesn't trust me.

Bethany left right after Lilly did. I let her say everything that was on her mind, and I listened to everything she said without arguing with her. I didn't feel the same way about her that I once did, and I wasn't ever going to again. That chapter of my life was over. She accepted this without making a scene and left quietly with tears in her eyes.

After Bethany drove off, I'd called my mom. Although my anger had subsided, I couldn't let her do this again. Giving out my address to Bethany was unacceptable, and I needed to get that straight. But when she'd answered the phone, she sounded older and somewhat frail, but more cheerful than she usually does. I don't think I noticed her aging as much before when I saw her every week before she moved, but now, it's been months since I've seen her, and the difference in her voice is noticeable today. I didn't bring up Bethany, and we talked for about half an hour. I can't even remember when we've had such a good conversation. Usually, our phone calls consisted only of her complaints, and I typically cut them short because she tends to use anything I say to somehow turn it against me negatively. But today, she had good things to share. She told me she'd made some friends, and they had a weekly domino tournament. I'd never known my mom to play dominos, or any games for that matter. She'd even met a man that has taken her to the movies a few times. I wasn't sure what to make of that news at first, but I decided I was happy for her. She deserved to be happy for once.

It was times like this when I missed having Liam around to talk to. I used to talk to him when I had problems with a girlfriend, or with Bethany. I still go to

Dallas to visit him in the nursing home as often as I can, but it isn't quite the same anymore and I wouldn't feel right talking about my relationship problems when he'd give anything to be in my shoes right now. I'd spent the last five years being a loner, but that came back to bite me because now I have nobody to talk about these things with.

Lately, my best friend has been Lilly. And as strange as it may seem, my next closest friend is a 77-year-old man, old enough to be my dad, or even my grandfather.

When I went back inside, I looked down at the box of odds and ends from the garage that I'd unpacked and no longer needed. If there was anyone that could make use of those things, it was Larry. I picked up the box and carried it over, finding Larry in his usual spot in the garage, piddling at his tool bench. A smile crept across his face when he opened up the box and found some fishing reels buried in there.

Years ago, I used to love fishing. I went with my dad a few times, but Liam and I used to go fishing fairly often. There was a lake we really liked to fish at, it was quiet, away from all the loud crowds. Fishing was a stress reliever for both of us. The thing about hunting and fishing is that you don't want to do a lot of talking because too much noise will scare away the animals or fish. When I fished with my dad, we caught fish. When I fished with Liam, we almost never had any fish. We'd start talking and laughing so much that our chances of catching anything were slim to none. I hadn't been fishing since the shooting. I kept one pole and some essentials for my tackle box, but I wouldn't be able to use everything I had. It seemed Larry was the perfect man to rehome these supplies to.

He walked over to his fishing pole collection which was propped up in a corner. "Oh, I sure love fishing, but I haven't been in about twenty years. I don't want to go by myself, and Alana never wants to go." He picked up a pole and wiped the webs off it. "You probably don't want to go fishing, do you? I mean, I know you're a busy man."

I looked at his hand, he still had a cast on his left thumb. "Can you manage the pole with that thumb?"

"You bet I can."

Tomorrow was my last day off until next Sunday. "Best time's before the sun comes up. I'll pick you up early tomorrow morning." Larry's face lit up like a kid on Christmas as soon as he heard that.

.....

I didn't sleep much last night. In my heart, I wanted to call Lilly, get us back on track. But in my mind, I couldn't do it. She said she was afraid to get hurt, but if she had trusted me, she wouldn't have had to worry about it. Trust is earned. I trusted Lilly and I thought I'd earned her trust by now as well. I'd let myself fall in love with her, every part of her. But that didn't take away that fact that it still rubbed me the wrong way when she questioned me about my feelings toward Bethany. I didn't need time to think about that, but she tried to insist on it, and I didn't need her to tell me what I did or didn't want. But I also wondered if I was being too harsh, which I have a way of being sometimes. I'd have some time to let that all marinate in my head while I fished with Larry this morning. Fishing does wonders for setting your head straight.

I loaded up my fishing gear and drove around to Larry's house to pick him up. He came outside wearing a fishing vest and a fishing hat that had lures attached all around it. A sharp contrast to what I was wearing, which was just a pair of athletic shorts and a T-shirt. Alana followed him with a thermal bag filled with homemade sausage, egg, and cheese burritos along with two travel mugs of coffee.

I drove us to a small lake just outside of town, one that Larry said was supposed to be good for fishing. We set up our chairs, opened our breakfast, and got our poles set up and cast the lines into the water. Sure enough, Larry did fine with the cast on his thumb, even though he was out of practice with the pole.

"So, Kade, not that it's any of my business, but word around town is that you and Miss Lilly have been seeing a lot of each other lately." The one thing I didn't necessarily love about a small town is that there wasn't much privacy.

I hesitated before I spoke. "Yea, we've gotten close."

"That girl, she's something. Sweetest thing you'll ever meet, but a little bit of a mess sometimes." He laughed. Yes, she's a hot mess for sure.

I could tell as soon as Larry started talking that we weren't going to catch any fish, but that was fine. I got the idea that it wasn't necessarily catching fish that Larry wanted, but more the male camaraderie thing.

He went on talking, "Alana and I met at the furniture store. She worked for me part time for a while. She didn't have any interest in me at first. I'm 15 years older than she is. But she finally came around. I asked her to marry me five times before she said yes. Can you believe that? But I was persistent, and I just couldn't give up on her. We've been married 30 years now and haven't regretted one day of it. Sometimes I think she's going to be the death of me, but I'd do it over again if I ever had the chance."

I smiled and took a bite of my burrito, glad that she put two for each of us since I didn't eat dinner last night.

Larry took a bite of his also, then went on talking. "She doesn't listen to a word I say. For example, four years ago she asked me if I thought we should re-wallpaper the master bathroom. We didn't know anything about wallpapering a bathroom, so I said no. And guess what she did? I was gone for about an hour and when I came back, she was on a step stool trying to scrape wallpaper off! And let me tell you, that wallpaper was stuck on like somebody's life depended on it never coming off those walls."

"So, what did you do?" I laughed, picturing the scene.

"Not a damn thing! I told her she was on her own with that. She tried every trick in the book to get that wallpaper off. Looked online, watched videos, nothing worked! There's wallpaper in some places, just bare drywall in others, it looks terrible! Four years later it is still the same! We'll have to hire a professional if it's ever going to get finished. She does this kind of thing all the time, keeps me in a state of panic every time I see her coming with a tape measure or a hammer. And it damn near gives me a heart attack if I see her with a ladder." He shook his head and smiled. "But darn it, I love her more than I've ever loved anyone. She's the world to me, even though she doesn't listen to a single word I say."

I'd been a jerk. Talking to Larry made me realize just how royally I screwed up. I had to see Lilly.

Chapter 23

Lilly

Es tut mir Leid...

It was a sleepless night. I hadn't heard from Kade, and I had a feeling I wasn't going to anytime soon. It was stupid for us to even argue about something like that, but we did. With any luck, Kade would be over it too and we could move on and forget the whole thing ever happened.

I'd gone to the bakery early this morning to start working on my Hire Somone Au-some campaign. It's funny how the bakery being vandalized had been the instigator of this campaign, but we were all in now, making it even better than I'd originally planned. Sydney and Lynette were also excited about the idea, and they both offered their services to help. Kennedy had been the one to help design the bracelets that I'd ordered. Jamie offered to make T-shirts. Ashley and Leanne also said they would help with anything I needed, which was great, because they are both much more creative than I am. The local news even agreed to do a segment on the campaign, and we had an appointment to go to the station next month, right before Jo and I left for Europe. Jo had some business contacts that she was going to try to get involved as well. It was really shaping up to be much bigger campaign than I ever anticipated.

Kennedy was going to be the star with this endeavor. They were going to send a camera crew to the bakery to film her in action.

"Kennedy, are you getting excited about your big news debut?" I asked her as she was setting up the classroom.

"Yep. It's gonna be my time to shine." That made me smile. I loved that she was excited about it. She wants to give the camera crew a tour of the bakery and show them what her job duties are and she'd already been doing some role playing with her mom to practice what she wanted to say. It's important to her to prove that she is a hard worker and that people with autism or other disabilities should be given a chance.

I'd kept myself so busy all day with work that I didn't have much time to think about Kade. But once I got home, I couldn't stand it any longer. I had to call him. That whole argument was just stupid. I'd gotten over my initial jealousy, and I was wrong to say what I said. Sure, he was quick to get mad, but he was probably already irritated by

Bethany showing up at his house. I wasn't going to let something like that get in the way.

I picked up my phone and tried his number. No answer. Crap. I waited fifteen minutes and tried again. Nothing.

Not wanting to harass him, I decided to take a long bath and try him again in about an hour and a half. I used my favorite lavender and sandalwood aromatherapy candles along with the matching body scrub, shaved everything, scrubbed my heels with a pumice stone, basically just wasting time to keep myself from calling Kade again too soon.

The water started to get too cool and as I was climbing out of the tub, the phone rang. I almost slipped trying to get to the phone, but then my face fell as soon as I saw it was only Caitlyn.

"Lilly, I had to come back up to the bakery because I'd left my phone here but there is something wrong with my key and I can't get the door to lock back up. Do you think you can run over here and lock up for me?"

What the heck? "Yea, let me get dressed real quick. I just got out of the bathtub." I blew out the candle and threw on a pair of jeans and a T-shirt. If anything, this would at least give me something else to do while I waited for time to try to call Kade again.

I pulled up to the bakery but didn't see Caitlyn's car. That's odd. Maybe she'd gone through the back. I used my key to open the front door. It was dark inside, but I heard music. Why was she playing music? I walked further into the seating area to get a closer look.

What is going on here?

There were lit candles placed around the table area. One of the small tables was covered in a simple white tablecloth. A single candle burned in the middle of the table. My heart started beating harder when I noticed the vase with freshly cut tiger lilies. Kade. He did this? There were two covered plates and two covered desert dishes. What was happening here and where was he?

I heard my phone ding from my pocket. It was Kade. **Es tut mir Leid.**

What? I was so confused. I texted him back: **I'm lost.**

Kade: **It's German for I'm sorry.**

Yes, everything was going to be ok. I texted him back, smiling at the phone: **Well then, Es tut mir Leid, too.**

Where was he?

Then there he was. He came from the back. He didn't say anything but stood there in jeans, boots, and a black dress shirt, holding at least a dozen red roses. He leaned up against the door frame and grinned. "Caitlyn's not here. She let me in and went home. She knew about this all afternoon. I'm sorry about yesterday, Lilly. I was an asshole."

My face softened as I let out a huge breath and bit my lip to keep from smiling. Struggling to find the right words, I slowly and teasingly made my way over to him and took the flowers from his hand. "These are beautiful," I said, smelling the roses. "And I'm the asshole, not you."

Kade took the roses and laid them on the counter next to him. "You're beautiful." He pulled me closer to him, put his hands on the sides of my face, and kissed me in a way that made my legs wobble. Then he led me to the table and pulled a chair out for me.

"I can't believe you did all this, Kade."

"You like surprises, remember?" He pulled the lid off my plate, and I let out a laugh when I saw what it was. "Nothing but the best for you." On my plate was a Thanksgiving Sandwich from Annie's Deli. "And Laurie put extra cranberry sauce on it for you." He chuckled.

Kade's plate contained a club sandwich, his go-to.

"May I ask what's on the dessert plates?"

"Remember when I told you I make a fairly edible pecan pie?" He uncovered my small plate, revealing the piece of pie. "For your drink, I hope I made it the way you like. It's a chilton." He'd thought of everything. This was incredibly sweet and so romantic. I loved that Caitlyn was in on it.

It's like we never had an argument. We basically picked up where we left off when he left my house Sunday morning. When we both finished eating, Kade turned the music up a little louder then reached his hand out. "Dance with me."

The bakery made the perfect dance floor, but we only needed about two square feet because we barely moved from the spot we started out in. I could feel his heart beating in his chest and being there with his arms wrapped around me just felt so right, like a dream I never wanted to wake up from.

Kade lifted my chin up and looked into my eyes. “You want to know a fun fact about me?”

I smiled up at him. “Of course, I do.”

He looked seriously at me, like he was about to reveal his deepest, darkest secret. “Fun fact about me... is I’m in love with you. So incredibly in love with you.”

Chapter 24

Kade

Free falling...

About a year after the shooting, Liam and I were both awarded with a Medal of Valor, the highest honor that a peace officer can receive in law enforcement. It's a medal that signifies exceptional courage and self-sacrifice that the officer exhibited, often involving imminent danger, when other lives were also at risk. The medals were presented to us by the governor at the state capital. We were two of about thirty officers that received medals that day. As I listened to each one of their stories, I remember feeling an overwhelming sense of pride to be included in that group of heroic men and women who had gone above and beyond to protect and serve.

I keep my medal displayed in a wooden shadow box, and it sits on my dresser next to a photo of Liam and I, in our dress blues, as our medals were presented to us. I ran my hand over the shadow box and then picked up the photo.

I miss the way things used to be with Liam. I miss the ridiculous jokes he used to tell, and the stupid pranks. More often than not, he was the only one that thought they were funny; they probably aggravated people more than made them laugh. Once, he dog-sat Peewee when Bethany and I went out of town. When we came back to town, he had wrapped every single dish in aluminum foil, including the ones in the dishwasher. Bethany had a fit when she opened up the dishwasher to find every utensil, plate, and glass carefully wrapped in foil. Then it just got worse when she opened the cabinets and every dish inside was also wrapped and stacked back neatly on their shelves.

It had been a few months since I'd been to Dallas to visit him at the nursing home. Normally, I went by myself, but I'd been thinking that a quick trip with Lilly might be fun. It's just a five-hour drive from Willow Creek.

A few days ago, Lilly agreed to take a quick trip with me. If we left early Sunday morning, we could have almost an entire full day and then come back on Monday. Those were already my normal days off, so it wasn't an issue for me as long as it worked for Lilly. I owed her a surprise, and

I lucked out by being able to book on short notice an activity that she was hopefully going to love.

.....

Lilly's parents were going to watch Beatrice and Larry agreed to come over and let Peewee out a few times a day. We'd decided to get on the road at 5:00 AM and I promised her a wake-up call at 4:00, which she claimed was inhumane treatment. She was still dead asleep when I called her, and by the sound of her voice, she was going to require another call to make sure she didn't go back to sleep. Sure enough, fifteen minutes later, she was asleep again.

"Ok, fine. I'm up. How are you so wide awake at this ungodly hour? It's not normal."

Even her sleepy, irritable voice still sounded beautiful to me. I put a pillow and blanket in the front seat of the truck and drove to her house to get her. If I'd been smart, I would have had her stay at my house last night.

Her front door was open when I got there. I knocked and walked inside to find Lilly gathering her things and throwing them into her overnight bag. Why do women need so many things for one night? Three cups. Three... One small one with coffee. One large one with water, then one with just ice, waiting for whatever drink she may come across along the way to pour into it. A jacket, even though it was going to be about 95 degrees, but she's always cold.

The other items were a mystery as they were all stuffed into her overflowing bag.

"I brought snacks. But don't worry, they are all mess-free snacks, so I don't destroy your truck's immaculate interior," she said, as she climbed in and found places for her things. Within thirty minutes, she was covered up with the blanket, her head resting on the pillow which she positioned on the console between us.

Two hours later, she was still asleep when I pulled into the parking lot for breakfast.

Her eyes grew wide when she sat up and looked out the window as I turned off the truck.

"The Bald Egg? You remembered!"

"Sweet cream pancakes are calling your name." After she'd told me about this place, I'd put a note in my phone so I could remember it. I'd been doing that off and on because I loved surprising her with little things like that.

She went from dead asleep to speed walking to the front door as if they were going to run out of pancakes if she didn't get there fast enough. Once we were seated, she didn't even open the menu. "Sweet cream pancakes, bacon, and scrambled eggs please," surprising the waitress on her excitement with her order. I ordered an omelet which seemed almost offensive to her.

She looked me dead in the eye, then shook her head. "Have you completely lost your mind? Have you learned nothing from what I've told you about the pancakes?"

"Can't help it. I'm an omelet guy." I laughed.

Once we finished eating, she began her interrogation of what activities I had planned.

"Well, first we'll run by and see Liam because the activity isn't scheduled until 1:00."

"And what shall I wear to said activity?"

"Comfortable clothes."

"Are we going bike riding?"

"No."

"Are we getting tattoos?"

"No, you already asked me that. I'm not getting a tattoo."

"You know, tattoos are beneficial. As a police officer, you should understand how important they are in helping to identify bodies."

"So, I should get a tattoo so they can identify my body?"

"I mean, it could be the deciding factor if that's all there is to go by." She cocked her head, seriously.

She had a tattoo of a cupcake on her ankle and one of Beatrice's ugly face on the other ankle. I wondered what the smiling face on her arm was for. "What made you get this smiley face?" I asked, tracing it with my finger.

"It just makes me happy. My family doesn't like my tattoos, but that's fine. I always say people should do what they want and be who they want because we only get one chance. Might as well live it the way we want. At the end of the day, I don't really care what anyone else thinks."

She smiled sheepishly at me. "I have other tattoos."

"Oh? Where might these tattoos be located?"

"Keep up these surprises and you might find out, Officer Wayland." Oh, hell yes. I could do that.

.....

Three hours later, we arrived at the nursing home and walked to Liam's room. He was sitting up in bed watching TV. His body was once thick with muscle from weightlifting, but now looked tiny and frail.

"Hey there, brother!" I said, walking up to shake his hand. The brain damage from the bullet had caused some cognitive-communication difficulties and it took a moment for Liam to process what I'd said, but finally his eyes lit up and he smiled as he held his boney hand out for me.

His once booming voice was now quiet and slurred, but understandable. "Hey man!"

"Liam, I want you to meet my girlfriend, Lilly." I'd never called her that out loud before, and I could tell by the look on her face that she liked it.

Lilly walked up to Liam and held her hand to shake his. "It is wonderful to finally meet you! Kade has had so many wonderful things to say about you!"

"How'd a dumbass like Kade end up with someone as beautiful as you?" The brain damage didn't change his sarcasm, which was still all there.

“I hit him with my car, so I owed it to him,” she said, smiling over at me, and taking a seat in the recliner.

“That’s actually true. I don’t advise being anywhere near her while she is operating a motor vehicle.” I winked at Lilly and sat down in Liam’s wheelchair, which was already next to his bed.

We stayed and talked with Liam for about an hour. It’s always hard to keep my emotions under control when I visit him in person. He couldn’t do much for himself anymore and even had to have help taking a shower or cutting up his food. Sometimes I had to fight back the feelings of guilt that I wasn’t able to react in time to prevent him from being shot in the first place.

His family had moved him to this facility so he could be closer to them, and they could visit him and check in on him more often that way. He also had a brother that lived in Dallas. I didn’t ask Liam if they’d been to see him lately, but I stopped at the nurse’s station on the way out and found out that visits from his family had slowly declined over the last couple of years and now he rarely had any visits at all from anyone, which made me not only sad for him but furious and disappointed in his family.

As hard as I try to hold it together for Liam, my eyes leak every time I leave his room. And as I looked over at Lilly, her eyes were also wet. “He seems like such a great guy, Kade. It’s just heartbreaking that you’re the only one that comes to see him anymore.”

I should have been asking about visitors all along, I just assumed his family was coming to see him pretty often and never thought they would stop visiting. They were always such a close family.

I wiped my eyes and smiled. “We’ll come back to see him soon. Let’s go get some lunch. It’s recommended to eat a light meal before the activity.”

“Would you stop calling it *the activity* and tell me what it is?” she begged.

“I can’t do that. It’s a surprise, remember?”

We stopped at a sandwich shop for a light lunch and then headed toward our destination. Lilly looked out the window at the lake nearby. “Ok, are we going canoeing? Hiking?”

I shook my head. A few minutes later we pulled up to the small airport that looked more like a large warehouse. “Here we are!”

“Is this an airport? Are we flying somewhere?”

“I’m sure as hell not. But you’re going skydiving,” I said as I got out of the truck.

She’d told me she always wanted to do this. There was no way that I was going to be doing it, but I’d be watching from the safety of the ground. I’d support Lilly in any adventure she wanted to do, within reason, but there was nothing that would make me jump out of an airplane myself.

Lilly hopped out of the truck and shrieked. "Seriously, Kade! I've always wanted to do this!" She ran to me and jumped up, wrapping her legs around my waist. "Is this you trying to find out where my other tattoo is?" she muttered into my ear before standing back on the ground.

"Yes, it's all part of my grand scheme." I smirked, taking her hand and leading her to where others were gathered around some picnic tables. The ones who weren't skydiving waited at the picnic tables. A van would drive the divers around to the plane and they would land back in this same area.

"Why aren't you jumping with me? It would be so fun to do it together!"

"Yea, well, unlike you, I possess the gene that makes jumping out of a plane seem like the exact opposite of fun. Plus, I don't think you can just do it without booking it in advance." I tried to use the lack of pre-booking for myself my main excuse.

As luck would have it, an instructor overheard our conversation. "Sure, you can! We had one cancel, and we have an open spot!" Dammit, he needs to learn how to mind his own business and stop eavesdropping.

"No, I think I'll sit this one out. I'd rather watch Lilly. It's more her thing."

"Pleeeeeeease, Kade? Come on, it will be so much more fun if you do it too." She looked up at me with her hands clasped, and a huge smile plastered across her face.

The instructor looked at me and shook his head. "Come on, man. You can't say no to that face." Does this guy not know when to stop?

I did the thing I told myself I would not do under any circumstances. "Fine." I muttered, and then I regretted it as soon as the word left my mouth.

Lilly jumped up and clapped. "Aaahh! Yes! Thank you!"

What the heck have I done? I'm going to freaking jump out of a damn plane. I've completely lost it.

"You're a bad influence on me." Since Lilly entered my life, I've felt like I was free falling. So, I might as well go for it.

Chapter 25

Lilly

My mother would kill me if she knew what I just did. Then, she would kill Kade for taking me to do it. But on the other hand, what she doesn't know won't hurt her and I'm 32 years old. I've always dreamed of skydiving, and now I'm wondering why it took me so long when it was such a simple process.

Kade had gone first, and I'll admit I had a twinge of guilt when I realized how nervous he really was and I never did anything to stop him from doing it. I wouldn't have pressured him so much if I'd known he wasn't just a little apprehensive, he truly seemed terror-stricken by the time we were up in the plane. He had such a wild-eyed look when the instructor scooted them both to the opening ahead of me. Then, after a few moments of talking to himself and trying to get his mind psyched up for what he'd decided was a huge error in judgment, he and the instructor finally went barreling over the edge.

I went after Kade, needing no time to prepare my mind. The instructor rocked three times as our legs dangled over the edge, then there we went, freefalling at ten thousand feet above the ground. It was the most exhilarating experience I'd ever had, almost a complete sensory overload until the instructor pulled the chute. The gradual glide back down to the earth below gave a freeing and euphoric sensation, like happiness on steroids.

Kade was on the ground waiting for me, with a huge smile plastered across his face. After we took our gear off, he was full of excitement, an emotion I really hadn't seen before from him. "That was awesome! I already want to go back and do it again!" This, the same Kade who I thought could very possibly have had a mild heart attack on the way down?

"You're serious? By the look on your face before you went out, I thought you were plotting my murder for making you do this."

"It was incredible! I mean, the initial shock and feeling of plummeting to certain death wasn't great, but once the chute came out, I was fine! I'd do it again for sure." Ok, this side of Kade I really liked, and my mind started racing on all the other adventures on my bucket list that he might also be willing to try.

"Well, in that case, I'm making it my solemn vow to continue to be a bad influence on you. Just looking out for your best interest, of course."

.....

After the skydiving adventure, Kade took me shopping at four antique shops where I lucked out with some great finds. One of them was a vintage cookbook that I'd been trying to find for months. Then we stopped at a coffee shop and sat at the outdoor patio with our drinks.

I watched as people walked by in front of us on the sidewalk, I'd always loved people watching. See what they were wearing, listen to what they were talking about, and try to imagine what was in their shopping bags.

"Have you been to Dallas very many times?" Kade asked, stirring his coffee.

"Yea, we used to come here about once a year when we were kids. There's so much to do and it's a quick trip from Willow Creek. My brothers and I always loved riding the roller coasters. It's strange, but in the summer when I can smell the melting asphalt in parking lots, it always reminds me of walking through the amusement park. It always smelled like fresh asphalt there." I took a drink of my coffee and smiled, remembering the last time I came to Dallas. "The last time I came, it was just me and my mom. She wanted a girl's trip. We flew instead of driving, and she booked a really nice hotel, it was more expensive than the budget allowed, but she didn't care. We went to the zoo, shopping, and ate at a fancy restaurant. I don't know why, but the thing that stood out the most on that trip was a simple trip to a candle shop. We spent so much time in there, laughing and smelling everything. We both fell in love with this one scent; it was orange and vanilla, kind of like the creamsicle scent, and we both bought a candle. For some reason, that was almost the highlight of our whole trip because we were just being silly and the shop owner probably thought we'd never been in a candle store before. I'm not sure why, but it's been years, and it just always makes me happy to think about us in the candle shop. Anytime I smell an orange and vanilla candle, it takes me back to that day." I didn't intend to get so sentimental about that story, but a tear fell out of my eye. "Oh gosh. Sorry, I didn't mean to get all emotional!" I wiped the tear away quickly, embarrassed.

"Don't be sorry, it's sweet. I love that you have those kinds of memories."

"So, what about you? Did y'all come here a lot when you were a kid?"

"No, we didn't really go on any trips when I was a kid. I'd actually never really traveled at all until I went into the military."

"I'm sorry." It made me sad to think of Kade not ever having some of those same experiences that I'd had when I was young.

"No, it's fine. I'm actually kind of glad that we didn't, because between my mom's constant bad mood and my dad's drinking, it wouldn't have been any fun for anyone." He laughed, but I could see a hint of pain hidden in his eyes. I decided it was a good time to change the subject, and we veered the topic to what was going to be for dinner. Kade did not take me to a restaurant. Instead, he took me to the grocery store where he bought prime rib from the meat market, along with potatoes and all the trimmings. It was fun to watch him shop, examining each piece of meat instead of just tossing the first ones he saw in the basket like I always do. I wasn't sure what he was inspecting it for, but he finally found two that he deemed suitable.

"Do you mind me asking where you plan to cook all of this?" I had no idea where we were even staying or if there would be a place to cook.

"You'll see."

We drove for about half an hour and turned onto a gravel road. I couldn't see it from the street, due to the clusters of trees, but as we drove a little further along the road, a peaceful lake came into sight. We pulled up to a small cabin. The wraparound front porch of the cabin was quite close to the water's edge and a small grill stood in the corner near a porch swing. There was a fishing dock right in front with two chairs. A few other cabins were in the area, but they were far enough away that it was still fairly private and somewhat hidden by trees.

"This place is beautiful!" I walked around the porch and examined the exterior of the cabin. It was so quaint and rustic, reminding me of the cabins I'd stayed at in New Mexico and Colorado before.

Kade had the front door unlocked when I went back around to the front. The inside was just as nice as the outside. The décor was a rustic, western theme with paintings of horses and cattle on the wall. One of the paintings had a black bull that looked just like the one Kip used to have, which he'd named Mark. Now, Sydney and Will have him on their property. On the end table was a lamp made from a brown cowboy boot with a cream-colored lampshade.

The cabin had one bathroom and two bedrooms; one with a king bed and one with a bunkbed. A million thoughts ran through my mind on what the arrangements could turn into. Instead of complicating things, I left my bag on the couch.

Kade gathered some supplies from the kitchen for the steaks and took them outside. I made myself at home looking through all the kitchen cabinets. Hanging on a hook along the kitchen wall was an apron that read "kiss the cook." I carried it outside and put it over Kade's head, tying it in the back for him.

"Perfect," I said, kissing him over the plate of raw steaks he was holding. "You look good in an apron."

He smiled and opened the lid to the grill. "How do you like your prime rib?" he asked, getting the fire started.

"The only way anyone should ever eat them. Medium rare," I replied, to which he cringed. Kennedy has warned me time and time again about the dangers of E. coli, but her lectures have fallen on deaf ears.

.....

Dinner was incredible, Kade is a genius at the grill. Afterward, we sat on the fishing dock and looked at the water. By then it was dark, and I didn't see anyone else around. For the end of September, it was still quite warm. The water would probably feel great.

I put down my drink and stood up, slipping out of my shoes. "Do you swim?"

"Yes, but I don't know if there's swimming allowed here." Always the cautious one, that Kade.

"I don't see anything telling us not to. And if I jump in anyway, are you going to arrest me?" I grinned.

"Don't tempt me. But we don't have swimming suits," he added, raising his eyebrows.

I didn't wait for him to finish his sentence. I jumped into the water, still wearing my tank top and shorts. "Come on! The water feels great!"

"You're crazy." He laughed, then took his shoes off. A few seconds later, he jumped in and scooped me up in the water. "But I love you anyway."

.....

We wrapped ourselves in towels and sat on the porch swing, listening to the sounds of the crickets and the trees softly moving in the breeze. I sat with my legs across Kade's lap. It had been a very long day, an amazing day, but also an exhausting one.

"Thank you so much for today, Kade. It's really been one of the best days of my life. I honestly enjoyed every second of it. The pancakes, meeting Liam, the shopping, dinner... and the *skydiving*!? I mean, come on. You have literally thought of every single thing, and it's been truly wonderful. I really don't deserve all this. You're spoiling me."

Kade ran his hand up and down my leg, then finally spoke. "I love spoiling you, though... seeing the look on your face when you're happy. I love the way your eyes twinkle, and the little dimple in your cheek pokes in. Everyone needs that. To be spoiled, to feel like they are the most important person in the world."

Nobody ever said anything like that to me. Kade was more than I'd ever even thought to even imagine. He was the whole package. Obviously, he was attractive, definitely more than attractive. He was just plain hot, sweltering hot.

But inside he was so much more than that: kind, generous, loving, brave, all the good things wrapped up with a bow.

I pulled myself up on top of his lap and kissed him, running my hands through his hair. I could feel his heartbeat speed up as he stood me up on the ground, then stood up and picked me up and started inside the cabin. "We need to get you out of those wet clothes."

Chapter 26

Kade

The sun was peeking through the opening in the curtain when I opened my eyes. I rolled over and found an empty spot where Lilly had been sleeping; one of her long blonde hairs remained on her pillow. I picked it up and twirled it through my fingers, thinking about yesterday and last night; I never wanted to forget any second of it.

Yesterday was amazing from start to finish. There was something about Lilly, I knew it from the second I saw her face the day of the dust storm. She was the real thing; she didn't put on a show or try to be someone she wasn't. She didn't even seem to know she was as gorgeous as she is, but beauty radiated from her both inside and out. She's been able to pull me out of my introverted shell and make me do things I'd never imagined myself doing before.

I looked at my phone to check the time. It was 8:24 a.m.; I usually didn't sleep this late, but yesterday was a long, tiring day. Excellent, but still exhausting. I could hear the clinking and clanking of Lilly puttering around in the kitchen and then padding her way back to the bedroom with a coffee cup. "I've got cinnamon rolls in the oven. They'll be ready in twenty to thirty minutes. The owners filled the freezer full of homemade goods along with the baking instructions to go with them! There's eggs in the refrigerator too if you want me to make some."

My God, she looked beautiful with her hair all a mess and no makeup on, standing there with nothing on but a long, thin white T-shirt. "Twenty to thirty minutes, huh?" She squealed as I grabbed her by the hand and pulled her over to me. "I can't quite remember what the tattoo looked like. I'm gonna need you to refresh my memory."

.....

Even though both of us would have loved to have stayed at the cabin longer, we had to work tomorrow and needed to get back to Willow Creek. Reluctantly, we got ourselves ready and started on our journey back home.

"I've heard about people getting altitude sickness from skydiving, but I didn't get any of that at all. How about you?" she asked, taking her shoes off and putting her feet up on the dashboard.

"No, I didn't get sick either, but you're going to have worse problems than that if the airbag deploys with your feet on the dashboard." I patted her leg, so she'd put them back down.

"We're out in the middle of nowhere; the airbag isn't going to come out," she complained. This girl was going to be the death of me.

"You never know. About a year ago, I worked on an accident scene where a woman's feet were on the dashboard while the car she was in was in a wreck. Her knee went through her eye socket. Trust me, it wasn't pleasant."

"Okay, okay, Officer," she said and put her feet back down. "You're a very *safety-first* kind of guy."

"Hey now, that's not entirely true. Remember, I jumped out of a plane for you... But back to the air bags topic, have you ever been in a wreck?"

"Nope, I'm proud to say I have an immaculate record. No tickets and no wrecks." It's funny how shocking that information was. If I was a jerk, I might have been tempted to run her name into the system when I got back to work to see if that was true.

"Nothing? Really? No fender bender? No hitting a parked car in the parking lot? No tickets for accidentally backing into patrol cars?" I teased.

"It's not that hard to believe!" She playfully punched me in the arm.

"Actually, it is, kind of hard to believe... Remember that field sobriety test?" She gave me the side eye. "Oh, and there was that one time when you ran over me." I couldn't help laughing at that.

"Well, yea, but if I hadn't run over you then you couldn't have met me and jumped out of a plane and had an amazing weekend with me, so it all evens out in the end." This was the truth. A lot of things wouldn't have happened if she hadn't run into me, so I'll be forever thankful for that little incident.

There isn't much to look at between Dallas and Willow Creek, making for a long, boring drive. We watched the almost non-existent and treeless scenery, consisting of brown cottonfields and expansive flat plains that go on forever. Then, I felt the truck start to rattle.

"Dammit," I muttered and pulled off to the side of the road. "I think we've got a flat." I got out and walked around to the back. Sure enough, the back right tire was flat as a pancake.

Lilly climbed out of the truck as I opened the back door to get the tools to change the tire.

This gave me an idea. "Have you ever changed a tire?"

"Why? Do you not know how to change a tire?" She looked at me in disbelief.

"Yes, I know how to change a tire. I'm trying to find out if you do."

"No, I've always called Will or Kip if I have a flat."

"Ok, well what if Will or Kip aren't around, then what?"

"Then, I'd call you?"

"Ok, and what if Will, Kip, and I are not around, and you are out of town in the middle of nowhere, stranded on the side of the road like we are now and it's going to take too long for the roadside assistance to come. Then what will you do?"

"Wave down a car to help?"

Just what I was afraid of. "No... That's not what you're going to do. Do you know how many creeps there are that prey on stranded women with car trouble?" She looked at me as if she were completely baffled. "So, here's what we are going to do. I'm going to teach you how to change a tire so you can change it yourself instead having to rely on some nasty pervert to do it for you in the middle of nowhere. Just to be safe. And because I'm a very *safety-first* kind of guy..."

She shrugged.

"Now, come on. Let's get started." Luckily, I had a scissor jack which was easier to use than a regular hydraulic jack because it doesn't take as much strength. Not that I thought Lilly was weak, but she certainly wasn't as strong as I am and likely needed the easier method. I showed her how to position the jack under the truck and walked her through doing it herself. She didn't complain about having to get on the ground to do this, and she looked damn sexy under there too. Bethany would have had a stroke if I'd even suggested she get under a truck on the side of a road. Once the truck was jacked up, I gave her the tire iron to loosen the lug nuts, but just as I suspected, she wasn't strong enough to even make them budge and I had to get them started for her. I made a mental note to get her a battery-operated impact driver to keep in her car to make it easier.

"I have a confession to make," she said, taking of the last bolt and sliding the flat tire off. "I know how to change a tire, Will taught me how a few years ago." She confidently rolled the spare over.

"And yet, you let me look like an idiot trying to teach you how to do it."

"And you assumed I was going to be a damsel in distress not knowing how to take care of myself, Officer Wayland." She smirked and hoisted the tire up on her own, resourcefully sitting on the ground and using her legs to lift the tire up.

I stood back while she put the lug nuts back on, correctly alternating in a star formation.

"Want to check to see if they're tight enough?" she asked scooting back. "That's the only thing I have a hard time with so I have an impact driver that I keep in my car." She grinned with smug satisfaction.

I checked and tightened them a little more.

She got up off the ground and dusted herself off. "Well? Did I pass inspection?"

"Yes, well played, Lilly. Well played."

"Never underestimate a woman, Kade. I also know how to change the battery."

"You can add an auto shop to your bakery. Your customers can eat a cupcake while they wait for their tire and battery. One stop shopping." I grinned at her and put away the tools.

"I'm not sure there's much of a market for auto shop and bakery duos, but I'll keep it in mind."

"So, what did you think of Liam?" I asked her after we got back on the road. We hadn't had a chance to talk much about it after we left the nursing home.

"He seems like a great guy. I can just imagine what the two of you were like back before he was shot. He still has a great sense of humor."

I would have given anything for Lilly to have known Liam back then. I could just imagine how much fun we would have all had together, especially with the two of them having such similar personalities. Bethany and Liam got along fine, but Bethany was easily annoyed by Liam's constant joking and sarcasm, even though it was friendly and well-intended. He used to tell me that he liked Bethany, but he thought she needed to lighten up and learn how to take a joke.

"I just can't believe his family doesn't go see him anymore. It's so sad."

When I found out that his family had slowly just stopped coming, it infuriated me. Their whole reason for moving him to Dallas was so they be close to him and keep an eye on him. That's got to make him feel like crap, to know his family is in the same city but not coming to see him. And all the while, he can't just get in his truck and go where he wants. He relies entirely on people coming to him. It made me want to call his parents and tell them what I thought about it. I used to love his family, I never would have thought they would do this to him, especially when he needs their support more than he ever has.

"I know. That's really bothering me. But he's improved so much, a huge change from what it was at first. Honestly, I wonder if he could upgrade to assisted living instead of the nursing home. I don't know much about that kind of thing, but it would be worth looking into, except I'm sure his parents would have to take care of it for him, and they don't seem to be too worried about him anymore."

"You know, Leanne is a social worker at a nursing home. She might be able to help if you want to talk to her about it."

I nodded, that would be a great idea. I'd heard about Leanne being a social worker, but I never put the connection there that she might be able to help with Liam.

We finally made it back to Lilly's house. I helped her carry in her bag, antique shop purchases, and her three cups. Of those three cups, I'd only seen her drink out of one of them.

“Well, I’d better get back home to check on Peewee. But thank you for the best weekend I’ve had in I don’t even know how long,” I told her as I pulled her to me.

“Well, thank *you* for the very best weekend I’ve ever had in my entire life. Seriously, Kade, you outdid yourself. It was literally perfect.”

“You are literally perfect, Lilly.” I bent down and kissed her, somehow finding the willpower to pull myself away and go to my own house when really, all I wanted to do was spend another night with Lilly.

Chapter 27

Lilly

The sound of my alarm was basically the worst sound imaginable because it meant that I was supposed to somehow pull myself out of my perfectly cozy bed and drag myself to work. I loved my job; what I didn't love was getting out of bed to go to it, especially on days when I could already tell that I was having a flare up. My legs felt like they were made of concrete blocks, sore and too heavy to move. I pushed my snooze button. Just a few more minutes and then I'd get up.

I couldn't miss work today; I had too many things I needed to get done, and I had some work to do on for the Hire Someone Au-Some campaign. Jo was helping with the networking side of it, and I had some calls lined up with some of her contacts this afternoon.

The snooze button was activated every nine minutes for an entire hour until I finally threw the covers off in defeat and forced myself out of bed. My concrete block legs were burning and every few seconds it felt like somebody was poking a sewing needle into them. As much as I loved every single moment of the weekend with Kade, it took a toll on me.

I stood in the shower under scorching hot water, hoping it would relieve some of the body aches. The shower did nothing for my energy level, so I lay down on the couch for about an hour and then finally left for work with a large cup of coffee.

Kennedy and Javier were behind the counter experimenting with new lemonade flavors when I walked in. Javier had taken Kennedy under his wing and liked to include her in as much as he could.

"Lilly! Just the person I wanted to see. Kennedy and I have found our next top seller. I just know it!"

"That's good," I said, not really paying any attention to them.

"Don't you what to know what it is?" he asked, seeming a little taken aback about my lack of interest.

"Sorry, what did you come up with?" I asked, sitting down in one of the bistro chairs, which suddenly seemed incredibly uncomfortable even though I'd sat in them hundreds of times before. All I really wanted to do was just lie back down.

"Cranberry, peach, lime! It's to die for. Just the right about of zip and a little extra zing!" he sang, adding a little jig when he said the word 'zing.' He was in way too good a mood for first thing in the morning, shimmying around fixing me a cup of the new creation. But then again, he'd already been at the bakery for a few hours, so this was basically mid-day for him.

"We call it the Javiken. Get it? It's mine and Kennedy's names mixed together," he said as he sat my drink in front of me then stood back as he and Kennedy both stared at me, anxiously waiting for my response to their new invention. I took a sip and nodded approvingly. It was quite good. I like a nice, tart lemonade and this was perfect. "Put it on the menu, Javier! It's perfect."

My eyes were heavy and if I blinked too long, I might just fall asleep sitting in that uncomfortable hard chair. I felt like the cartoon characters I watched when I was a kid, the ones that put toothpicks in their eyelids to keep themselves awake. "If y'all need me, I'll be in my office. I'm not feeling very good." Kennedy's eyes grew wide with that news.

"What are your symptoms? Have you been checked for covid, flu, strep, and sepsis?" She backed a few feet away from me when she said that.

"It's not covid... or sepsis. I just had a long weekend. Come get me if you need anything," I told them both and walked off to my office, closing the door behind me.

It's always cold in my office. Refrigerator cold. I could probably keep a tuna sandwich out on my desk all day and not get food poisoning by eating it for lunch the next day. The entire rest of the bakery is perfectly comfortable, but my office of all possible locations was the one with the extreme temps. And cold makes everything hurt. This is why I keep not one, but two blankets in there and an electric heater. Maybe just a little power nap was what I needed. After turning on the heater, I folded one blanket to use as a pillow, pushed my computer keyboard out of the way, and placed the folded blanket on my desk so I could lay my head down. Then I covered up with the other blanket. Just 15 minutes, that should work.

I woke up to the sound of a knock on my door and Kennedy walking in. "Um... Javier needs something."

"Oh crap. What time is it?" I looked at my phone. I'd been asleep for an hour and a half.

"Are you ok?" she asked me, looking like she in no way thought I was ok.

"Yes, just tired. Needed a nap I guess." I got up and found Javier to see what he needed. He'd just had a question about the cake decorating class schedule, one of the classes was conflicting with a sourdough class. I got that situated but felt overwhelmingly weak, like I had weights hanging off my shoulders, making my body too heavy to hold up. I went back into my office, but this time I put my blankets down on the shaggy rug on the floor. I lay down right there on the rug, hoping nobody would walk in and see me. But at the same time, I didn't really care who saw me.

My excuse to everyone else when I feel like this is always the standard 'I'm just tired.' It's simple, easy, and accepted by almost everyone. Say anything else and the eyes start to roll, the subject quickly changes, and they think you are a hypochondriac. This is the problem I come across all the time. I get this way very randomly and with no warning, body aches, weakness, extreme fatigue, just overall not good. It's a similar feeling to the flu; however, when you have an autoimmune disorder, it's hard to know if you are actually sick, simply tired, or if it's a flareup. However, this time it probably was a flareup due to my adventures in skydiving. But that's neither here nor there, the 'I'm tired excuse' still works.

Of course, Kennedy of all people was the one that came in and saw me lying there on the floor in the fetal position looking like a preschooler at naptime.

"This is not normal. Do you need to go to the hospital? Where's your thermometer and blood pressure cuff?"

"I don't have a thermometer here and I don't own a blood pressure cuff. I'm just tired."

"Normally, people don't sleep on their floor at work." Ok, she doesn't need to be the voice of reason right now. "I'm getting Javier." She turned and swiftly marched out of the office.

I just stayed there, too tired to care. I was the boss; I could lie on the floor at work if I wanted to.

About a minute later, Javier and Kennedy were both standing in my office staring down at me. Javier spoke like he was talking to a child. “Lilly? Why are we lying on the floor?” Oh, good grief. Why do I have such nosey employees?

“Just a little tired. Kade and I went to Dallas over the weekend and jumped out of a plane. I think it wore me out more than I realized.”

Kennedy and Javier said in unison, “You did what?!”

Immediately after them, I heard another familiar voice from my doorway. It was Will. “You jumped out of a plane?” he asked, walking into my office. “Why doesn’t this surprise me. And what are you doing on the floor, is it naptime?” He raised his eyebrows, looking down at me.

Now I had Kennedy, Javier, and Will all staring at me as I was still curled up on the floor of my office with a blanket. I let out a deep breath, frustrated that nobody was just letting me sleep. Yes, this was a respectable workplace. No, I didn’t care at that particular moment. I got up off the floor and sat in my office chair with my blanket around me.

As expected, Kennedy put in her medical recommendation. “If you are prone to fainting or have other serious medical conditions, I would have recommended contacting your medical provider before risking life and limb. Also, you might suffer from low iron anemia." Good ole Kennedy, always ready with a diagnosis, but she's the only one that I don't mind hearing it from.

I put my computer keyboard back in its place. "Well, anywho... I'm going to try to get some work done." I looked over at Will. "Did you come to get some lemonade for Sydney? Javier and Kennedy came up with a new flavor, the Javiken." Sydney was a lemonade freak, and he was always coming in to get lemonade for her.

"Of course. I need a gallon. And six teacakes... So, I guess you and Kade are pretty serious? I mean, since you're jumping out of planes together and all?" He sat down in my other chair and picked the brown, crunchy leaves off the plant that had once been green and healthy when Sydney gave it to me.

"Yea, we're getting pretty close."

"I'm glad; he seems like a good guy... Does he like football? I ended up with an extra ticket to the game next weekend." I loved that he thought of taking Kade. It would be fun for the three of them to become friends. I'd never had a boyfriend that was friends with either one of my brothers or with Kip. Will despised Harrison, and he wasn't particularly fond of any of the others before him either, certainly never offered to take any of them to a football game.

"Oh, a man date! That would be so fun for y'all. He needs to have friends to hang out with. He's really not very social." My mind started racing. The guys could do their man things together, we could have group dates, vacation together, Friendsgiving... oh, the possibilities.

"Not a man date. We're going to a game..."

"Same thing."

.....

If ever there was a miracle, staying at work all day was one of them. I even managed to get all the calls that I'd planned. I'd sold a crapload of T-shirts, sent bracelets and flyers out, and had several businesses wanting to partner with me on the campaign.

Kade called me during his lunch, and I told him how I was feeling today; however, I immediately regretted telling him. The last thing I wanted was to make him feel bad for taking me to have the most amazing weekend of my life. And I also didn't want to give off the vibe of always having something wrong with me either. He'd already dealt with my projectile vomiting on his shirt, my unsightly eye and lip fiasco, and now this.

I'd only been home a few minutes when Beatrice barked at the door. Kade was standing there with a shopping bag and a bag from The Crunchy Chicken. He was wearing a black T-shirt that was just form fitting enough that it showed all the definition of abs. How is it legal to look that way?

"What's all that?" I asked as he kissed the top of my head and walked to the kitchen, setting everything on the counter.

"I have come to the rescue. I brought food and some goodies for you." He started unpacking the food bag and placing everything on the table as I sat down. As glad as I was that he was here, taking care of me, I felt guilty at the same time.

"Thank you for this! It's a lot better than the peanut butter crackers I would probably have eaten."

"I feel bad for cramming so much into the weekend. You overdid it and now you're paying for it. I should know better. The same thing happens to my sister," he said as he leaned down to give Beatrice one of his fries.

"What? Oh, no, no, no, that's not it. I read online that skydiving can cause fatigue. It's probably totally normal! Not your fault at all, so don't even think that way, weirdo." I took a bite of my chicken sandwich and then remembered what Will said about the football game. "Will has an extra ticket to the football game for this coming weekend if you want to go with him and Kip. He told me about it today. Maybe you'd like a little male bonding?"

He nodded his head while he chewed his bite. "Male bonding? I don't know about all that... but yea, I'd love to go." I was glad he agreed, I'd really been afraid he'd say no.

“So, what’s in the bag?” I asked, looking over at the bag still on the counter.

He got up and picked it up. “I need to go to your bathroom.” A few moments later, I heard the bathtub running. Then, he came back to the kitchen. “Bathroom’s all yours!”

“Um... Ok... why is the water running?”

“I wanted to make you feel better, so I hope it works. I’m going to get out of here so you can rest and get to bed early.” He gave me the gentlest hug and kiss.

“Have I told you how much I love you?” I asked him, resting my head against him and not wanting to move away.

“I love you too, more than you know... Now, go get in the tub and I’ll call you tomorrow.”

The bathroom lights were off. He’d prepared for me a cozy vanilla scented hot bubble bath with Epsom salts added in for my aching muscles. On the side of the tub, he’d put a brand-new loofah with vanilla scented shower gel. And in the corners were three orange and vanilla scented candles, the same scent that I’d told him about from the trip with my mom.

I sank down into the tub, letting the bubbles come up over my face. Why did Kade, someone so different than me, love me so much when I hadn’t really done anything to impress him. All I’d done was ridiculous random things, taping bread to his door, hitting him with my car, throwing up on him, getting upset about his ex-wife, nothing particularly endearing... But here he was, spoiling me and loving me anyway.

Chapter 28

Kade

Earlier in the week, I'd called Leanne to talk about Liam. She is the social worker at Meadow View which has both nursing and assisted living options. She said they could do an assessment on Liam to see what services he would need and which setting would be most appropriate. She did agree that it sounded like an upgrade to assisted living might be a good idea but couldn't say for sure until they could get an assessment done. The barrier would be his family, but it wasn't going to make much difference to them if he was in Willow Creek since they weren't going to visit him anyway.

I was going to have to call his parents, but how do I tell them that I want to move their son to a facility five hours away from them because they don't care enough about him to visit him? There isn't really a good way to put it.

I had some time before leaving for the game. Now was as good as time as any. I pulled up Liam's mom's number on my phone, took a deep breath, and pushed the green button. She answered on the second ring. I always had so much love and respect for Liam's parents, especially his mom, and thought of them as my second set of parents. His mom always called me 'mijo.' She was loving and always gave me tight hugs, treated me like her own son, and scolded me when I did something stupid. But now, hearing Gloria's voice, it unnerved me to think they could just forget about Liam the way they had.

"Hi, Gloria, it's Kade." It felt weird calling her by her first name, I used to call her 'mama.' She insisted on it, and she wasn't the kind of woman you argued with.

"Kade? Oh! It's been so long!" Her voice, even though I wasn't happy with her, still had such a calming effect on me. When I was younger, especially in high school, she always made me feel like no matter what happened, she would have my back even when my own mother might not have cared so much. I'd missed that after they moved away to Dallas while Liam and I were in the military.

How could I start this conversation? Asking to move her son to live in my town because he doesn't get visited by his family in their own town? There had to be an explanation for this; the people I knew and loved wouldn't have done this to him.

"I went to visit Liam last weekend. He looked good, really good."

She got quiet for a moment. "Oh, that's good to hear."

"In fact... I'm no expert on this, but since he's improved so much, I'm wondering if an upgrade to assisted living would be better for him. Maybe feel a little more homelike and less like he's in a hospital." Even though the facility he's in is a nice one, it still feels very institutional, like he's in a hospital room.

She was quiet for a while then spoke again. "I didn't think... I mean, I didn't know," she stammered, seeming to not know what to say.

"Look, Gloria, I don't know how to put this and I'm not trying to be rude. When I saw Liam last weekend, I stopped at the nurses' station to talk to them about him. They said he hasn't had any visits from family in a long time, that y'all used to visit him, then it slowly just stopped altogether. What is going on with that?"

I heard her take a deep breath and then exhale it. "Liam's brain damage changed him; he isn't the same with us anymore. I don't know how he is with you, but he doesn't want us to visit. We tried, we kept thinking he didn't really mean it, that it was something that would pass when he recovered more. But when we'd visit, he wasn't nice, Kade. He isn't the same Liam that he used to be. I couldn't do it anymore; I couldn't see him that way and my visits just seemed to stress him out. I feel guilty about it, I really do. It eats at me every day, but I haven't seen him in a year."

"I don't understand; he doesn't act that way with me. At all, in fact, he was making jokes and everything. And he was fine with my girlfriend also." How could he be acting this way with his own family? They were so close, basically the perfect family, the kind you see on TV sit-coms.

"I don't really understand it, either, but I didn't want to continue visiting if it was triggering for him and he just always became so angry when we were there. He's fine with his brother, but he moved to Wisconsin and hasn't been back to town in a long time. It isn't that I've just forgotten about him. I call the facility to check on him, and the social worker calls me when there's a problem."

My heart broke for them. It's not what I was expecting, and I felt guilty for assuming they had just abandoned him. "I'm so sorry, I didn't realize..."

"It's ok. I'm just thankful that you can visit and he still wants you to."

"So, that's kind of what I wanted to talk to you about. I've moved to Willow Creek. It's in West Texas, about five hours from Dallas. I have a friend that's a social worker at the nursing home there, but it also has assisted living. I talked to her about Liam, and she said they could do an assessment on him. If it's ok with you, I'd really love to move him here. He'd be just a few minutes from my house, and I could visit him as often as I wanted. I'd keep you up to date on him."

Gloria agreed. Then she cried, a cry that was a mixture of relief, sorrow, and gratitude all combined.

.....

Will, Kip, and I were all going to ride together to the game; it was a thirty minute drive to the football stadium. While we were at the game, the girls were going to do some sort of girls' night.

They'd be picking me up in a few minutes. I texted Lilly while I waited.

Me: **Have fun tonight doing whatever it is girls do on their girls' nights.**

Lilly: **We're painting pictures and drinking wine! Have fun male bonding!** What was it with her obsession with male bonding...

Me: **We'll be watching a game...**

Lilly: **Yes, it's called male bonding.** I could picture her smiling when she said that.

Will's truck pulled up in front of my house. I pet Peewee on the head as I walked out the door and then climbed into the backseat of Will's truck. I hadn't been to a game in person in years. It's something Liam and I used to do, different team of course, but we used to enjoy the college football games. We'd make a whole day of it with tailgating first before the game.

Will looked back at me. "So, I heard about the skydiving expedition you and Lilly went on."

"Yea, well, the plan was just for Lilly to do it. I wanted to surprise her with it, but she ended up talking me into it too. I *really* did not want to do it, but your sister has a way of making it hard to say no to her." Kip and Will both nodded.

"One thing about Sydney and Lilly is they are exact opposites. Lilly isn't afraid of anything. At all. Sydney is literally afraid of anything and everything. Get this. She's even terrified of escalators, avoids them like her life depends on it. And don't ever even think about telling her there could potentially be one single bear anywhere in the vicinity of an entire town or she will not be traveling there. Needless to say, between avoiding escalators and bears, it's hard to find a place to go to on vacation, camping is sure out of the question. Lilly, on the other hand, I'm pretty sure she would do just about anything."

Judging by Lilly's next text, she had already gotten into the wine.

Lilly: **Y'all are all going to be best friends by the end of the 2nd inning.**

Me: **How many glasses of wine have you had? Football has quarters, not innings. That's baseball.**

Lilly: **Well, same thing. Anyway, have fun! I love you!**

"Will, your sister texted me something about the second inning. I take it she hasn't been to many football games." I chuckled.

He and Kip both laughed at once. Kip looked back at me. "Now, that's something Sydney and Lilly *do* have in common. Neither one of them are football fans. We took them to a game one time and they both took books to read."

We arrived at the stadium and found our seats. Will and Kip had season tickets, and I decided next year, I might think about getting some too.

About halfway through the third quarter, or inning as Lilly would call it, a man a couple of rows in front of us, who'd clearly had too much to drink started being handsy and inappropriate with the woman sitting next to him; she made it obvious that she did not welcome it and kept trying to scoot farther away from him. I knew there were officers there, but I was closer and could handle it until I could get one of them over to take over. I took out my cell phone to call the campus police department and let them know that I was there and would take care of the situation until they were able to take over.

I stood up and told the guys, "I need to handle something. I'll be back." I made my way down to the man and woman, stepped between them and showed my badge. I could see the relief in the woman's face when she realized who I was. "I'm Officer Kade Wayland with the

Willow Creek Police Department." I looked at the man, trying to stall until the other officers got there. "I've noticed you being inappropriate with this woman. She doesn't act like she likes it." I looked over at the woman. "Am I correct that you do not want him to touch you, ma'am?" She nodded her head, trying to not make eye contact with the man. I'd worked in this field for long enough to know to keep my eye on the guy, so I wasn't surprised when I saw his fist rare back. I was able to block the hit and put him in an arm bar hold, taking him down between the bleachers before he ever knew what hit him. Just about that time, the two uniformed campus police showed up, subdued the man, and checked my credentials. After they took my story and got my information, I walked back up to sit with Kade and Kip who were standing up, watching the scene unfold, along with everyone else around.

"What was that all about!" Kip asked when I got back to my seat.

"Just some drunk jerk trying to get his hands on the woman next to him. Now, not only does he face attempted sexual assault and public intoxication but also assault on a public servant."

"Well, I guess I don't have to worry about anyone messing with Lilly. You'd kick their ass for sure," Will said as we sat back down.

"Yea, they might want to leave Lilly alone," I replied, with one hundred percent certainty that anyone messing with Lilly would not be enjoying their day after that.

It was a good game, we won 24-22. It was fun hanging out with Will and Kip; we found out the three of us had quite a bit in common.

Kip looked back at me after we got back into the truck. "So, I don't think Lilly ever said how the two of you met."

"The first time I met her, I was pulling her over and had to do a field sobriety test. Oddly enough, completely sober. The second time we met was after she hit me with her car in a dust storm. I guess it was fate. On the first date, she threw up on me. That just sealed the deal." I chuckled, thinking about those times.

Will nodded his head and grinned. "It's disturbing how none of that surprises me... The thing about my sister is it's always going to be something crazy like that, but she's the real deal. What you see is what you get with her, but that's not necessarily a bad thing."

Just talking about her made me want to see her. It was getting late, but not too late after Will dropped me off back at my house.

Me: **You still up?**

Lilly: **Yes, about to watch Schitt's Creek.**

Me: **Care for company?**

Lilly: **Of course, but can't find Penny. Giving up looking until tomorrow.**

Me: **Change of plans, I'll pick you up in 15 minutes.**

Chapter 29

Lilly

Penny made an appearance just before Kade got to my house; I found her crawling out from behind my dresser just as I was about to leave. I'd let her out to walk around freely while I tidied up her aquarium. I usually put her right back, but I got sidetracked and forgot she was out. But even though she was safe and sound, back in her home, Kade still took me to his house. He even let me bring Beatrice with me.

My house is usually our hang out place, so I'd only ever been to his front door. You can learn a lot about a person from their homes. His taste was very different from mine. Where I had a vibrant, eclectic style, he had a very minimalistic décor. Clean. Very clean but with a warm and cozy vibe at the same time. He had a weight room. I mean, of course he did with a body like his. The reading room was what shocked me. It was like something you'd see online but never in real homes. The room was decorated with rich, dark tones, but it probably didn't seem dark during the day because of the huge picture window. The bookshelves he built using branches of a real tree were phenomenal; I loved that he designed it himself and built it with his own hands. And the plants, there were so many; large bushy ones, cute small succulents, tall prickly cacti, vining ones hanging from the ceiling, and rare exotic plants that I'd never seen. I knew he had a green thumb, but I didn't realize he was basically a horticulturist.

"Syndey would be drooling all over your rug if she saw this room. She's a plant lady, as she calls herself." I took out my phone and showed him the picture. "Look at this, it's her pride and joy. She calls her Big Bertha. They use the dining area just for Bertha's room now that it's gotten so big." Kade's eyes grew wide, and he took the phone from me to get a closer look at the beastly monstera.

"Damn! It's probably worth a ton if she ever wants to sell it."

"Trust me, she doesn't. I'm almost positive it's in her will... as a beneficiary." I smirked, but seriously, Sydney treated that plant like it was one of her children.

He hesitated for a moment and almost walked past what I could tell was his bedroom.

I stopped and peeked in. "Is this your room?"

"It is." He stepped in and turned on the light and as I walked in, I felt myself flush at the thoughts that raced through my head.

His bedroom was moody and dark with the only bright color being the green from the plants grouped near the window. He's the kind of man that takes care of things, takes pride in his home. I like that. A lot. He's even the kind of guy who makes his bed. Of course he was. I don't even do that. He had nothing out of place. His nightstands had nothing on them other than a lamp, his charging station, and a clock. On his dresser was nothing but a plant, a shadow box containing a medal, and a photo of him and Liam.

"What's this medal?" I asked, running my hand over the top of the box.

"It's my medal of valor. Liam has one too. The governor presented them to us a year after the shooting." Looking at the photo of the two of them made my heart swell.

After the bedroom tour, he showed me the rest of the house and the firepit he'd been working on in the backyard. I don't know why being in his house and seeing his things had such an effect on me, but it did. I loved seeing what he did when he was here by himself, the things that made him happy and were important to him, that showcased who he was. Strangely, just seeing where he cooked his dinner, did his laundry, and went to bed made me love him even more, in a much deeper way. And it made me want to be here more, a lot more.

I wasn't the only one that felt at home in Kade's house.

"Beetle Head is already the boss of Peewee, it seems." Kade laughed, pointing at Beatrice, who was curled up on Peewee's monstrous, fluffy bed acting like she owned the place while Peewee lay next to it on the hard floor.

I wasn't sure what to expect with Peewee and Beatrice meeting each other. Beatrice is only twelve pounds compared to Peewee's hefty one hundred fifty. However, I quickly found out that there was nothing to worry about. Peewee acted as if Beatrice could annihilate her at any given moment and Beatrice, being the queen she is, promptly assumed her position as the alpha dog.

"I'm kind of hungry; do you want a snack?" he asked, opening the freezer.

"I always want a snack."

He pulled out a box of frozen taquitos and dumped some in the air fryer. I took the empty box to the trash can. At the top of the trash was a birthday card and some pictures of Kade and Bethany spilled out to the side of it, in plain sight. Both of them smiling and clearly very much in love with each other.

"What's all this?" I pointed into the trash can.

He shook his head and sighed. "More of Bethany's crap. She sent me a birthday card and some pictures of us as if that was going to make any difference. I just took one look and trashed them. If I'd had a fire going, I would have just thrown them in."

"First of all, I didn't know it was your birthday. Second of all, is she some kind of psychopath? I thought she understood that there's no chance in hell for the two of you to get back together." At first, I kind of felt sorry for her, but this just really made me irate.

"She doesn't have a choice; she's going to have to understand." He shrugged. "I had to block her on my phone and on social media. It's crazy, I never would have thought she would be acting this way. I don't know what has gotten into her. But don't worry about her. She'll have to just get over it."

"I'm not worried. She needs to find herself a new man, this one here is taken." I poked my finger in his chest. "And when is your birthday? Did I already miss it?"

"My birthday is actually tomorrow, the big three-five," he groaned like thirty-five was teetering on senior citizen status.

We turned on the TV and ate our taquitos on the couch, sharing a container of sour cream.

Kade's eyeballs grew wide staring at the large heap of sour cream balancing on the end of my taquito.

"Can you even taste any of the taquito with that much sour cream piled on?"

"The taquito is simply the delivery system to the sour cream. Just a tastier option than eating it with a spoon." I quickly ate the bite, savoring the creamy, cold goodness with a hint of taquito. “Don’t judge,” I muttered, still chewing.

We ate our sour cream and taquitos in silence while we watched TV for a few minutes, then I remembered the plans for tomorrow. “My mom wants to have everyone over to her house for dinner tomorrow. She thrives on cooking family dinners. I think she’s making chili and cornbread. I was specifically instructed to bring you with me. Just beware. They can be a lot.” My parents had been nagging me about bringing Kade over. I hadn’t wanted to put him through their inevitable interrogation, but it was going to happen sooner or later.

“Tell me about your parents. What was it like growing up with them?” That was sweet of him to ask. I don’t think most guys gave a flying flip about their girlfriends’ family.

“Well, they’re great. I have a good family. They are the kind of people that like to laugh and have fun, but at the same time you have to watch yourself because if you accidentally say so much as “dammit” or imply that you or any of your friends have ever done anything that the church preacher wouldn’t approve of, then it gets awkward real fast. My parents are as old-fashioned as you can get. You should have seen them when I got my first tattoo. They acted like I’d plummeted into a life of street drugs and gangs. All because I had a cupcake tattoo on my ankle... If that isn’t scandalous, I don’t know what is.

Obviously, the other tattoos didn't go over well with them either.

"They don't drink, cuss, dance, stay up late, or drive too fast. They think if you can detect an outline of a bra under your shirt then it's too revealing. Your shorts shouldn't be too short, and your pants shouldn't have holes in them. Basically, I don't fit in with my own family. But they love me anyway, and I love them. They're really the best. They're the kind of people that no matter what is going on in the world, you feel safe with them."

"Good to know. I won't wear my short shorts to dinner." He chuckled. "Are you closer to one or the other? I was always closer to my dad."

"Yea, me too, I'm closest to my dad. He just kind of gets me a little more than my mom does. Maybe it's just a daddy's girl thing. My mom is closer to my brothers. But my dad thinks anything I do is better than anyone else in the world has ever done it. If I make a cake, it's better than any cake that's ever been made before. If I give him advice on his store, it's the best advice that anyone has ever given. He's just that way. He still keeps a picture of me when I was two years old in his wallet, and he still shows it to people. And the funny thing is, he doesn't have any pictures of my brothers in there." I smiled thinking about that picture. It's all ratted and the ends are curled up. I'd given him recent pictures to replace that one with, but he still held onto that one.

"You're really lucky, you know?" He pushed his empty plate aside and sat back.

"Do you want to tell me about your parents? I don't know much about them." I knew enough to know it wouldn't be the same wholesome, Hallmark movie kind of situation I'd grown up with.

"I loved my dad. I told you he was an alcoholic, but nobody outside of his family knew it. He wasn't mean or abusive or anything like that. He got up on time every day, went to work, and he was well respected at the same job for over thirty years. But the minute he stepped inside the door when he got home from work, he opened his first beer. I hated hearing the pop of the beer can. Then the sound of the empty can falling into the trash, followed by the pop of another can opening. After a few beers, he moved on to whiskey, always mixed with soft drinks in a red solo cup. And by 8:30 he was slurring so badly we couldn't understand him. I tried to stay in my bedroom after dinner, so I didn't have to witness it. My mom always tried to get him to bed by 9:30 or else he would drink so much that he could barely walk to his bed without falling. Sometimes he did fall, and I had to help my mom get him into bed. Even with all that, he was still my hero. I hated his drinking because I felt like it robbed all of us, including him, but I loved everything else about him."

I let that marinate for a moment in my head. I'd never even seen my own dad drink a beer, not even a glass of champagne at a wedding. "What about your mom?"

"Grouchy. Seriously, never happy. She and my dad fought all the time. But when he died, she was still grouchy. She could ask me to do something; I'd do exactly what she asked. Then she'd be upset because I did it wrong. There was no winning with her." He looked puzzled suddenly. "But you know what's weird? I called her recently and she sounded happy. It was really... odd... She has friends all the sudden, and they play dominoes? She's never played games. I don't think she ever even had friends before. And apparently, she has a boyfriend, too. So, I guess things are looking up for her."

"Your mom's just out there living her best life now, I guess! Maybe she just needed a change of scenery, a fresh start."

He smiled and pulled me over closer to him. "Fresh starts are just the thing sometimes."

Kade kept a blanket neatly folded over the arm of the couch. I covered up with it and curled up with my head on his lap. He played with my hair, without me even asking him to do it. I used to have to beg Harrison to play with my hair, and he would complain and then stop after just a few minutes. Not romantic. But Kade playing with my hair? It was just so intimate, romantic, so different. I don't know why I thought I was going to watch the next episode of Schitt's Creek, because within minutes, I was too relaxed to hold my eyes open any longer.

At some point I felt him pick me up, but it seemed so effortless that I didn't fully wake up. And in the morning, I woke up in Kade's bed, still in my T-shirt and leggings, with him wrapped around me.

I met Kade in July. I thought he was a grumpy police officer that needed to lighten up, and I'd hoped I would never see his face again. Now here it is October and I'm in his bed. He played with my hair until I fell asleep, carried me to his neatly made bed, and cuddled up with me in his freshly washed fabric softener scented sheets.

Last night was pivotal, like we'd dived deeper into more of an emotional, deeper closeness. Nothing and nobody can change what Kade and I have, especially not a deranged ex-wife.

Sydney and Will have told me their story countless times, and both of them always say "when you know you know." I'm not a love at first sight kind of girl, but I'm madly and deeply in love with him. I knew it with the tiger lilies. I knew it with the candlelit bakery date. I knew it with the skydiving. I've known it probably all along. But it's this moment right now, without a single shred of doubt, that I know that I will never ever love another person like I love this man for as long as I live.

Chapter 30

Kade

I woke up to the sound of soft snoring next to me. I rolled my eyes and smirked because Lilly swears that she doesn't snore. But when I rolled over toward her, it was Beatrice's homely face that rested on what would have been Lilly's pillow. When I first met that dog, I couldn't imagine even Lilly sleeping in bed with it, much less myself. Now here she was lying her ugly head on a pillow next to me in my own bed. The little mutt has found a place in my heart even though I never thought it would be possible. Over the sound of Beatrice's congested nasal passages, I could hear Lilly moving around in the kitchen.

This was going to be a good birthday. I thought about last night. Something about it seemed different, like Lilly and I were somehow closer even though all we did was eat taquitos and talk about our parents. Lilly had fallen asleep on my lap, and she was so peaceful that I didn't want to wake her up, so I'd carried her to my bed. We could have stayed on the couch all night, but I wanted to sleep next to her in my bed.

After I got up and walked into the kitchen, she immediately sang happy birthday to me and made birthday pancakes. After we ate, I took her and Beatrice back to her house so she could get ready to go shopping with Jo for the things they needed to take on their big European Extravaganza, as they called it. Now that the trip was right around the corner, I really wasn't all that excited about the two of them going to another country, I'd be in a state of panic until they returned home safely. I felt better when she was close by where I could get to her quickly if she needed me.

"I know what I'm getting you for your birthday! I'll bring it over later!" she said as she kissed me and jumped out of the truck with Beatrice.

I don't really like to compare Lilly and Bethany. I used to love Bethany, or I thought I did, anyway. I don't think I ever truly understood what real love was until Lilly came along. Well, practically vehicular assaulted me, that is. Bethany is beautiful; that's what attracted me to her at first. But her problem is she knows she's beautiful and she bases her entire identity on that. I didn't realize how annoying that is until after she left me. Lilly doesn't even realize how freaking gorgeous she is. And from what I've seen so far, she doesn't spend hours in the bathroom with bottles and jars of who knows what kinds of expensive products scattered all over the counter. She doesn't care who sees her without any makeup or with her hair a mess. She will boldly go out into public dressed as a bottle of ketchup for Halloween. I know this because she has already bought and modeled her ketchup costume for me. She also presented me with the mustard costume that apparently, I'll be wearing. Bethany wouldn't dream of stepping foot out of the house without full makeup and hair, and she definitely wouldn't be caught dead in a Halloween costume.

And of course, Bethany hates surprises. She didn't even like gifts unless they were selected from her very specific list she created. I'd tried buying gifts for her that weren't on her approved gift list, but they were typically exchanged. When Lilly told me she liked surprises, I made it one of my life's missions to surprise her as often as possible because there's nothing better than that look on her face when she gets excited about something she wasn't expecting.

Since I knew she would be out for a while with Jo, I decided it was the perfect time to give her flowerbeds a facelift. The tiger lilies that I'd planted for her were through for the year and needed to be cut down until they could come back again next year. Meanwhile, she needed something new and colorful for fall. I thought a vibrant mixture of yellow, purple, and orange chrysanthemums would be perfect for her.

After a surprisingly pleasant happy birthday call from my mom and from my sister, I went to the store to get enough plants for my own yard and for Lillie's, but I'd do Lillie's first before she came home.

First, I stopped at the bakery to plant some of them in the planter box and pots that were in front of the window. The bakery is closed on Sundays, so there was nobody there. The new flowers gave a pop to the front of the bakery that I knew Lilly was going to love. Then I headed to her house to do her flowerbed. Liam used to make fun of me for being so particular about flower placement, but I see nothing wrong with wanting it to look good. I carefully arranged them so there would be a good balance of color throughout the flowerbed. Then I poured fresh, black mulch down on top of the dirt which made the colors really stand out. I also replaced the dying flowers in the pot on the porch, then swept up the mess. Doing things like this for her made me happy because I knew she was going to love and appreciate it when she saw it, and I wanted to make this my thing that I'd always do for her. Maybe for Christmas I'd surprise her with hanging multicolored LED lights on her roof and decorating her front porch with snowmen. I imagined she was probably the kind of girl who loved going into the city at night, listening to Christmas music with a cup of hot chocolate while driving around the neighborhoods looking at Christmas decorations. She probably likes having her own house decorated too.

I was loading my supplies into the truck when a car pulled up in the driveway. A man got out of the car with a vase of flowers. “Hello, sir. I have a delivery here for a Lilly?”

“Sorry, she isn’t home right now.”

“Mind if I just leave them here with you?” He smiled and handed me the vase.

“Uh, sure. I’ll give them to her.” Who could be giving her flowers? Maybe it was something from her dad. He seems like the kind of dad who would do things like that for his daughter.

After the driver pulled away, I looked at the card which was clearly marked and not in an envelope. It read, ‘You are my everything. Love, Harrison.’ Excuse me?

First of all, why the hell was her ex-boyfriend sending her flowers? Second of all, what was I supposed to do with these flowers? Give them to her and say, “Here are the flowers that Harrison sent for you?” She is his “everything?” How can that even be? Lilly wouldn’t be seeing somebody else, especially not her ex-boyfriend. She just wouldn’t do that. She loves me, not some prick named Harrison. She made birthday pancakes for me after sleeping in my bed last night. She’s made me fall so deep in love with her that I can’t even process what is happening right now holding this damn vase of flowers from some jerk named Harrison. Just the name alone was making me mad. Harrison. *Harrison?* Really? My grip on that vase was so strong I was going to break it, so I set it down by the front door. What kind of name is Harrison, anyway? It's a last name, not a first name unless you're a millionaire Hollywood actor. Could he not go by Harry or Harold? It makes him sound like a stuck-up twenty-four-year-old that wears boat shoes with khakis while he's playing chess on his dad's yacht. That's seriously not the kind of guy I can see Lilly with.

I didn't even know what to think. I'd literally just planted flowers for Lilly and these show up while I'm still here? How freaking convenient. This is either a practical joke, not a funny one in the slightest, or Lilly had been seeing *Harrison* on the side. Was this a test or something? Was I supposed to call Lilly and ask why this Harrison character was claiming her as his everything? Should I throw them away and she'd never know they ever existed? No, I was going to leave them on the porch by the front door and wait to see how this played out. It was a mistake. It had to be. I couldn't even imagine Lilly not being honest with me and we were way past the point of dating other people being a thing, especially not dating exes.

I drove home and tried to release some of my anxiety by planting my own flowers while I waited to hear from Lilly, sure she would be calling when she got home and hoping this whole thing would turn out to be a huge mistake.

Two hours later, my phone dinged with a text from Lilly. **Hey! Just finished shopping! I'm going to run home to let Beatrice out and then I'll bring your gift over!**

I couldn't really respond to it. I was so confused; still not sure what to think. So, I waited.

About fifteen minutes later, the phone rang.

Her voice sounded happy and confused at the same time. "Uh, Kade? Did you happen to plant flowers at my house? Because if you did, thank you! They are absolutely beautiful!" Did she think Harrison might have planted them?

I took a deep breath and exhaled. "That would be me. I'm glad you like them." I struggled with my tone because I had no idea how to react to what was going on.

There was a long pause. Was she going to bring it up or was I going to have to do it?

We finally both spoke at once.

"Your flowers arrived when I was there," I said flatly.

"Harrison sent me flowers," she said at the same time.

"Lilly, I'm kind of confused. Why is your ex-boyfriend sending you flowers and claiming that you are his everything? The delivery driver handed them to me while I was loading up after I planted your flowerbed." At least she was telling me about it rather than keeping it a secret as if I didn't already know.

"Your guess is as good as mine. I haven't talked to him since we broke up and I'm certainly not his *everything*. I wasn't his everything when we were together and he would never say something like that."

I believed her. Her voice said it all. There was no way she was doing anything with Harrison or anyone else behind my back and I hated that the idea even crossed my mind.

"Wait, did you think I was cheating on you?" She sounded hurt.

I stammered, trying to find the words. "No, I didn't think you would do that. I... I really didn't know what to think. I've been wondering if this was a bad practical joke."

"You poor thing! I'm so sorry. Here you were being the best boyfriend on the planet, planting flowers at my house, and then somebody shows up with flowers for me from another man? I can't even imagine what was going on in your head. I don't even want to know."

"Yea, it wasn't much fun. I can tell you that much."

"But I honestly do not think Harrison sent them. He didn't send me flowers when we were together. He's not a romantic kind of guy. I texted him to see if it was actually him, which was awkward. We'll see what he says."

"Ok. I feel like somebody else is behind it."

"Wait, do you think somebody would be trying to break us up? Like to make you jealous or something? I don't know who that would even do that, though, because nobody cares if we are together. Harrison sure doesn't give a damn who I'm seeing."

Could it actually be somebody trying to break us up? We aren't in junior high. I couldn't imagine anyone doing something like that.

"Harrison is typing. Hold on," she said and waited a few seconds. "Oh my gosh. I'm so embarrassed. He just said no with a question mark like I'm stupid to even ask. I guess that answers our question."

It isn't that I didn't believe Lilly, but I felt a huge rush of relief knowing it wasn't Harrison that sent them. "I think I know who did it." It had to be Bethany. I never would have thought she was capable of doing anything like that, but lately, I'm not sure I could put it past her. Maybe she decided that if she couldn't get to me any other way, she'd just try to break me and Lilly up. I'm not sure how she found out where she lived though, or that her ex-boyfriend's name was Harrison, and that bothered me.

"You have got to be kidding. Your deranged, psychopath ex-wife?"

"I don't know who else it could be."

That got Lilly fired up. "That's it! I have had it with her! What is her phone number? I'm calling her. At first, I felt sorry for her, but she sure better not show her stupid, perfectly contoured, overly botoxed face around here again or she will regret it. And you and your police people just better not be anywhere around while I'm kicking her butt because I'm not going to jail because of her, either."

I couldn't help but laugh. "There's no need for any butt kicking or jail time, and you don't need to call her. We don't even know for sure if it's her. But I'll handle it. Now get over here, you've got a gift for me, remember?"

Chapter 31

Lilly

Catastrophe by cupcake...

When Sydney found out that Kade liked plants, she had a great idea for his birthday gift. There was a boutique plant store in town, and they had something called a Variegated Monstera Albo Halfmoon that Kade, being a fellow plant enthusiast, would go crazy over. I took her advice and bought it for him and to go along with it, printed and framed a photo of the two of us still in our skydiving contraptions. Sydney knew what she was talking about; he loved it. He also loved the photo, and he put it on his dresser next to the photo of him and Liam. I came back home afterwards; I had a lot of things to do before the news crew came to the bakery today.

It was cooler in the mornings now, but I drank my coffee on the porch anyway so I could look at the flowers

Kade planted. When he planted tiger lilies in my yard during the summer, I thought it was the sweetest thing a man had ever done for me. And he didn't even stop there; he'd checked on them when he was here and watered them if they looked dry. The new flowers and the fresh black mulch look amazing. A man who buys a woman a bouquet of flowers does not even come close to comparing to a man who plants a woman an entire flowerbed. He's one of those good guys that you can take home to your parents and not have to worry about it. It's a whole other level unlocked that I've never gotten to experience before Kade. We were having dinner at my parents' tonight, and I didn't even have to give him a list of dos and don'ts because there was nothing they wouldn't approve of, and that's saying a lot.

I took a picture of the flowerbed and texted it to Jo. **Look what Kade did while we were shopping.**

She texted back immediately: **They don't make them like that anymore. He's like a collector's item.**

I picked a pink, long sleeve button down shirt to wear to work today but also took two other shirts for Caitlyn's opinion since she was the fashion expert. Normally, I'm not too picky about what to wear, but since we'd be on the news and all, I wanted to give off the best impression. I even did full face makeup instead of my mostly natural look which is usually just a little blush, lip gloss, and mascara on any other day.

The first thing I noticed when I pulled up to the bakery were the colorful mums. He'd even planted flowers here? He was just too much, a true gem. Or a collector's item, as Jo called him earlier. And the timing could not be more perfect with the news crew coming today.

Kennedy was inside cleaning tables. Her hair was as neat as a pin, all tied up in a perfect bun.

"Are you ready for this?" I asked her. The camera crew was coming today, but our interview at the station wasn't until Friday, right before Jo and I leave for the airport. It was going to be a huge day.

"Yea, I think so. What are they going to want me to do?" We'd already been over this many times and we'd even done a little roll playing to prepare.

"Remember? They just want to see what you do at work. You can show them how you get things ready for the classes, clean, organize, just all the different things you do during the day."

"Ok." That seemed to satisfy her, and she went on with the vigorous scrubbing of already spotless tables.

Caitlyn was behind the counter, setting out cupcakes, teacakes, and lemonade for the camera crew.

I twirled around once and asked, "Is this shirt ok? Or else I have these two." I held up the other two shirts I brought with me.

She nodded approvingly at the shirt I was wearing. "Oh, yes. That one is perfect. It's very bakery owner-ish." Relived that I passed inspection, I took the other two shirts to my office.

While I was still in there, I heard a woman's voice asking for me. And when I walked back to the counter, the voice belonged to none other than Little Miss Manipulator, Bethany. She made me sick standing there all tall and cocky with her spray tanned self, acting like she was in charge of something. It's ok. I could handle this like a civilized human being. I could be the bigger person here.

"Is there something I can help you with?" I politely asked, with the most professional smile I could muster.

"Yes, there is. I'm going to need you to stay out of Kade and my relationship. We are trying to reconcile, and it seems you are continuing to get in the way of this. I'd appreciate it if you would stay away from him." Who did this broad think she was? She can't traipse into my bakery ordering me to stay away from *my* boyfriend? Oh, hell no.

Caitlyn and Kennedy stopped what they were doing and stared at Bethany and I.

I kept my fake smile plastered across my face and spoke in an overly sweet tone, totally opposite to how I felt. "Oh dear. I can see how this is quite a dilemma for you. And I just hate that for you, especially since you are so delusional that you believe there is any chance at all of reconciliation between the two of you. But it seems that Kade loves me very, *very* much and doesn't want to give me up for anyone, much less someone who is as deceptive and obnoxious as yourself." Through all of that, I kept a smile on my face. It felt good, really good to confront her like that. She didn't have a chance in hell with Kade ever again. I had no doubt about that.

I heard a gasp come out of Caitlyn while Kennedy audibly stated, "Oooohhh."

There was a deep, death stare going on in Bethany's deep brown eyes, under her annoyingly thick, perfectly curled lashes. She looked over at the cupcakes, then back at me. Then gracefully reached over and picked up a blue buttercream topped cupcake.

I froze.

She wouldn't.

She did.

Blue cupcake in hand, she lunged forward and pushed the cupcake right into my face, then slid it down my neck. I stood there speechless, wiping cupcake off my eye and trying to process what just happened.

"Stop it, right now!" Caitlyn yelled, positioning herself in between us.

Bethany licked some of the icing off her finger. "I've had better frosting."

Scratch the part about me being the bigger person. That was all I was going to take. I picked up a green cupcake.

"Lilly, don't," Caitlyn warned.

I walked around Caitlyn, smashed the cupcake it into Bethany's face and slid it around on the top of her head, vanilla cake crumbling all through her long, dark hair.

And then it was on. Bethany reached across and grabbed a hold of my hair, right at the root. I screeched, "Let go, you freak!" trying to pull her hand off my hair, but doing so made her squeeze tighter.

Caitlyn jumped in between us again and tried to get Bethany out of my hair. Meanwhile, I grabbed Bethany's hair, sandwiching Caitlyn in the middle of us. "Stop it, both of you!" Caitlyn yelled, having no effect on the hair pulling.

Kennedy wasn't having it. The next thing we knew, she picked up a full glass of Raspberry lemonade and poured over Bethany's head, some of it also landing on Caitlyn's head. Then, red faced and holding an empty glass, Kennedy yelled, "Let go of her hair and get out of this bakery! I'm giving you five seconds or I'm calling the police!"

Everybody stepped away from each other. Bethany's hair was dripping and stuck to her face with a big clump sticking out from where I'd had a hold of it. The pink lemonade mixed with the icing created a liquidy green substance running down her neck and onto her dress. Her non-waterproof mascara was running into the mix as well creating black streaks.

I stood there with blue icing and cake smashed all over my makeup and my cute, Caitlyn approved shirt. Icing and crumbs clung to the wispy pieces of hair falling around my face.

Even Caitlyn was covered in a mixture of green and blue icing and parts of her hair were wet with lemonade. It wasn't a good look for the news clips we were about to be making.

Kennedy had clearly assumed the role as the only civilized person in the group. She hit her palm against the counter and yelled, "Everybody out of this bakery! I just had this place looking spotless and now it's a disaster! The news will be here in like half an hour!" We all stopped and looked at her. Poor Kennedy, she'd worked so hard to make everything perfect and not only was the floor a total disaster, but so were Caitlyn and I.

With that, Bethany stormed out of the shop, but before going to her car, she stopped at the flowers and pulled them all out, throwing them down on the sidewalk. Kade's flowers! She just yanked them out like they were trash! I started out the door after her.

"Have you completely lost your mind? What kind of person does that?! I'm calling the police. This is property destruction." But I didn't even have to call the police, because Kade's patrol car pulled up just in time. He stepped out of his car with a very unhappy and confused expression on his face, similar to the face he'd made when he pulled me over. First, his eyebrows furrowed as he looked at Bethany and I, then he looked down at the flowers dumped on the sidewalk.

"What the heck is going on here?" he asked us. I couldn't imagine what must be going through his head at the sight that was before him.

"Kade, I can explain," Bethany spoke first, acting innocent like she's a victim in all this.

"No, I can explain," I interrupted her. "Bethany showed up here telling me to stay away from you because I was interfering with your reconciliation. Then she shoved a cupcake in my face and pulled my hair, and it all went downhill from there. She also dumped my flowers out." I gestured at all the flowers and soil scattered around.

Caitlyn stuck her head out the door. "Lilly, hurry up! We have to get this place cleaned up before the camera crew gets here!" Crap. She was right. The camera crew would be there in about fifteen minutes, and we looked like we'd just stuck our faces in our first birthday cake.

"Kade, I've got to get cleaned up. The news is going to be here any minute."

"Yes, go get cleaned up. I'll clean this mess up out here and I'll deal with her." He looked toward Bethany who had a stupid, sad puppy expression on her face.

"Thanks." I walked back inside where Kennedy was mopping up the mess on the floor.

"Kennedy, I'm so sorry. I really am. Let me get cleaned up and I'll help with all this."

She stopped mopping and looked up at me, grinning slightly. "That witch deserved it."

I breathed out a loud sigh. Ok, this was going to be ok. It's fine. Everything's fine. I ran into the bathroom and joined Caitlyn in fixing our hair and makeup and changing into clean shirts. How could we have been so lucky that I had two extra shirts in my office and Caitlyn wore the same size as me.

Caitlyn finished before I did and went out to put more cupcakes and lemonade out from the little mishap. I heard a tap at the door.

"Can I come in?" It was Kade.

I opened the door. "Officer, you realize this is the women's restroom. What would people say?" I said, innocently as he walked in and closed the door behind him.

"It's important police duty. I've come to do a welfare check on you."

"Ok, as long as it is official police business. I'll allow it."

He smirked. "You look a lot better than you did a few minutes ago. I can't believe I just happened to drive up when I did. I came over here to watch the big TV debut and to wish you and Kennedy good luck and didn't expect to see the tail end of a cat fight." He snickered.

I laughed. “You should have seen Kennedy, Kade. Bethany had a hold of my hair and Kennedy poured a glass of lemonade over her head. Then she ordered her out of the bakery. Well, she kind of ordered everyone out after that. I think she almost fired me. She wasn’t putting up with any of this nonsense. She was great.”

“Well then, that just adds to the whole reason for the campaign, I guess. She’s got potential, that girl. By the way, I cleaned up the sidewalk and put the flowers back in the pots. The soil was still so loose from planting them that the roots were still on. I think they’ll be fine.”

“Aww, thank you so much. You always save the day.” I gave him a good, thorough inspection of his uniform. “Are you allowed to look like this? I mean, are women purposely breaking the law when they see you?”

He turned my head to the side with his hand. “You have a little icing on your neck. Let me get that for you.” He bent down and licked it off.

“Is this how you treat all the women during welfare checks, officer?”

There was a knock on the door, interrupting our restroom rendezvous. “Um, what are y’all doing in there? The camera people are here!” she hissed from the other side of the door.

“We’re just doing drugs,” I joked back to her which made Kade laugh as we walked out.

The whole thing with the news crew went fabulously and I couldn't wait to see the clips. Kennedy went above and beyond what I expected. She was confident, proud, and poised. She went into an in-depth explanation of her job title, her day-to-day duties, and the importance of a germ and hazard-free environment. She demonstrated setting up the workspaces for the classes, showed them where she keeps her cleaning supplies, and most importantly, the first aid supplies cabinet and the Choking and CPR chart. By the time it was over, you would have thought she owned the whole bakery. She even told the camera crew that there's no way we could run the place without her. It was obvious that she was going to win everyone over during the interview at the news station Friday.

.....

After work, I went home and waited for Kade to come pick me up to go to my parents' house. Will and Sydney and the kids would be there too, along with Harriet... For some reason, my mom always felt the need to invite her sister to all our family dinners even though somebody always ended up offended by something she said or did.

Dinner was about what we'd expect. My dad made jokes about my mother's cooking, even though her food is always incredible. Harriet didn't have anything outlandish to say, which was a first for her. Kade turned out to be amazing with kids. Micah, Elsie, and little Kendra all loved him immediately. Seeing him with children was the sweetest thing I'd ever witnessed. Kendra was just a baby and seeing her perched on his lap, squealing and smiling at him was the cutest. Micah tried to arrest him, and Elsie put him in charge of burping her baby doll. Kids had never been at the top of my wish list, but my reproductive system was telling me it wanted to procreate just at the sight of him with those kids.

.....

Back at home, Kade and I settled into the couch with Beatrice. "Have you ever wanted kids?" he asked, totally catching me off guard.

I thought about it for a moment. "I mean, I've thought about it. I've been kind of scared to get pregnant because I think it might be high risk for me, but I've never actually talked to my doctor about it. What about you?"

"Yea, I've always wanted kids. Playing with the kids tonight just made me think about it. Bethany and I tried to have kids, but it just never happened. And now, I'm glad for that."

"Especially since she's psycho. I can't believe I got into a fight with her! You should have seen it! She had a hold of my hair and wouldn't let go. Then I grabbed her hair and Caitlyn wedged herself between us. And the best part was Kennedy pouring the lemonade over Bethany's head. It was a whole crap show." I still couldn't believe what happened. I'd never been in any kind of physical altercation before.

"It sounds like you're ready for cage fighting now." He laughed. "But seriously, I'm sorry she did that to you. I wish I'd gotten there sooner and none of that would have happened."

"Well, I'm terribly frightened," I teased, scooting closer to him. "I may need police surveillance until tomorrow morning."

He put his arm around me. "Oh yes, you definitely do."

Just as he was starting to kiss me, the phone rang, interrupting the romance. It was Jo. "Hey, um... I have some bad news. I may have to back out of Germany. Actually, I really do have to back out of Germany." Nooooo. No, just no. She can't.

"Excuse me, what did you say? You're kidding, right?" She had to be. We were going in just a few days. Everything was booked, paid for, it was all set.

"I wish I was kidding. I was riding Frankie and she threw me off. I broke my leg, I'm in the ER right now and I'm going to have to have surgery." Crap. Frankie is her horse. She's never thrown her off before.

"What??!! Are you ok? Well, I mean, of course you aren't ok. What the heck, Jo? Surgery? I'm so sorry! Well, I'm not going without you. This was our trip, we can reschedule, right?"

"Lilly, we didn't get the travel insurance. Everything is paid for, nothing is refundable because we did everything the cheapest way possible. Can you get somebody to go in my place? Maybe one of your parents or another friend? Or better yet, Kade could go with you. I'll be mad if you don't go."

"I'm not going without you, Jo. I'd feel terrible being there without you. It wouldn't be right." I just can't imagine leaving Jo here when we'd plan this together.

"Lilly, this was the only time for at least a year, maybe longer, that I'd be able to do it. I know how badly you've wanted this trip. It's paid for. Just do it. You can face time me as often as you want. You've been so obsessed with this trip. Please, I'll feel so guilty if you miss out on it because of me."

I thought about it for a while and decided to go. Jo wanted me to do it and although I'd probably not find anyone to go in her place, I'd been on solo trips before, and I could do it this time too.

Chapter 32

Kade

When you know, you know...

"I don't know if they allow dogs in the facility, Lilly," I told her as she climbed into the truck with Beatrice.

"She's a therapy dog, Kade."

"Yea, I don't think so. Willow Creek's ugliest dog can't be a therapy dog. I mean, they will need more therapy to recover from the trauma of seeing her face." I smirked. "But she's perfect for Halloween."

"I brought a big tote bag. I'll stuff her in there until we get to his room. I just thought he'd like to hold a dog in his lap for a while. It's therapeutic even if she isn't a therapy dog. You told me he used to have a dog before the shooting." That was true. Liam had a miniature schnauzer named Tiger. He was having him treated for cancer. His parents took him to their house after Liam was shot, but he didn't live much longer after that.

Liam agreed to move to the facility in Willow Creek. Leanne was a huge help and facilitated the whole thing. He'd moved in this week, and Lilly had decorated his room for fall. I told her I didn't think he would care about seasonal decorations, but she said she wanted his room to be cozy for him, and I'd say she succeeded. Liam was propped up in his recliner with his soft new fall colored blanket, and his pumpkin printed pillows. He wore his brand-new fleece pajama pants, and his socks with spiders printed on them that Lilly picked out with me in mind.

"See? He's cozy, right, Liam?" she asked him as we walked in to see him. He had a nicer, bigger room than he'd had in Dallas. He'd been able to move into the assisted living section which was a big upgrade from the nursing home he'd been in before. He even had a small kitchenette which Lilly and I had stocked with snacks and drinks for him.

Since he'd improved so much and was closer to me, I was going to be able to take him out of the facility sometimes. I thought it would be nice to take him to my house for a couple hours, bring him over for holidays, just hang out and do guy things sometimes. He hadn't been able to do that in years.

Liam adored Lilly. I think he looked forward to seeing her just as much as he did me. But Lilly felt the same way about him, and I knew she would continue to check on him even if something happened to me. He gave her a thumbs up and smiled at her, then his face lit up even more when she pulled Beatrice out of the tote bag.

"I wanted you to meet my dog, Beatrice." She sat her in his lap. "She's really sweet."

"She looks like Kade," he joked. Beatrice licked Liam's face and then snuggled into his blanket as he patted her head. Liam looked up at me. "You're a dumb ass if you don't marry this girl." This made Lilly laugh out loud, and her face matched the pink in her shirt.

"Hey man, you need to mind your own business or I'm sending you back to Dallas," I teased, even though he was right.

One of my favorite things about Lilly is when she puts her mind to something, she doesn't back down. She'd proven that with her quest to "cozy-up" Liam's room but also with the Hire Someone Au-some campaign she'd been working on. She had made the campaign even bigger than I ever thought she would. It all started with that kid being a butt head at the bakery and saying mean things about Kennedy, and Lilly knew then and there that she was going to turn it into something positive for Kennedy and she did. That kind of determination was one of the most attractive things about her.

When we left Liam, we dropped Beatrice off at Lilly's house. Then, I drove us to the news station. I'd promised

Lilly that I would be there to cheer them on. Kennedy's mom and Sydney would be there also. I would drop her off at the airport a few hours after that. Alone. Sending her off to another country by herself wasn't something I was excited about doing, but she insisted.

On the ride to the news station, I mentioned how I wasn't crazy about the idea. Lilly matter of factly stated, "I'm going alone and that's all there is to it. It isn't the first time I've gone on a solo trip, and it isn't like it's unheard of. Vacationing alone can be very relaxing. I already checked and I'd be losing too much money if I cancelled and this was the only time Jo could even go so it isn't like we could have rescheduled it anyway. Nobody else can go on a few days' notice, that would be ridiculous to even ask them. I'll still have fun, and I'll be facetiming Jo, so she'll still be with me in a way. Don't worry. I'll be fine. It'll be fun!" It isn't that I didn't think she would be fine, I just thought she would have more fun with somebody to share the experience with. She was right, though; nobody could go with her on a few days of notice. I know this because I already tried and couldn't pull it off.

"Ready for the big TV debut?" I asked, knowing full well she was more than ready.

"Of course! But Kennedy is the big star on this, not me. So many businesses have gotten on board with this! Laurie from Annie's Deli just hired a guy that goes to Wacky Wednesday with Kennedy. She interviewed him last week for her dishwasher opening and so far, he is doing a great job. And Dr. Ramos came into the bakery the other day and said her office manager has been working with a case manager at Shell's Place to interview a couple of their clients for some positions they created." Her eyes lit up as she beamed with pride at the progress that was happening because of this project.

"That's great! Looks like your campaign is a big hit."

We pulled up to the station and saw Kennedy, Lynette, and Sydney all waiting for us in front of the building, wearing their matching campaign T-shirts.

We all went into the building and the news reporter, Courtney Mansfield, led us to the interview area. It was much smaller than it appears on TV. There was a small red couch, a chair, and coffee table with the News logo behind it. Just a few feet in front of that was the camera. Lilly and Kennedy were directed to the couch and the rest of us stood back to the side to watch.

Lilly radiated confidence in front of the camera, as if she'd done this a hundred times before. It was when the reporter asked her why she started this campaign that she really nailed it. "Everyone deserves a chance, an opportunity, a way to provide for themselves, to learn new skills, and to have a sense of accomplishment. Humans need that, no matter what their situation is. It isn't a matter of spreading awareness. How many times do we see people mindlessly sharing posts on social media about disability awareness but then they don't take the time to learn anything about it, and they are still just as ignorant about it as ever. Awareness doesn't mean anything if people aren't also going to show acceptance and inclusion and willingness to give people opportunities. It's not ok to discriminate because somebody is different. They could be the best employee you've ever had, maybe even a friend for a lifetime. Kennedy here is a prime example. And quite honestly, we have learned every bit as much or more from Kennedy as she has from us. She just needed a place to fit in. The bakery wouldn't be the same without her. She's practically running the place now." Lilly smiled at Kennedy and patted her on the knee.

I looked over at Lynette and Sydney, both with watering eyes as they listened to Lilly.

Then it was Kennedy's time to shine. She'd trained for this, as she had been saying. She didn't look at the reporter but looked straight into the camera and spoke like she was giving a State of the Union Address at the White House. "I just want to say that I started out as cleaning captain, and I was promoted to Director of Sanitation and Infection Control, and I've been told I'm the best one in Willow Creek. Now I'm starting to learn some other things, and I want to learn to bake. I've never been in trouble at work; I'm always on time, and I follow all the rules. I can't use the cash register yet, but Lilly says that's ok because not everyone uses a cash register in their jobs. I've had other jobs, but they didn't work out for me because they were always yelling at me to hurry, or they would get mad at me if I didn't understand something. I felt like they didn't like me because I was a little different from everyone else there. Just because somebody has a disability doesn't mean they can't do anything. They might do it differently, but that's ok. I know a lot of people that don't have a job because they can't find anyone that will hire them and that makes me sad. I just want to thank Lilly for giving me a chance and I hope other businesses will give other people like me a chance too. Who knows? They might be surprised." She looked back at Lilly to see what she thought of what she said. Lilly nodded and beamed with approval.

Lynette and Sydney were wide eyed with their mouths open wide. When Kennedy finished talking, they looked at each other as if they were totally shocked that she pulled it off as well as she did. Once the camera stopped rolling, they jumped and clapped and squealed with excitement then ran over to congratulate Lilly and Kennedy.

I looked at Lilly, amazed at how much I loved this woman. Lynette watched me staring at Lilly and then walked back over to me. "You know, you better hold onto her. She's a good one."

She didn't have to tell me that. "Yea, that's what I keep hearing." I nodded and laughed, even though I already knew this.

"You don't know how hard we have tried to help Kennedy find a job that she could actually keep for more than a couple of months. All it took was Lilly meeting Kennedy one time, and she knew immediately that Kennedy would do well at the bakery. Kennedy had been to a cake decorating class with Sydney and Lilly saw her potential. She created a position and offered her a job that very same day even though Kennedy hadn't even applied for a job. And she was right; this has been the best thing that has ever happened to Kennedy. But as Sydney always says, when you know you know. Lilly knew, and she was right. So, I guess it's true."

"Sydney knows what she's talking about," I agreed. I'd heard Sydney and Will use the 'when you know you know' phrase a few times since I'd met them.

I drove Lilly home after we left the news station, gathered up her luggage, and went to eat at Annie's. Her plane would leave at 4:00 PM and she would arrive in Frankfurt at 9:30 AM their time; it was a seven-hour time difference. Then she would take a train to Wiesbaden where she would be staying for five days.

"Lynette really likes you. She told me about how you offered Kennedy a job after just meeting her one time at a cake decorating class. You changed her life with this job apparently."

“Yep, you should have seen the way she just started cleaning and organizing things during the class. I just knew she would fit in.”

“When you know you know, I guess.”

She stopped and looked at me for a moment, then nodded her head. “That’s right. When you know you know.”

When we arrived at the airport, I took her luggage out of the truck and set it on the sidewalk. “I’m going to miss you this week. I wish I could go with you.”

“I know. I wish you could too, but it’s ok.” She poked me in the chest and added, “And stop worrying about me. I’ll be fine.”

“I know you will.” I lifted her up off the sidewalk as I hugged her.

“Did I ever tell you how much I love you?” she asked.

“No, I don’t recall you ever mentioning that to me before.”

“Hmmm. Well, I do,” she said and kissed me before grabbing her luggage. “See you in a week!”

I watched the love of my life happily walk through the double doors as if she had not one single care in the world. But then she glanced back at me and collided right into a lady walking out, causing the woman to slosh her iced coffee all over the front of her designer shirt. The woman made a look at Lilly and muttered some things that I was sure were not pleasant, but I couldn’t help but laugh. That gorgeous, carefree, although sometimes careless adventure seeker was all I wanted in the world.

Sometimes you get an idea that you can't put it aside and you must figure out a way to make it happen. I had some calls to make and somebody that owed me a favor.

Chapter 33

Lilly

The ten-hour flight to Frankfurt was utterly horrific. Not only was there a wailing baby in the row behind me, but I was sandwiched between two rather heavy-set men who both intruded onto my own middle seat, creating a kind of sardine can affect. The man in the window seat had not only presumably eaten a few bean burritos before the flight but also needed to use the restroom about every hour, resulting in me having to continuously wake up the snoring aisle seat man so we could stand up and move out of the way. How he was able to sleep is a mystery to me. Then, I accidentally squeezed my bottled water, sending water squirting all over both me and window seat man which I did feel bad about at first but decided he deserved it due to the excessive restroom visits and frequent offensive odors. Since sleeping was not an option, I was able to watch four of my favorite rom coms which were the silver lining of the whole thing.

It was 9:30 AM, and regardless of my lack of sleep, I was ready to experience Germany. I breezed through customs and picked up my luggage, then hopped into an uber for what was supposed to be a thirty-minute drive to the Airbnb in Wiesbaden but ended up being quite a bit less than that. I'd told Kade about the autobahn, but I didn't realize the traffic would really be this fast. The Uber driver acted like he was either a Nascar driver, or we were involved in a high-speed police chase. We had to be going well over 100mph which was exhilarating for me but would have sent my mother into a fit of sheer terror. I wanted to face time Jo, but it was only 2:00 AM in Willow Creek. That was going to be the hard part with the time difference. I'd just have to make some videos and send them when she woke up.

Even though Jo hadn't seemed as excited about this trip as I had been, she would have loved this town! The architecture alone was unlike anything I'd ever seen in America, with baroque buildings and elaborate details. And the little streetside cafes! It would have been so much fun to sit there with Jo, sipping our wine or coffee and sampling each other's food. Jo and Kade had both told me that most of the menus at the restaurants, particularly in the touristy spots, might be bilingual. This proved to be true with the lunch spot I chose. The menu was written in German with some English in each description. I'd really wanted to order something at random, having no idea what it was, but it was ok because I couldn't believe how good the pork knuckle was that I ordered. I took a picture of it for Jo. I also ordered a beer because you can't go to Germany and not drink beer, it's practically the law.

Later in the afternoon, I walked along the brick paved streets lined with little shops, bakeries, and restaurants. I bought a little hand carved cuckoo clock, a hoodie, and of course a Christmas ornament to hang on my travel theme tree. It was great, but I had to admit, I was a little lonely. I FaceTimed Jo while I walked along the street, pointing my phone at the buildings and the pastries and sausages and intricate figurines in the shop windows. I showed her my clock which she immediately told me I should be glad I live alone because she would seriously hurt me if she had to live in a home with a cuckoo clock going off at the top of every hour.

Even though it was supposed to have been a trip with Jo, I wished Kade were here. The town is so romantic. I could just imagine being here with him, walking hand in hand along the brick paved streets. We could have sat outside one of the little outdoor restaurants drinking beer or wine and sampling food off each other's plates.

A few hours later, I went back to the Airbnb and sat out on the patio. I'd lucked out on this Airbnb, it was tucked away behind some thick trees near a beautiful botanical garden. There was rattan patio furniture with green ruffled seat cushions, and string lights along the top and down the sides of the deck. It would be a perfect place for me to read the books that I brought with me. I took a photo of my view and posted it on my story. Almost immediately, Kade called.

"Having fun?" he asked. It seemed crazy that he was halfway across the planet from me.

"It's even more amazing than I thought it would be. I just wish Jo could have come with me. I feel kind of guilty being here without her, but she insisted." I was quiet for a moment. "I wish you were here, too. You would love it, Kade. We could have had so much fun here together."

"I wish I could have come. I tried. I really did."

"I know you did. It was just so short of notice."

"So, what kind of exciting things do you have planned for tomorrow?"

"Oh, lots of things! I'm starting out with breakfast at this cute little bakery that has the most amazing looking pastries and coffees! Then I'm going to go for a walk around town. I found a Croatian restaurant for lunch that I want to try. And in the evening, I made a reservation at this winery that's on a mountain! You can take this funicular railway up to it and it just looks like it will be so beautiful. It's something Jo and I had been really excited about."

"Sounds like a fun day. Wish I could be there with you."

"Me too. Everything is just so beautiful, I wish you could see it. Pictures don't do it justice."

"Maybe someday we can go together, until then, don't do anything I wouldn't do."

"But you only live once, Kade. I mean, what happens in Germany stays in Germany, right?"

"Um, no. I don't think that's how it goes." He laughed. "I've got to get to work. I love you, Lilly. More than you can even begin to imagine." Something in his voice sounded different. Sweeter, more emotional than normal.

.....

I tried to call Kade again before I went to sleep last night, but his phone went straight to voicemail. With the seven-hour time difference, he would have still been working and must have been busy.

I waited to call Kade again until noon the next day. Again, it went straight to voicemail. He would be on duty. I couldn't help but worry about Kade when he was at work, maybe not as much as I probably would have if we lived in a town with a higher crime rate, but when he didn't answer his phone, I couldn't help but wonder if something had happened. Especially after what happened to him and Liam. I knew the danger was always there and it was something I'd have to deal with as long as I was with Kade.

A while back, we'd shared our locations with each other on our phones. I usually forgot that I had the app on my phone because I never looked at it. I frowned at the phone when I saw that his location was turned off. That didn't make any sense. Why would he turn off his location and it just happened to be when his phone was going to voicemail? So, when I called him before I went to bed, it would have been about 3:00 PM his time. Now, it would be about 7:00 AM his time and it was still going to voicemail on the first ring? And with his location turned off. He sounded different last night. Maybe I misinterpreted it? Maybe if something happened to his phone, it would make it to where the location didn't show up.

I called Jo. She could talk through this with me. "Ok, Jo. Please tell me I'm not overthinking. Kade's phone keeps going straight to voicemail."

"And? Maybe his phone is dead? Maybe he turned it off so he could not be interrupted at work? Maybe he is sick and wanted to sleep?"

"And the location on his phone isn't working. What if something happened to him and that's why his phone isn't working? Like a car accident... or worse?"

"You're being ridiculous. I'm pretty sure if somebody's phone is dead or turned off, their location also won't show up."

"Oh, I guess you're right." I was being ridiculous. If something bad had happened to him, somebody would have heard about it by now. Or it would have been all over social media. He was fine.

I walked back to the Airbnb, carrying a shopping bag full of more souvenirs in one hand and my vanilla latte in the other. From across the yard, I saw something stuck to the front door. Something brown that wasn't there before. As I got closer to the door, I saw what it was. There was a large pretzel wrapped in plastic wrap, taped to the middle of the door. Next to it was a note that read, ***"Fun fact about pretzels is they represent the origin of the phrase 'tying the knot.'"***

I froze. I'd taped the sourdough to Kade's front door after I ran into him with my car. Kade is the only one that would have done this since the sourdough thing had become a joke between us, so had the fun facts. But Kade was back in Texas. Who else would have taped a pretzel to my door? He could have asked the Airbnb host to do it? Jo could have given him the contact info. I looked around, but there was nobody there.

I pulled the pretzel and note off the door and walked inside, then tried to call Kade again. It rang this time.

"Hello?"

"Hey there. Something really weird happened. There's a pretzel taped to my front door with a note next to it with a fun fact. Did you have somebody do that?"

"Who would I have asked to do that? I don't know anybody in Germany, Lilly. Maybe the Airbnb hostess did it? Might be customary in Germany."

"I kind of doubt that it's customary." I looked at the note.

"Well, I have no idea, then. Oh, I want to see your patio. You told me how nice it was out there. Can you face time me?"

"Oh, yes! Hold on." I opened the back door and walked out onto the patio. "See? Isn't it cute out here?" I pointed the phone around so he could see the view.

"It's nice! And you said there was a botanical garden too? You know I have to see that."

"You're going to love this." I walked down the pebble path to the botanical garden. "It's literally breathtaking," I said as I approached it.

"Yes, it is." His voice didn't come from the phone. Standing next to the water fountain, wearing a navy suit, holding a bouquet of fall flowers was Kade.

I put my phone down, speechless.

"How many times have I heard lately that when you know you know? I think it's the Willow Creek slogan. But it's also true. My life isn't complete unless you're in it, every day, for the rest of it. I knew it when you assaulted me with your vehicle. I knew it when you taped a loaf of bread to my door. I knew it when you projectile vomited on my shirt." He smiled, but his eyes were watering. "And I've known it every time your green eyes lit up, every time I heard your laugh, and every moment that I've lived since I met you. I hated the dust in Willow Creek, and when that haboob blew in, it made me want to move back to Austin. But then you came barreling through like a beautiful, crazy whirlwind and changed my life. You were something good in the dust and I thank God every day for that storm because without it, I wouldn't have you."

By that time, tears were falling out of his blue eyes. He was going to do it. This is it.

And there it was. Kade handed me the bouquet of flowers, dropped down on one knee and opened a small black box that he pulled out of his pocket.

"Let's make every day your biggest adventure. Marry me, Lilly." He didn't wait for my response before slipping the ring on my finger, because he knew what I'd say.

.....

Kade, my fiancé, and I rode the little wooden train up the mountain to the winery. The crisp autumn air was chilly, but not terrible. The entire place was more beautiful than I anticipated. We walked hand in hand along the paths to the Neroberg Temple, a large white gazebo, and then up the hill to the winery. The view was everything. Past the rows of golden vineyards, the town could be seen below. The buildings and church steeples mixed in with a vibrant mix of greens, yellows, and orange foliage. We found a woman that offered to take pictures of the two of us, our first pictures as an engaged couple.

I'd been looking at the ring on my finger and then looked up at Kade, who was already looking at me. "So, how were you able to pull this off?"

"I pulled some strings at work and got a few days covered. I'll repay the favor when I get back. I turned off my location in case you were spying on me. I didn't want you to see the airport."

"What? Spy? I'd never..." I laughed. And that also explained why his phone went to voicemail. He was on the plane. "I can rehome Penny for you."

"No, you can keep her. It's a price I'm willing to pay."

Epilogue

Kade

September, a year later...

The wedding turned out beautiful. Lilly wasn't picky about the wedding; her main concern was that our family and friends were there. So many people in Willow Creek love Lilly and they all jumped in to offer whatever they could to help with the planning. Ashley made all the floral arrangements as she had also done for Sydney and Will's wedding. Leanne made Little Elsie's flower girl dress. Food was catered by Annie's Deli. Guests had their choice of a club sandwich or a Thanksgiving Sandwich. And of course, Caitlyn and Javier made the cakes. We told them they could do whatever they wanted, and they did not disappoint. The bride's cake was flawless white buttercream with perfectly handmade tiger lilies covering the top and flowing down around the base. The groom's cake was a police theme.

I wish I could sing, but I can't. The next best thing was her brother. I'd heard Will sing before; we were thrilled when he agreed to sing during the wedding. Lilly had asked me to choose the song and let it be a surprise to her. I picked the song that we danced to at the bakery, and she cried while he sang it.

Lilly and I stood in front of rows of our closest family and friends. Liam by my side as my best man and Jo next to Lilly. Who would have thought that Larry would have been an ordained minister, but there he was, standing in front of us with a bible in his hand.

"Kade, you may kiss your bride," he announced. Our first kiss as husband and wife. She's my wife. Lilly Wayland is my wife. The crowd clapped and cheered and I heard a few whistles from the back, most likely some of the officers that I'd become friends with.

Walking hand in hand with my new wife past the rows of my new family and friends, I've never felt so at home and so loved by so many people. In the past year, I'd removed my protective coat and allowed myself to make friends, to be close to people. I'd made friends with the other officers and some of the firemen and paramedics. My best friends were Liam, Will, Kip, and Ashley's husband Antonio who's a fireman. I'd become very close to Larry and Alana, but mostly Larry. He was like a father to me, maybe even a grandfather. We'd gone fishing a few more times, and the last time, we actually caught some and cooked them together.

Liam had been making progress with physical therapy and continues to live in his assisted living room. Lilly takes Beatrice to see him anytime we visit, and we've taken him to our house several times for a few hours at a time.

Lilly sold her house and moved in with me a few months after I proposed. She's made a few minor changes to the décor, actually, she's completely redid every inch of the house except for the reading room which she said was already perfect. The only change is that it now has two chairs in it instead of one and her books have been added to the shelves. I love seeing her things in the house, her makeup and hair clips spilling over to my sink, her cup collection taking over the cabinet, and her vast supply of unused candles piled high on the dresser.

Her tarantula died of old age shortly after she moved in. Fortunately, she didn't replace it with another spider. Instead, she has a hairless rat which she named Philip. She isn't the kind of girl that would be happy with a fish or a bird; she likes the ugly pets. Her quirky and unique personality is what attracted me to her in the first place. I'm definitely not going to complain about her interesting choices in pets.

Lilly has a way with people; they all love her. I knew my sister would love her, but she made my mother laugh. My mother, the grouchy one. I don't even remember the last time I heard her laugh. She even hugged Lilly and she's not a hugger.

I watched as Lilly danced with Liam out on the middle of dance floor. She spun his wheelchair around and held onto his hands as she danced in front of him. Leanne, Sydney, and Ashley all joined in too. Liam had a blast with them.

While they were all dancing, I found Kennedy, sitting alone eating her sandwich. "May I have this dance?" I extended my hand. She accepted and I led her out onto the dance floor. Kennedy had made some great strides at the bakery in the last year. She had started doing some baking and Lynette was dropping her off at the bakery early to help Javier get things ready for the day. She was usually on cupcake duty, but Lilly was working with her on teacakes now. She'd also earned another raise.

Kennedy had become very comfortable with me in the past year, and she'd even started making jokes. "I'm glad you married Lilly. I was getting tired of her talking about man hunting at the hardware store."

I laughed at that. "I'm glad I could be helpful." When the song was over, I walked Kennedy back to her table. Her mom was sitting there and she stood up and hugged me.

"Congratulations, Kade! Kennedy and I are so happy for you and Lilly. I haven't seen two people more in love since Sydney and Will got married. I can only hope I can find somebody that loves me like you and Lilly love each other."

"Oh, I'm sorry, I thought you were already married?" I asked her.

"Oh, I was. We've been divorced for more than a year. I don't think I've really talked about it to anyone. We were only married a few years, and Kennedy never had much of a bond with him so she probably hasn't mentioned it to anyone. I'll know when I find the right one for me. I just hope he comes along before I'm too old and senile to realize it." She laughed.

"He will. And thank you so much for coming tonight. I've got to go find my bride."

I found Lilly, laughing so hard she was crying, talking with Jo and her date. "Excuse me, I need to borrow my wife for a moment." I told them as I took Lilly by the hand and led her to the dance floor.

"Hi, wife," I told her, looking down at her into her emerald eyes, the eyes that I'll be looking into forever.

"Hi, husband," she replied and kissed me as if nobody else was watching.

We forgot about everyone else and danced as if we were the only two people there, as if time had stopped and nothing else in the world mattered. And it all started with a West Texas dust storm.

The End

Acknowledgements

Thank you to Lee Ortiz and Darrell Campbell. Your insight, experience, and bravery in law enforcement were overwhelmingly inspirational and instrumental. Your expertise was invaluable to me. Thank you also to Lee for assisting with some of the wording pertaining to law enforcement. Thank you to Tom and Katy for your assistance in areas related to law enforcement and dispatch.

Thank you to Erica Ramos for once again, reading my chapters as I finished them. Thank you for being my cheerleader while enduring my countless texts and emails regarding this book.

Thank you to my husband, Mike, for your lack of complaining while I rotted away on the couch, writing my book, instead of doing almost anything else.

Thank you to my kids for your patience and unwavering support in this writing adventure.

www.ingramcontent.com/pod-product-compliance
Lightning Source LLC
Chambersburg PA
CBHW030243120726
47903CB00005B/1599

* 9 7 9 8 9 9 2 4 6 8 3 4 2 *